PRAISE FOR

The Paris Affair

"A wonderful, entertaining story with a cast of compelling characters on a wild and crazy romp through the hangouts of Paris. It's got more twists and turns than Monet's brushstrokes. Pure enjoyment."

Don Pugnetti Jr.,
author of *A Coat Dyed Black:*
A Novel of the Norwegian Resistance

"*The Paris Affair* is an art-filled caper through San Francisco and Paris, rife with delicious food, delectable wines, and delightful romance mixed with mystery. Make sure you have a glass of wine and a snack handy; this book will whet your appetite."

Laura Moe,
author of *Breakfast with Neruda,*
Blue Valentines, and *The Language of the Son*

"Filled with plot twists and revelations that unfold like a carefully curated art exhibit, *The Paris Affair* promises to keep readers guessing until the very end. Don't miss this funny, sexy, and delicious tale of art, love, and deception in the City of Light."

A.C. Fuller,
author of the *Crime Beat* series
and the *Alex Vane* series

The PARIS AFFAIR

DIANE W NAAB

MUSE
PRODUCTIONS

THE PARIS AFFAIR
© 2023 by Diane W Naab

ISBN 979-8-9883038-0-0
ISBN 979-8-9883038-1-7 (ebook)

This is a work of fiction. Names, characters, places, and events are products of the author's imagination, and any resemblances to actual events or places or persons, living or dead, is entirely coincidental.

Cover and Interior Design: Bookery
Editing: Kathy Burge & Kara Aisenbrey
Author Photo: Joel and Mary Levin
Printed in the United States of America

To every creative visual artist and wordsmith:
I am in awe and inspired by you all.

*"Quand vous arrivez à
un embranchement
dans la route, prenez-le."*

"When you come to a fork in the road, take it."

—*Yogi Berra*

2015

Alex entered the Galerie d'inspiration and lifted a glass of champagne from the tray the attendant was carrying. *"Merci."* He smiled and nodded to associates and clients he knew as he scanned the room.

"Excusez-moi. Is that a Derain? André Derain?"

Alex turned to see before him an exquisitely dressed woman in her late fifties. The heady scent of her perfume, Bvlgari, aroused his senses. The small Hermès bag on her shoulder, the signature *H* on the flap, gave him a sense of her style and taste.

"Oui. From the Fauvism period. His colors are marvelous, aren't they?" he said.

The woman came closer to reveal simple gold jewelry. Her long, slender legs were caressed by a white silk skirt, the Louboutin heels with their signature red soles setting off a spectacular vision of wealth.

Alex, aware of every detail of extravagance, also saw a woman without a clue about art or even the importance and history of André Derain. Her reference was strictly information from the brochure she was holding as she fanned herself, obviously attracted to the man before her, the Derain painting of little importance in the moment.

Alex sensed an opportunity, not only for himself, but also for his brother Pierre.

"Alexander Marshal." He reached for her hand. "Art agent for several collectors, mostly here in Paris."

"Nice to meet you. Sonja Reid, visiting from San Francisco."

Their hands lingered for a moment, then she slowly slid her hand from his. He produced a business card and invited her to contact him at any time. Seduction was not completely on his mind. Opportunity had just presented itself.

Chapter 1

Alex left the gallery, glanced at his watch, and punched Pierre's number on his phone. It was early afternoon in Washington DC; Pierre would no doubt be at a café in the upscale Adams Morgan neighborhood where he lived with their mother. The thing that was most on Alex's mind could not be discussed on the phone. He focused instead on a detail he knew his brother would be delighted with—his idea that Pierre should move back to Paris.

"Pierre, I have a couple of things I'd like to discuss with you." He suggested the idea of moving. "We could share my two-bedroom apartment until I find something else for myself. I'm barely there as it is. Besides, aren't you tired of living with our mother? The second thing . . . well, we can discuss that once you arrive. What do you think?"

"What do I think? You have no idea how often I've thought of moving back to Paris. *Merde!* I hate my life here. Memories of our father's condescending voice ringing in my ears. The constant belittling. Paris is where I belong." Pierre knew it wouldn't take long to pack up a few items, mostly art supplies, and be on his way "home."

"Excellent. I'll make travel arrangements for you in the morning."

Alex picked Pierre up at Charles de Gaulle airport a few days later. After arriving at the apartment, they sat at a table with a bottle of pinot noir, a fresh baguette, and a wedge of Camembert cheese.

He eased into his proposal. "Remember, Pierre, when you created those paintings for my friends back in college? A Picasso, a Kandinsky—I can't remember the other two. They were amazing copies, with your signature cleverly disguised under the artist's name. My cheapskate friends only paid you a hundred dollars each." He laughed and shook his head. After a moment, he became serious. "I propose that you do one more—in the style of André Derain. It would be sold as an original that had never been on display or on the market before. Obscure, with no provenance."

Alex poured more wine and continued. "No one, certainly not the art patron I have in mind, would question the authenticity of the piece. She would simply HAVE to own it, no questions asked."

Pierre tapped his fingers on the table, then stood. "So basically, a forgery. What do I think? Illegal comes to mind, for starters." He began to pace. "I'm not on anyone's radar. Pretty low-key as an artist these past few years. But you? You would risk your career for this?"

"I'm telling you it's practically risk free. The patron is a rich social climber. She's utterly clueless."

Alex knew they both had an aversion for wealthy snobs with no appreciation for fine art, whose only goal was to show off and impress. Pulling off this simple forgery would be a delightful secret between them.

Pierre studied Alex for a long moment. "Okay. I'm in. A one-time stunt!"

Once settled, Pierre began to research Derain intensely: the details of his life, all of his known paintings, his particular stylistic traits, and the influences of Cézanne, Matisse, and Monet. Vivid colors in both landscapes and portraits. He also proceeded to experiment—duplicating the paints Derain used, scraping old canvases and practicing the tedious methods of "aging" the finished work. The goal was to recreate to perfection the color, stroke, and vision of the original artist. Pierre's natural abilities and his art degree gave him an edge on all of this. Moreover, not only was he an extraordinary artist, but he also had the rare intuition to channel the artist he was mimicking. To sense who Derain was. How he perceived life and his surroundings. This gave Pierre the edge in the game of forgery.

Chapter 2

2017

It was three o'clock in the afternoon, and the prestigious Brauleigh's annual art auction had concluded its final day at the landmark Fairmont Olympic Hotel in Seattle.

Joi Pascale and Monica Graham, partners in Muse Fine Arts Gallery, were there from San Francisco, not only for business, but also on the chance of adding to their personal collections.

In 2001, Joi and Monica had received their art degrees from the highly regarded Pratt Institute in New York, along with their friends Sam Robson and Phillip Edwards. Now the four of them were partners with the successful art gallery and the associated events planning company Chic.

Alex and Pierre were also in attendance at the auction. For Alex, it was an opportunity to meet up with gallery friends and associates, collectors, and—always—prospective clients. He had invited his brother so they could enjoy some brother time. Something they rarely did nowadays due to Alex's busy schedule.

The place buzzed with conversation. Gallery owners, collectors, and longtime friends connecting to discuss the world of art.

"I see Andrea over by the champagne table," Monica said. "I'm going to talk to her about a fundraiser she wants Chic to arrange."

Joi said, "Okay. I need to pay the cashier and pick up my painting." She fumbled in her purse and retrieved her credit card just as Alex approached.

"Congratulations on your winning bid. The piece is a wonderful example of Forain's depiction of ballet subjects."

"Thank you. My first acquisition of Impressionist art." Smiling, she reached for Alex's hand. "Joi Pascale. I'm part owner of a gallery in San Francisco."

Alex took her hand. "Alex Marshal. Art agent from Paris." They shared a mutual attraction—smiling eyes lingered for a moment.

Joi slowly withdrew her hand and continued, "I've always loved Jean-Louis Forain's work. Especially the ballet paintings, which evoke his close friendship with Degas. I studied ballet for a few years, so this has a special meaning for me."

Alex continued in his art agent mode. "An astute buy, given the current rise in the market for Impressionists as a whole, not to mention the so-called 'lesser painters' of the movement, like Forain."

Alex saw Pierre approaching. "Excuse me for a moment. I need to speak with my associate." He stepped away and told Pierre that he might be going for a drink.

Pierre buttoned his jacket and adjusted the gray wool scarf around his neck. "And I'm going for a walk. I want to check out some of the downtown galleries, see some Northwest Coast art." Smiling at Alex, he indicated Joi with a nod of his head. "I assume you'll be late getting back to the hotel." Pierre rarely attended auctions with Alex, abhorring the pretentious art collectors and the absurd amount of money that exchanged hands. He wasn't a promoter like his brother. He was simply an artist.

Alex smiled. "Yes. Probably late." He checked the schedule on his phone. "I have an appointment in the morning with a curator at the art museum, and I need to check in with a couple of clients. We can go to Pike Place Market when I'm done. I hear the fishmongers put on quite a show. And there's a wonderful little French restaurant I think you'll like." He also checked the reminder text from the airlines. "Our flight to Portland is tomorrow evening. Then San Francisco and finally home to Paris." He smiled and patted Pierre's back. "Have fun, *mon frère.*"

Meanwhile, Joi had gotten in line to pay for her painting. Once the piece was wrapped and she had the documentation in hand, she made her way back to the main room and found Monica just as Alex approached.

Monica glanced at Alex. "Monica Graham, Joi's business partner." She shook his hand, then said, "Joi, I'm heading back to the hotel. Time for a nap."

Joi shifted the painting in her arms. "Would you mind taking this with you? I won't be long."

As Monica departed, Joi turned back to Alex, hoping they could continue their conversation. He smiled and said, "Looks like we've both been abandoned. My associate just took off to check out some local galleries. Why don't we go for a drink. The Metropolitan Grill is close by."

Monica returned to the hotel and made a quick trip to the parking garage to check out her "new ride." Before their flight to Seattle, she had found her dream car listed online in the Seattle area. A black Mazda Miata. The price was right, so she'd had it checked out by a local mechanic and delivered to their hotel. Joi thought they would be getting a rental for the trip home. The Miata was a little surprise on Monica's part—cruising home in a hot little sports car.

Around five o'clock, Monica decided to text Joi regarding dinner plans. Just as she started her message, a text from Joi popped up saying she was going to stay over in Seattle and had already booked a flight home for the following day. Obviously, the surprise mini vacation would not be happening. The drive home would now be solo.

Trying to stay calm, Monica responded with: *Oh, okay. Well, have fun. I'm out of here now. Checkout for you is at eleven tomorrow. I'll have the hotel put your painting in their vault.* Monica realized if she kept texting, the words would not be so congenial. She was furious. She grabbed her bag and Joi's painting and headed to the front desk. By five thirty, she was on I-5, radio blasting, top down—headed for Astoria, on the Oregon coast—alone.

Chapter 3

The winding Oregon coast highway, so stunning in daylight, had a foreboding, claustrophobic feel in the fog and darkness, making it hard to see and breathe at the same time. It was past midnight, and Monica's solo drive from Seattle had been nonstop. A range of feelings overtook her. Exhausted was in competition with hungry and miffed—and worried over Joi's impulsive decision to stay in Seattle with a man she had just met.

Through the gloom, she spied a small 1940s-looking café ahead. A neon sign, "Millie's All-Night Diner," flickered in the fog, the *n* missing from *Diner*, giving a vision of film noir. One old car, a blue 1950s Chevy, was parked beside the building. She pulled in and made her way up the weathered wood steps. Struggling to open the door, she was startled by a face peeking through the window.

"Sorry. We're closed."

"But your sign says 'all night.' Please? Coffee and a donut to go?"

The waitress, in her late sixties, put down the half-read James Patterson paperback a customer had left behind, sipped the last of her beer, and unlocked the door. She eyed Monica in her expensive city clothes and, with a raised eyebrow, decided her late customer was okay. "It may say 'all night,' but with this fog I haven't seen a soul for hours." Then, with a warm smile, she added, "Well, unless you count Gary at the gas station. He's here almost every night for a burger and a brew." She grabbed a sponge and began to wipe down the worn Formica countertop.

Monica studied the woman. Deep crow's-feet and smile lines marked her face. Frizzy gray hair tucked into a bun at the nape of her neck completed the visual of a woman who had struggled in life. But right now, she was smiling like a contented woman.

"Thank you for letting me in. I'm starving, and I really need to use your restroom." Slipping off her coat, Monica looked around at the aging tables and booths. Red plastic tablecloths, a jukebox in the corner, and faded posters and memorabilia covered the walls. "Are you Millie?"

"What? No, I'm Wanda. Millie passed a couple of years ago. I kind of inherited this place. Cooking and busing tables all day is not my idea of a dream career. It was once—when Millie and I bought the café. Kind of a new start for both of us." She shuffled off, grabbed a day-old powdered sugar donut, and poured the last of the coffee into a paper cup. "That'll be six dollars. Go ahead and sit down. I need to clean up here anyway. Where you headed?"

"Um, the restroom . . . ?"

Wanda nodded toward the hallway.

The doors marked "Gulls" and "Buoys" completed the scene of an old beachside café. Startled by her image in the murky and cracked mirror, Monica dabbed at her makeup and skewed spikes of hair, in wild disarray from having the Miata's top down earlier. Realizing the futility, she gave up on her primping.

Back at the counter, she found Wanda mopping the floor beside the grill. Humming what vaguely sounded like "Crazy," the old Patsy Cline tune.

"In answer to your question, I'm headed to San Francisco. I've been in Seattle for a couple of days and thought I'd take my time driving home. My friend was supposed to be with me, but, well . . . not to bore you." Arms crossed and talking mostly to herself, Monica turned and walked to the front window. The fog had become an eerie shroud. Speaking louder: "She's so impetuous. And I'm pretty much fed up with her thoughtlessness." She let out a deep breath. "Is there a motel nearby?"

"You okay, honey?" Wanda approached Monica and tentatively patted her shoulder as they both stood looking out the window, as if viewing the splendor of the Grand Canyon. "If she's your friend, be careful not to turn away. Us girls need to stick together, you know."

Monica muttered, "She's been my best friend since grade school. I'm worried, that's all. What I really need right now is a place to sleep."

"Down the road a bit is the Bayside Motel. Not fancy by a long shot, but they usually have a few rooms available."

Leaving a ten-dollar bill on the counter, Monica grabbed a book of matches with the café logo—a collection habit she'd had for years—and thanked Wanda for the snack and the girl talk.

Getting back into the Miata, Monica wondered if she should call Joi, then decided she didn't need to play mother hen to a grown woman.

Pale lights blinked from the vacancy sign on the Bayside Motel, a typical two-story concrete-brick building painted light blue, with hanging flower baskets desperately in need of water.

She entered the small office and found a young man intently watching TV, sipping a can of Mountain Dew—seemingly unaware of her presence.

"Excuse me. I need a room for the night."

Startled, he turned and greeted her with the enthusiasm of an awkward schoolboy.

The TV played an old black-and-white movie, Anthony Perkins uttering, "We're all in our private traps." She glanced at the attendant and back at the TV, wondering if he was aware of the cliché. Shaking her head, she signed the register, grabbed the key, and headed down the hall.

Her stuffy, cramped room was brown. Bedspread, chairs, carpet, and lamps. Brown. The only hint of color was in the two small, faded prints—one of seashells and the other a moose—hanging askew on the brown fake-wood wall paneling.

She slumped in one of the brown chairs, took off her shoes, and thought about the auction. Brauleigh's had done well, as usual, due in part to Joi's purchase. But the man, Alex—there was something about him. Too smooth and charming, in a young Alain Delon sort of way. And she could swear his colleague looked familiar.

Exhaustion jumbled her thoughts as she lay fully clothed on the bed. Anthony Perkins . . . shower curtain . . . Joi . . . stale donut . . . Frenchman . . . familiar stranger . . .

Zzzzz.

After a few hours of sleep, Monica was ready to hit the road. No longer in a mini-vacation mood, she headed east to I-5, punched the Miata into high gear, and headed home.

Chapter 4

Monica arrived in the Marina District by early afternoon. Her apartment had floor-to-ceiling windows facing north over the bay and showcased simple white modern furniture, white walls, and enormous panels of abstract art created with a palette of bright orange, red, celadon green, aqua, and black.

She planned to call Sam later for an update on business over the last few days. He'd been working on the promo for the upcoming X6 exhibit, which was to feature some of the best contemporary art in the area. The gallery and Chic were situated in a historic building in the South Beach area. Both businesses were lucrative, with well-attended art openings and ongoing corporate events. They were able to promote and represent known and unknown artists using a fairly basic plan of media promotion and themed opening receptions. The events business was a little more detailed, requiring more production, more staff time, and travel out of town.

Head wrapped in a towel after her shower, she put on yoga pants and a Chic T-shirt and drifted to her state-of-the-art kitchen in search of sustenance. The fridge was filled with packages of food from restaurants and delis, a bowl of grapes that now looked like raisins, and a container of something she couldn't identify. She grabbed her phone. "Hello, Huang Fu. It's Monica. I'd like to order my usual. Yes. And two egg tarts. *M goi.*"

After a fabulous meal, she slipped on running shoes—even though she had no intention of running—stopped at the corner deli for a newspaper and bottle of water, and continued down the hill to Aquatic Park by the Maritime Museum. There was a feeling of community here; drummers sat off to the side and engaged those who walked by, children played in the sand, and old men chatted about politics and fishing. The park had a stepped concrete seawall that overlooked a horseshoe-shaped lagoon and sandy beach.

Just as she started to call Sam, her phone rang. "Joi? Where *are* you? Are you okay?"

"I'm fine. I'm at the airport ready to catch my flight. I should arrive home at about four. Would you pick me up? I've so much to tell you. Oh, got to go. See you soon. And thanks."

"What's going on?" said Monica to no one. Joi had already hung up.

Chapter 5

Joi's plane was due to land any minute. Monica paced, anxious and full of questions. She took a deep breath, slapped a smile on her face, and mentally zipped her lips. She would be patient and let Joi explain herself.

Joi approached, all smiles and waving.

Any calm Monica tried to muster went straight out the window. She crossed her arms and tapped her right foot. "What in the *hell* is going on? You have some explaining to—"

Joi rolled her eyes and pulled Monica to the side. She hugged her short, ranting friend and whispered, "Calm down!" She grinned. "I have so much to tell you. Well, maybe not everything."

Joi grabbed her bag and asked Monica to carry the piece of artwork. They locked arms as they walked the short distance to the car. Joi tried to make light of the situation, babbling about the crying baby on the flight and the second glass of wine she finally ordered.

Monica announced, "Here we are," as they approached the Miata.

Joi said, "What? Is this yours?"

Monica nodded and tried to contain a grin. Once inside the car, she took a deep breath and spoke with slow, precise diction. "It's a nice car. A lovely car." Looking around. "Perfect in every way." She faced Joi, voice now elevated. "It was meant to be a surprise. I had it delivered to the hotel in Seattle so we could have a nice drive home." She shook her head. "Okay. Enough of that. So, what's up with you?"

Joi sighed. "After you left the auction, I went for a drink with Alex, the art agent. He's extremely intelligent and knowledgeable about art, especially the Impressionists." She closed her eyes and sighed again. "We walked a few blocks to a place on Second Avenue. Had drinks, talked about art, his travels, and my life in San Francisco. Then I texted you with my plans. I'm really sorry about that, by the way."

"Yes, yes. I get the picture. Continue with Mr. Intelligent Art Man. The one that's apparently swept you off your feet. Him."

Ignoring the remark, Joi continued. "We ate steak and crab. Drank wine. By that point, we could barely keep our hands off each other." Joi's face flushed from the memory. "We ended up at his hotel a couple of blocks away."

"Good God."

Joi continued. "Monica, he asked if I would go to Paris with him. He has business there and thought I would enjoy seeing the museums and experiencing Paris to the fullest. I said yes."

Monica erupted. "You are so—I don't know—naive? First of all, you don't even know this guy. Second of all, you have responsibilities here. The X6 exhibit, the auction in Monterey next month, and the two corporate events we've still got to put together. You can't leave us hanging like this."

"Monica, this is an amazing opportunity for me. I've never been to Europe. I've had a squeaky-clean passport for five years, just waiting to be stamped for the first time. I'll be with someone in the art world who can show me the most incredible collections on the planet." Anger took over. "And you know what? You are not my mother. I'm going! And I won't let you down. I'll take care of it. I'll find extra staff. Not a big deal. And we have a week to figure out the rest."

Monica began to relax, but still in her maternal mode. "The X6 exhibit was your original concept. Are plans in place?"

Joi patted Monica's shoulder. "It will be okay. I promise."

After dropping Joi at her apartment in the Haight-Ashbury district, Monica called Sam. "Can you meet me for a drink? We've got a problem."

Sam put his phone on speaker while he retrieved a file on last month's exhibit budget. "Sure, for a little bit. See you at Buena Vista around six? What's up?"

"I'll fill you in later."

Monica arrived at the Buena Vista café, not far from her apartment, at a quarter past six. Situated at the bay end of Hyde Street and the cable car turnaround, it was one of their favorite hangouts and practically their second office. A noisy yet calming place to discuss the next event, exhibit, or personal trauma. Weaving through the café, packed as usual, she found Sam at a small table by the window, sipping a brew and scanning his phone. She ordered the bar's famous Irish coffee then pushed her way through the crowd to join him.

Sam cocked his head. "You okay?"

"No. I don't know. Joi is taking off for Paris next week. I don't know for how long, but I'm worried. She's going with a guy she just met at the Seattle auction. Geez, he could be a serial killer. He could be a rapist. He could be—"

Sam smiled. "Hey, slow down. Why is she going? And who's this guy—"

"I don't know about him. I met him briefly. He's an art agent from Paris. His associate was just leaving, and I swear he looked familiar." Monica paused, thinking about the tall man with Alex, then took a sip of her drink. "Whoa. Double shot. Anyway, she won't listen to me. She's enchanted with this charmer. I'm wondering about her lack of responsibility, which brings me to part two: she's walking away from her exhibit. Her baby. Which leads to part three: we don't have the staff. We can ask Dani and Trev to put in more hours, but . . . wait." Taking another sip. "We need Phillip!"

Sam grinned. "You crack me up. You rant about a problem, and in less than five minutes you have said problem solved, barely coming up for air." He leaned back in his chair and finished his beer. "Glad I could be of some help. I've got to go. Jenny's waiting for me at home. Her folks are in town, and we're meeting them for dinner, which will no doubt lead to something crazy like Club Fugazi or Chinatown. God, I hate doing the tourist thing. Don't they know I've got to work for a living, in order to take care of their princess? Even though she makes more money than I do working for Mr. Attorney Man with hundred-dollar bills shooting out his . . ." Sam looked around. "Ass."

"See you in the morning." Sam left, but Monica kept talking. "I'll call Phillip, then drag my butt home, pour a glass of wine, and whine to myself, since I'm the only one living there!"

Fog on the bay began to roll in, soothing Monica as she walked back to her apartment. Once home, she turned on the gas fireplace, loving the atmosphere the fire brought, making the room alive—as if she weren't alone. She kicked off her shoes and headed to the kitchen for a snack. Stress had become a normal part of her life, and she didn't like it. She didn't eat right, and she'd gained weight. And how ironic that her ex-husband Ben was chef and owner of one of the top restaurants in San Francisco, but she came home to inedible food.

Returning to the living room, she curled up on her white leather sofa, thinking of options to enhance her personal life. Single and thirty-eight gave her pause. *Maybe I should get a cat.* She looked around the room. *And a huge floor plant.* She glanced at her shoes by the front door. *Maybe I should actually go running in those shoes. I could join a health club. Ha! Health club? Yoga. I could do yoga.* She took a sip of wine. *I could sign up for online dating.* She ran with that idea. She'd heard it was safe and candidates were screened well. *Who knows? Maybe it's my turn to meet a Mr. Intelligent Art Man.* With that thought, she fell asleep on the sofa, a half glass of wine still on the coffee table.

Chapter 6

The next morning, Sam entered Monica's office with two cups of espresso. "Your coffee, ma'am."

"Thank you, Sammy."

One thing they'd all agreed on was that a quality espresso machine would be at the ready. A coffee nook in the reception area invited visitors to relax and enjoy a cup and a conversation. Informal, like a Starbucks, but with great art. It also served as a station for exhibit receptions.

The building had a huge open space on the main floor with interior brick walls. Off the gallery was a large room where Dani and Trev created the "magic" for both the gallery and events business. The mezzanine afforded separate offices for Monica and Sam, and another office Joi and Phillip shared. Joi spent most of her time in her home studio creating art, and Phillip worked at a hair salon on Union Square when he wasn't helping out at the gallery.

Even though Sam was the only one in the room, Monica tended to speak as if to a large audience about new information. A sort of TED Talk. "I didn't bring this up yesterday because I was so wound up about the exhibit. Next month's auction in Monterey—I'm assuming Joi will still be in Paris, so we need to push forward on our own." Monica stood and began pacing. "We're in real trouble if we don't pull this auction off in a spectacular way. Being awarded the restoration project for this building and its fundraising event was a coup for us. We can't fail."

Amused, Sam let her rant. He said, "Good news. Phillip called. He's going to free up some time at the salon and help as much as possible. The exhibit will be a piece of cake for him."

"Perfect!" Monica now visualized a giant checklist. "That will give us time to concentrate on the auction in Monterey. Publicity and preliminary PR has been released. We need to firm up the staff working the event and the usual details." She turned to Sam, who had basically stopped listening. He was used to her ranting. "I want this auction to show some class. Not the same predictable event. We need entertainment, building restoration storyboards, women swinging from chandeliers—whatever. And, of course, incredible food and a full bar. Speaking of pizzazz, maybe Phillip could help with the auction as well. He'd love the chance to go to Monterey. What do you think?"

Sam shook his head. "Huh? Oh, yes, sounds good. When he gets here, we'll meet down in the gallery. First things first."

Monica decided to confide in Sam about her latest personal revelation. "Hey, Sam. What do you know about online dating?"

"For who? You?" He flashed her a grin.

Monica flipped her head back, stared at the ceiling, and then at him. "Yes, me. I was thinking about signing up and seeing what happens. I need a diversion in my life."

Sam's smile faded, and he leaned forward.

Monica took a deep breath and continued. "I can't just exist for the gallery. My personal life is . . . well, I don't have one. 'Monica's personal life.' Has a nice ring, don't you think?" She drifted off, fantasizing about romantic dinners, long walks on the beach, impromptu weekends in the wine country.

Sam stood and gave her a hug. "Can't hurt to look into it. Just promise you'll keep me informed of your progress. I want to know exactly who you're dating and . . ."

She squinted at him. "Hey. You're not going to be lurking around while I'm having coffee or a drink with Mr. Intelligent Art Man, are you?"

"Who?"

Not seeing his friends in the gallery, Phillip went upstairs to Monica's office. "Good morning, darlings." He was his usual dapper self, dressed in cream-colored linen slacks, a pale pink silk shirt with a periwinkle scarf draped around his neck, and shiny loafers with no socks. His slightly overweight body could still pull off a classic European style.

"Well, you're looking alert and loaded for bear." Monica smiled.

"Oh, I could never be with a bear. Hairy beasts. I'm more the quiet lamb type."

"Well, get your sweet lamb's tail over here and give me a hug. We've got a ton of work to accomplish in a very short time."

Phillip was eager to work with his friends whenever possible. He was the fourth in the group during their Pratt days but had spent the last few years managing a beauty salon on Union Square. His talent, however, was with art exhibit design and presentation, he managed details down to coordinating what everyone should wear on opening night. Not that anyone followed those instructions, but it was a revealing aspect of his vision.

They all went down to the gallery space, where the artwork still hung from the last exhibit. Phillip said, "Okay. What do we have so far?" He walked to the far end of the room and began sketching and taking notes.

Monica followed Phillip. "Joi has the basic plan. That's all we know at this point." Not completely confident that was the case, she emphasized, "And just to be clear, she's still in charge of this exhibit." She changed her tone and the subject. "Want an espresso?"

Monica sighed, once again, about Joi's decision. Leaving her responsibilities—all on a romantic whim—and knowing so little about the man she seemed to be entrusting her life to. Her safety. Just like that. *Oh God. I could never have children. I can't take the stress.*

Just as Monica was about to call her in-house techies, Dani and Trev, to the meeting, Joi sauntered in looking relaxed and fabulous in her black pantsuit and Jimmy Choo designer heels. Her innate sense of style, gleaned from previous employment at a high-end clothing boutique, showed in her stunning presence now. Even when painting in her studio, she looked chic.

Joi gave Monica a hug. "Phillip's here. What's up?"

"What's up, darling, is that he's taking on your exhibit. I'm still having a hard time with this, you know," Monica whispered. "Your timing is shitty—and that's all I'm going to say." Monica's face reddened; she hadn't meant to come across so abrupt.

"I'm truly sorry. I explained that. But just so you know, I bought my return ticket. I'll only be in Paris for two weeks." Joi squeezed Monica's shoulder and subtly brushed a piece of lint off her jacket. They were so close, except visually. Joi tall, elegant, and calm with long, dark, wavy hair. Monica short, stylish, and definitely carrying the mother-hen gene—organized and in control—with short, spiky hair. Their hairstyles revealed their personalities to a tee.

Monica said, "Fine. But what you can do right now, so I can concentrate on Monterey, is meet with Dani, Trev, and Phillip and get them up to speed. I need to know this is going to work before you leave on your romantic, fun-filled trip to Paris." She smiled and blew her friend a kiss in hopes of calming the churning waters that she herself had caused.

Joi said, "Bringing in Phillip was perfect. He'll make the opening what it needs to be. And it doesn't matter if it was my baby. He's doing the work. Let's let it be his now. Okay?"

"Yes, of course. Sorry." Monica knew she needed to back off.

Monica's thoughts drifted to Alexander the charmer and his associate. Who in the hell were they? She needed answers, but they obviously weren't going to come from Joi—who no doubt didn't know either.

Later, Phillip went up to Monica's office and tapped on the door. "Darling, do you want to hear the fabulous plan we've come up with?" Not waiting for a response, he continued. "Well, I've contacted all six artists who will be represented in the show. Of course, they will be here with their dates and . . . arriving in limos, dressed to the nines."

Monica looked up and said, "Who's paying for that? We're already putting out a lot of bucks just for the basics."

Phillip flipped his hand in the air. "Not to worry. My friend Brandon works for a limo company. He can get us a good deal on three cars—two artists and their dates per car. We also, and I hope this won't be a problem for you, asked Ben to cater from the Purple

Puffin. He was delighted that we asked and will be emailing over some food options. I also think we should have champagne, don't you?"

Before Monica could respond about hiring her ex-husband to provide the food, Phillip continued throwing both arms in the air. "And the flowers. Oh, flowers will be everywhere. Everywhere! I'm thinking all white. Gorgeous against dark aubergine walls."

Monica tried to interject. "It sounds lovely, but—"

He cut her off again. "And finally, the music. Instead of the usual classical ensemble, we should have a soft jazz group. Moody, sexy jazzzzz." Phillip hugged himself and floated into a reverie.

"Phillip, Phillip, Phillip—Hold on! Before you implode. I want you to give Sam a detailed outline, with anticipated expenses, before I even consider saying yes. Please, sweetie. This afternoon. And before you go, would you consider helping us out with the auction next month? It really needs your touch. And it includes a trip to Monterey. What do you think?"

Phillip came out of his reverie with a big grin. "Of course, I'll help you out! What are girlfriends for? Muah!" He blew her an air kiss and left the room, arm held high, waving.

Opening receptions could be as small and pedestrian as cheese and crackers and a fruit plate. Coffee, tea, and fruit punch. This was never the case at Muse Fine Arts Gallery. Never. The type of art being shown dictated the event's decor. Music and catered delectables were geared to the ambience of the event. All staff, which amounted to four, plus Phillip on this particular opening, would be on deck to play host and hostess to the attendees.

Later that afternoon, they all met in Monica's office. Sam presented the details and projected expenses Phillip had given him.

With one minor tweak to the menu and hiring two limos instead of three, Monica signed off. Everyone cheered with a happy dance and left her office and the gallery for the day. Let the weekend begin!

With a good night's sleep, hot shower, and espresso, Monica was ready for a personal change. She would start her diet immediately. Salad, fruit, and yogurt.

Wanting to spend some time with Joi, she gave her a call. "Hey, girl. Want to go for a walk in Golden Gate Park and maybe take in the de Young Museum?"

A little stressed, Joi said, "Oh, I don't know. I've got a ton to do before next week. What do I pack for Paris? Or do I just grab a toothbrush and go shopping when I get there?" She smiled, then changed her mind, thinking Monica probably wasn't smiling. "Yes. Okay. That would be great. I can meet you at the museum in an hour, and we can walk after. I love the Asian exhibit they have going on now. I could see it a hundred times!"

Waiting on the steps of the de Young gave Monica time to think about what was going on. She had known Joi since grade school—a shy and awkward girl—and had stood by her and tried to help her make her way socially. Joi's parents were kind, wonderful people but also extremely protective of her. The decision to attend Pratt had been a big step for Joi in cutting the apron strings, as her parents had wanted her to stay closer to home. Now Paris. Same situation. Joi was standing up for herself.

"Good morning." Joi pulled Monica to her feet. "One of my favorite pieces here is the *Three Attendants* sculpture in the Asian wing. It makes me weep—every time. Let's go to that room first."

Later, stopping for a glass of wine at the museum café, Joi confided that she had done a little research on Alex while in Seattle before her flight home. She'd found that he was indeed respected in the art world for his intelligent and businesslike approach to promoting art and helping galleries, corporations, and private collectors with fine art acquisitions. She didn't know much about Pierre but assured Monica that he was an associate of Alex's and that all was well. At least Monica now had a name for the mysterious but familiar-looking man—Pierre.

"I can't explain it, but I feel totally comfortable with Alex. No inner warning signals about safety. Our evening in Seattle was magical. He treated me with respect and wanted to know all about me and our gallery and my aspirations as an artist." Joi took a sip of wine. "And he told me about his family. Growing up in Paris, his dad with the French Embassy, his mom an artist. And later moving to Washington DC and becoming a part of the art scene." She shook her head and shrugged. "I think he's wonderful." Joi looked at Monica, pleading for her to understand.

Monica said, "I'm happy for you, sweetie. But spending one romantic evening with someone doesn't warrant flying off to a foreign country for two weeks—which in itself is a concern. Your family and friends are here. People you could call if something went terribly wrong." She added, "By the way, this Pierre character. Did he look familiar to you? I saw him for only a moment, but a bell rang. I don't know. Maybe nothing."

"Pierre? Yes, maybe." Joi shrugged. "Anyway, I'm trusting my instincts on this. I promise to stay in touch, especially if I'm not feeling safe. I can always catch the next flight home." She kissed Monica's cheek and smiled. "And thank you for fussing."

"The other thing I wanted to ask you about is the painting you bought. That's quite a chunk of money. Have you done any research on the piece?"

"Not exactly. But it has been authenticated, and Forain is one of my favorite artists. I couldn't resist. I have it hanging on that little wall by the bookshelves. The lighting is perfect."

Monica shook her head. Ever skeptical, she would research the painting herself.

Chapter 7

After a few days meeting with colleagues at several galleries in Portland, San Francisco, and Sausalito, Alex and Pierre arrived at the SFO airport and made their way to the Icelandair check-in kiosk, where they were to meet Joi for the two-p.m. flight to Paris. With Joi busy putting together the art exhibit at her gallery, they hadn't seen each other since Seattle.

Alex adjusted his shirt collar and popped a breath mint. He spotted Joi and stood back a moment and watched, fascinated by her beauty and mannerisms—so elegant but obviously nervous about the trip as she squirmed in her seat.

Joi knew her decision to take this trip was right. The gallery would certainly survive her absence. Closing her eyes and visualizing Paris put her in a dreamy mood—until a screaming child ran past, almost tripping on her carry-on. Back to reality, she pulled her bag closer, rummaged in her purse for mints and her boarding pass, loosened her large white scarf, and began reading the Paris travel guide she had purchased a few days before. She softly pronounced words she knew would be important . . . *Oui, s'il vous plaît, merci, bonjour.* Then, out of the corner of her eye, she saw Alex.

He grinned. "Hello there, beautiful."

Their embrace and slightly innocent kiss felt awkward. Quite different from their romantic night only a short time ago.

She noticed Pierre standing a few feet away just as the call for first-class boarding was announced. She smiled and motioned for him to get in line with them.

He stayed where he was. When the brothers traveled together, they kept their distance. Not walking or sitting together, and getting their own hotel rooms. A habit Alex insisted on should a problem arise regarding their art dealings—to protect Pierre.

Joi held up her small carry-on bag. "As you can see, this is it. Shopping is pretty much at the top of my list when we arrive." She imagined elegant shops and boutiques touting famous designers.

Alex smiled. "I think that can be arranged." He envisioned taking her to the fashion center of Paris—a place she belonged.

Once on board, they settled into buttery-soft gray leather seats and were immediately welcomed with a glass of champagne. And there, next to Alex, finally heading to Paris, she began to relax. A new chapter in her life? Maybe.

Alex took her hand and gently kissed it. "Happy?"

Joi closed her eyes and purred. "Mmm. Yes." She faced him. "Thank you so much for inviting me."

The attendants were friendly, offering more champagne and later bringing steaming damp cloths for cleaning their hands. Beautifully plated meals were served on linen-draped trays, and a nice bordeaux was poured.

They chatted about places to see in Paris, Alex's work schedule, and a little about his childhood in France.

"You must have loved growing up in Paris. Was it hard to leave and move to America?"

"Yes, I did love it. My memories of Paris are mostly of school, friends, piano lessons at Les Harmoniques, and spending time in the country in the summer. Then later studying at the Sorbonne. I was eighteen when we moved to Washington DC."

Joi smiled at Les Harmoniques, visualizing him playing piano. His school uniform of gray wool shorts, white shirt, and dark blue sweater with the school emblem. She turned to him. "Did you have a pet growing up?"

Alex hesitated, not wanting to talk about his childhood. A painful time. Serious now, he said, "We had a wonderful French spaniel named Pétillant. We called her Pet. She was basically my dog, and I loved her. When it was time for us to move, I had to give her away. That was the hardest thing I've ever had to do. My best friend Jacques wanted Pet, so that's where she went to live." Suddenly thinking of his cruel and overbearing father, Alex became quiet, suggesting the conversation was over. "The flight to Reykjavík is a little over eight hours. You should sleep now." He closed his eyes—memories flooded back of his father's abusive ways, not only with family, but also with Pet. *Bastard* crossed his mind.

As Joi slept, Alex continued to reminisce about his childhood. Fond memories of Paris and the countryside, and his beautiful artist mother. They would spend hours hiking around the many vineyards and small villages. She would sit and paint with Pierre as Alex ran off on his own adventures. Memories of his father, however, were not as fond. He was an overbearing man who had little time for his family, but did have time to carry on affairs with other women. Alex had known at a young age that he would eventually break from his father's grip and pursue the life he wanted. After college, his social contacts and business education put him on the track that he found himself on now. He learned the acquisition of art was becoming a commodity, making it easier to find new art collectors willing to purchase without concern for paperwork and auction house appraisal.

Landing in Reykjavík in the middle of the night allowed for a short walk and a peek into elegant boutiques and the airport guest lounge. The walls were illuminated with panels depicting ice caves—tables, chairs, and a bar all solid ice. Joi felt as though she were in an ad for a travel magazine, dressed in fur and sipping icy blue concoctions.

Back on board, she slipped off her shoes and curled up in her seat. Alex reached in his carry-on and pulled out a small package. "I have something for you." He handed the gift to Joi. "It's something you'll need to have with you at all times: *The Little Black Book of Paris*. A guidebook divided into sections by arrondissement, which are areas, or neighborhoods. Each chapter has its own map with listings of places to see, eat, stay, and shop."

"Thank you. So much better than the huge tome I brought." They scanned the pages, looked at maps, and found their hotel in the 8th arrondissement, between the Opéra Garnier and the Jardin des Tuileries. Once again, she snuggled against Alex's shoulder and fell asleep.

A flight attendant announced they would soon land at Charles de Gaulle airport. Joi made her way to the restroom, fluffed her hair, applied a touch of makeup, and finished with a little evian spritzer. She was ready for Paris!

Alex noticed Joi's phone, with the black-striped case, lying on her seat. It must have slipped out of her purse. He tentatively looked toward the restroom then slipped it into his pocket.

Joi returned and smiled at Alex with the look and beauty of a model. Having promised to call Monica when they landed, she dug through her bag for her phone. No phone. "Oh my God. Where's my phone?" She searched between and under the seats.

Alex pretended to be concerned. "Well, that's unfortunate. Don't worry. Once we check in to our hotel, we can buy a smart phone for you."

As they were about to depart the plane, Joi alerted the flight attendant of the missing phone. "My life is on that phone!"

Alex gave his cell number in case it was found.

Joi was stressed as they arrived at the baggage claim area. Alex was tense and quiet. Pierre, as always, stood back as if traveling alone.

"May I borrow your phone, please? I need to call Monica."

Alex hesitated. "What's her number? I'll place the call for you."

Just as Alex began to key in the numbers, a man bumped into him and knocked the phone to the floor near the baggage carousel.

"Hey. *Fais attention!*" Alex said.

The man apologized, bent down, and quickly switched Alex's phone with one he had in his hand. He nodded his apologies and hurriedly walked away. Luckily Alex's phone was still unlocked. He quickly downloaded a hidden spy app on the phone and returned to the baggage area in search of Alex.

"*Monsieur. Excusez-moi.* There may be a problem. Our phones are alike, and I believe I handed you my phone by mistake. *Je suis désolé.* You see, my phone has my initials inscribed on the back right-hand corner. Please check the phone I gave you."

Alex pulled the phone from his pocket and checked for the initials. The letters *MG* were indeed inscribed on the back. A little annoyed, he frowned at the man as they exchanged phones. It was all done so fast that the call to Monica was forgotten. Alex and Pierre retrieved their bags and joined Joi as they all made their way out to the curb and the prearranged Uber.

Joi tried to appear nonchalant, even though she was still stressed about her phone and yet ready to burst with excitement. She hoped Alex would end his grouchiness.

The drive into the city was long and quiet with a typical airport-to-city view and heavy public transportation. Occasionally, Alex would point out the landscape, dotted with typical stone cottages intermixed with small industrial businesses and community restaurants. "Paris, like all big cities, is a mix of small, unique villages. You'll see neighborhoods that look a little different. People dress a little different. And a range of wonderful food aromas unique to their culture."

They arrived at the Hyatt Madeleine in early afternoon. Alex walked around the car to Pierre. "I'll call you later."

Once Alex and Joi entered the hotel, Pierre hailed a cab. "Pecquay, off rue Rambuteau."

The Hyatt lobby was polished with a subtle elegance. Fresh bouquets of lilies and white roses adorned tables and pedestals. Alex went to the front desk to register as Joi stood and admired the decor. A mix of traditional and modern.

Alex said, "Just so you know, I booked us separate rooms." He slung his bag over his shoulder, retrieved Joi's bag in one hand, and reached out for her hand with the other. "Shall we?"

They arrived on the fifth floor and found suite 512. Alex handed Joi her key and bag and said, "Your room, *mademoiselle*." He kissed her cheek and said his room was right down the hall. "Take a nap if you like. We'll meet a little later. I've made dinner reservations at a terrific restaurant." And with that, he strolled down the hall.

Though surprised, Joi was also grateful she had a suite to herself. A romance could go either fast or slow—in any direction.

Her suite was lovely. A terrace and a sitting area with tall windows, and white orchids placed around the room. The furniture, carpet, and duvet were all white. The bathroom had a shower and a separate soaking tub, black-and-white tiled floor, fluffy white towels, and a robe hanging on a bronze hook. As she stood on the terrace mesmerized, she softly whispered, "Paris!"

Not wanting to stay inside, Joi decided to take a walk and search for a place to buy a phone. The concierge directed her to an ATM and an electronics salon a few short blocks away.

Once the phone was loaded with a minutes plan, she called Monica. "Hi there. It's your best friend who happens to be calling from 'Gay Paree.'" Before Monica could respond, she continued. "We just checked into the Hyatt Madeleine. Alex is resting, but I couldn't stand staying inside with this glorious city to explore. I'm out walking around."

"I'm so glad you called," Monica said, blurry-eyed. *This time difference thing is going to be a pain in the ass.*

"How is everything going with the exhibit?" Not waiting for a response, she practically screamed into the phone, "Listen, I lost my phone and I'm freaking out. Please go to my apartment and see if you can find it. I just bought a new phone. Here's the number." Joi continued to walk and talk, exhausted but hyper. In awe of her surroundings and starving.

"You lost your phone? What the hell? Um—exhibit plans are in place. I hate sounding like a parole officer, but please call me every day. I need to know you're okay. Promise?"

"I promise. It's strange, but when I realized I had lost my phone, I asked Alex if I could use his. He said that he would make the call and then hand me the phone. What am I, five? Oh, and to what you're probably thinking, we do have separate suites at the hotel."

Monica fell back to sleep before the call was over.

Unaware, Joi continued talking. "Okay. I'm going across the street to my first Paris café for a glass of wine and a croissant. Talk to you soon. Muah."

Sitting outside at La Palette, Joi soaked in the experience. Crushed together with other singles, couples, and handsome waiters dressed in black slacks and vests, white shirts, and long white aprons. Shops snuggled together in a puzzle of color. Notre-Dame peeked above the trees on Île de la Cité. She felt like she was in a scene from the film *Midnight in Paris*.

A polite young waiter took her order and she replied, "*Bon. Merci beaucoup.*" Speaking to a Frenchman, in Paris, with her limited vocabulary, was beyond exciting.

She walked the streets, absorbing her surroundings. The smells of sweet and savory, the buzz—mostly in French, with an occasional rude comment by a tourist. She couldn't help but grin as she peeked in shops—small and intimate, with an old-world feel—and window displays, tasteful and unique. Classic architecture with brightly painted double doors, iron gates revealing small gardens, and a blanket of cobbled streets throughout the city. Stopping at a small boutique on rue Saint-Denis, Joi made her second purchase—a black beret—and promptly adjusted it on the side of her head. Passing the iconic Centre Pompidou with its colorful industrial-techno facade, she vowed to visit it another day.

Chapter 8

Joi sauntered into the hotel, with the intent of taking a nice long nap. She was immediately confronted by Alex.

"Where have you been? It's not wise for you to go off by yourself."

Stunned, she said, "Well, I went for a walk. I bought a phone and called Monica. I stopped at a café." Lowering her voice, she added, "And why, exactly, are you so angry?"

Alex softened. "I'm sorry. I feel responsible for you, that's all. Do you want to walk somewhere? Get something to eat?" He noticed her hat and smiled. "Very charming on you." It always amused him that first-time visitors to Paris found it imperative to purchase and wear a beret. He reached over and made a slight adjustment. "There."

She cocked her head and fluttered her eyelashes playfully. "Thank you. With the long flight and the excitement of being here, I think I need to rest for a bit. And I want to shower and change."

Alex said, "Of course. It's three o'clock now. Why don't we say six! Call me when you're ready. By the way, what's the number to your new phone?"

She gave him the number, nonchalantly kissed his cheek, and headed up to the fifth floor, feeling slightly *puissant*—powerful.

Joi stretched and rolled over in bed. It was five o'clock, and the room had taken on a lovely golden glow. She added lavender oil to her bath and laid out her one nice outfit. A simple emerald-green silk shift and black linen low-heeled shoes. She definitely needed to shop the next day.

Her phone rang. "*Bonjour*, Alex. Yes, I'm revived and starving. Will Pierre be joining us?"

"No. He has other plans." He hesitated. "I'm working on something. Give me fifteen minutes. See you in the bar downstairs."

Alex entered La Chinoiserie and found Joi by the fountain. She looked lovely as she sipped her wine and perused the guidebook he had given her. She smiled at her accomplishment as she mouthed words. Yes. She was the right choice for this trip. The perfect attraction for his art dealings. Playful, confident, intelligent—and slightly naive.

He approached and kissed her cheek. "Are you studying for your exams?" he teased.

"*Mais oui.* Where are we going for dinner?"

"I made reservations at a lovely restaurant called Verjus. You will love it."

"Sounds wonderful. I'm a little hungry now—"

"Of course." Alex loved her enthusiasm and innocence, loved the idea of showing her his Paris. "Wine and a snack you shall have." He admonished himself. *Be careful. Don't fall for her.*

They arrived at Verjus a little early, entering through the downstairs lounge off Passage de Beaujolais. The small, intimate, dimly lit bar with its rounded brick ceiling was packed with patrons waiting to be seated upstairs. Alex ordered chardonnay as they settled onto their barstools.

Joi had sensed sadness when they spoke earlier about Alex's childhood. Not something she would soon bring up again. "Will you be working tomorrow? We haven't talked much about what you will be doing here and why you invited me. I'm intrigued." She blushed, embarrassed at her own naivete.

Alex half smiled and nodded. "Well, my business is buying and selling art, as you know. I work with auction houses, mostly here in Paris." He took her hand. "I thought you, as an artist, would love to see this incredible city and spend time in the museums and galleries. I enjoy your company and would like to get to know you better. Very uncomplicated." He kissed her hand and said playfully, "I don't usually pick up girls and whisk them off to Paris, you know. I met you and thought you would love it. That's all."

"What about Pierre? Who is he, exactly?"

Alex hesitated. "Pierre and I have known each other for many years. He's my business partner and an extremely fine artist. I do what I can to promote his work."

"So, if he's your business partner, what—"

"Time to go upstairs. Our table will be ready."

They entered the dining room by way of a circular metal staircase from the bar below. Three crystal chandeliers bounced soft lighting off the white walls, tall windows, and stemware, adding elegance to the room. Everything was white—candles and small bouquets of flowers graced each linen-draped table, and large arrangements of lilies sat on pedestals throughout the room.

Alex explained how the meal would be served. "Verjus only offers an eight-course tasting menu, with appropriate wine served with each course. The portions are small, and the length of the meal long, to allow for digestion. Such a lovely way to eat, don't you think? Notice the other diners enjoying each bite and savoring the moment. The French respect their food and wine. Conversation is quiet and intimate. Sensuous."

The meal began with the first course: a cold soup of tomato, melon, and cucumber, beautifully served with a single nasturtium on top. The wine, a chilled vouvray.

Next, *escargot* with grilled carrot and lemon, perfectly paired with Grand Cru Riesling. Joi hummed with delight. Tasting a variety of wines was a new experience. At home, buying a bottle of wine on sale at Safeway was the norm.

Alex watched as she tentatively took her first-ever *escargot* out of its shell, closed her eyes, and took a bite. Wide-eyed, she gulped it down and sipped the last of her wine.

As they discussed their plans for the next few days, Alex leaned forward and whispered, "I want to show you everything. You belong here in Paris."

A waiter appeared and removed their plates and wineglasses. Behind him a young waitress announced the next dish. "Scallops, mozzarella, *cédrat* with black truffle." She placed the small plates in front of them along with a sliced sourdough baguette and salted butter. Cuvée Raipoumpou was poured into fresh glasses.

As they gazed at each other, Alex smiled, stabbed a scallop, and eased it into Joi's mouth. Feeling warm and playful, she took a small piece of baguette, slathered it with butter, nibbled the crust, and then pressed it into his mouth.

They sipped their wine, leaned into each other, and chatted about everything, about nothing—it didn't matter. The evening was enchanting.

Potatoes, watercress, marrow, and caviar were served next, and soon after, wild trout with beetroot and almonds. The chosen wine, Corbières Clair.

Every bite and sip were luxurious, beautiful, and opulent. And Joi was feeling all of that.

The waitress appeared with pork, pickled peppers, and spring onions. She poured Doucinello into their glasses, then brought Chaource cheese, sourdough crackers, and onion confit.

The finale, and the night's most exquisite dish, consisted of summer berries, yogurt sorbet, and *gâteau d'entonnoir*. Muscato was served in small chilled glasses. They slowly fed each other bites and sipped the last of their wine. A perfectly glorious meal in the City of Lights!

"Such a lovely evening. I want to walk and see the magic of Paris at night." Floating on the experience of culinary perfection, more wine than she was used to, and the undeniable attraction she felt for Alex, Joi leaned into him as they strolled toward the Seine. Passing the Louvre, they approached the Pont des Arts, and right there before their eyes, the Eiffel Tower, glittering and pulsing with golden light in sync with Joi's heart. Tears welled in her eyes as she turned to Alex, held his face, and kissed him hard and long.

The morning sun streamed through the windows like a golden dream. Joi rolled over and saw Alex asleep beside her. She snuggled closer and fell back to sleep. *Alex.*

Later that morning, Alex entered her room, dressed and ready for the day. "Hey, sleepyhead. It's almost noon. Get your sweet self up, and I'll take you to lunch before the Louvre."

Groggy and jet-lagged, Joi was not ready to leave her newly christened magical bed. "Mmm. What? What time is it? Why are you dressed?" She stretched out her arm. "Come back to bed." Memories of last night made her feel warm and tingly as she stretched her long legs around the covers. Lovemaking with Alex was like nothing she had ever experienced. Ever.

Amused, he slowly repeated, "It's almost noon. And I'm dressed because I'm taking you to the Louvre." He threw the covers off her, pulled her to her feet, and kissed her forehead. "I'll get you a latte."

Revived from her shower, Joi looked at herself in the mirror and giggled. "The Louvre, for God's sake." She pointed at her reflection. "You, my dear, are going to see the *Mona Lisa!*" She dressed in the only other outfit she had brought but decided against the beret, remembering that Alex seemed to smirk at it yesterday.

They lunched on foie gras, grilled bass, salad, and chardonnay at Café Marly, adjacent to the Louvre. Joi couldn't keep her eyes off Alex. He was so comfortable with himself and with her. They sat close and found subtle moments to touch, both savoring the intimacy of the previous evening. Lunch was delicious, the atmosphere beautiful, the company sublime.

She wondered where this relationship was going. She would only be in Paris a few days.

Smiling, Alex reached over and brushed her cheek. "Let's go."

The lines for the museum were unbelievably long. Joi thought this visit was probably not going to happen today. Standing in awe of the enormity of the Louvre and the famous glass pyramid designed by I. M. Pei, she stood like one of the stone statues before her, unable to move.

Alex took hold of her hand and whisked her past the long line of visitors waiting to enter. As they reached the attendant at the gate, Alex flashed his badge.

The gatekeeper smiled and nodded. "Nice to see you, Mr. Marshal."

And that was it. They went in, grabbed a map, and headed to the many galleries. Room after room, staircases, hallways, every surface and pedestal filled with amazing art. Pieces she had seen only in her art history studies at Pratt.

As they climbed the Daru staircase that highlighted the marble statue of the winged goddess Nike, Alex said, "It would take a lifetime to see it all. Take it slow, savor the moment, and come back every day if you want. Study your map and make a plan for your next visit."

After an hour and a half of viewing extraordinary art, accompanied by Alex's extensive knowledge of the artists, Joi said, "I'm overwhelmed. Every corner I turn, I'm looking at art I've seen only in a classroom or my parents' collection of art books. They would love this." She thought of them and felt sad. They could easily afford to visit Paris, but their frugal ways wouldn't allow it. She reached out her arm to Alex and said with a theatrical flourish, "Take me to the *Mona Lisa!*"

They made their way to the Denon wing, where the famous painting was on display. Smaller than she had imagined, it was barely visible through the tiers of visitors standing before it, all taking photos with their phones raised high. She noticed one smiling young man toward the front. He was facing the crowd, taking a picture of all of them taking a picture of Mona. It was a ridiculously funny scene. Joi raised her phone and took his picture as he waved at her.

They strolled the Jardin des Tuileries adjoining the Louvre. Benches, sculptures, and fountains were surrounded by well-manicured gardens in full bloom with the promise of the Arc de Triomphe in the distance. They walked past vendor after vendor selling small paintings, old books, scarves, bags, and T-shirts—not unlike any tourist town in America, or the world. But this was Paris, and chic, and somehow so much better. Down the steps to the Seine, they saw river barges converted to houseboats lining the shore. Many with whimsical herb and flower gardens, patio chairs and umbrellas arranged on top. Tour boats drifted, runners jogged, and lovers sat on benches, content with their place in the world.

Joi took Alex's hand. "Let's stop for wine and . . ." She hesitated. "*Casse-croûte.*" I'm not ready to go back to the hotel just yet."

Alex smiled at Joi's penchant for *le grignotage*—snacking.

Walking arm in arm in the direction of their hotel, they stopped at Café de la Paix. Alex said, *"Rosé, s'il vous plaît, et fromage."*

Chapter 9

On opening night of the X6 exhibit, the gallery looked fabulous with freshly painted accent walls in deep plum, an almost black hue. Large bouquets of white magnolias were strategically placed around the room, and overstuffed furniture had been arranged in intimate seating areas. Servers were ready to work the room with trays of champagne and hors d'oeuvres. Phillip's attention to detail, right down to the multicolored feather pen at the guestbook table. It was the perfect backdrop for the edgy works by the six new artists—everything from panels splashed with bright, textured paint to smaller, more intimate landscapes. Traditional sculptures next to an installation hanging from the ceiling, with canvas, chains, and torn strips of paint rags.

"Doors open in fifteen, darlings." Phillip passed through the room, adjusting flowers, napkins, and Sam's collar.

Monica and Sam grinned. They adored Phillip.

"I took Joi to the airport this morning. She's beyond excited. She promised to keep in touch." Monica rambled on. "I'm really happy for her. A little envious. Kind of worried . . ."

Sam didn't respond. He was okay with Joi's Paris adventure but preferred to keep the focus of their conversation on the exhibit that was about to open.

"Now we wait." Sam said, looking around the gallery. "Wait and pray this show is a success. Doors open at six. Phillip instructed Brandon to have the limos arrive at exactly six fifteen. A grand entrance by the artists and their escorts."

"Nice touch, Phillip!" Monica was delighted with the look of the gallery. "Joi would have loved this. I'll text her some photos. She'll like that."

Sam looked hesitantly at Monica. "I forgot to tell you: Ben donated the hors d'oeuvres from the Purple Puffin. He insisted."

"Yes, Phillip told me. That was generous. I'll call him tomorrow."

Monica and Ben's breakup had been hard on both of them. Separate career demands—his with the restaurant, hers with the gallery and events business—simply didn't allow time for a stable relationship, a strong marriage, or a family. They continued to support each other, and the love remained, but the time and attention did not.

On this balmy Friday night, the doors opened to several regular gallery patrons. The usual suspects, attending to admire and partake of food and drink, but not necessarily to purchase art. They were like props in a play, and they gave the gallery interest for the passers-by. Others began to arrive, and soon the place was buzzing with activity and conversation. Per Phillip's instructions, the two limos arrived at exactly six fifteen, and the X6 exhibit was officially underway.

The artists were dressed in wonderfully bizarre styles—some in boots, leather jackets, and multi-strands of jewelry, all with carefully revealed tattoos. Others in bright, painterly outfits to match color-streaked and spiked hair. As they sashayed in, the jazz combo upped its tempo, and the gallery exploded with applause. Patrons were delighted with the fanfare, the food and champagne—so delighted, in fact, they gladly opened their wallets, swiped their credit cards, and added to their personal art collections.

All of the artists stood next to their work, engaging patrons in conversation, answering questions, and wowing them with stories of creation, from start to finish.

Sam was in the process of selling one of the new pieces. A six-foot-tall sculpture depicting what the artist described as *Urban Angst*. He expressed his enthusiasm not only as a salesman but more importantly as an artist and sculptor himself. "I can't tell you the time and effort that goes into creating a piece of this size and complexity. I'm personally in awe of his work. You have made a wonderful choice."

Monica smiled as she observed Sam. She made her way over to him just as the customer drifted away.

"We do have a successful event here, Mr. Robson." Monica handed him a glass of champagne. "You are an excellent salesman."

Sam beamed. "You know, even with all the planning and hard work, you never know until the doors open—and the wallets as well."

It was late, nearly eleven, by the time Monica locked the gallery doors and Ben's team cleared away the remaining food and wine. Ben had also arranged for three servers to work all evening, giving Monica, Sam and Phillip the needed time to mingle with guests and promote the art. The opening had definitely been a success. Every artist sold five or more pieces, with an additional two commissions. Good for them and good for the gallery.

Trev and Dani, their two behind-the-scenes gurus, left as soon as was appropriate. They were booked to play music at a small club down the street from the gallery. Playing music, no matter what time of night, was their real passion.

Phillip hung around with Monica and Sam until Brandon came by in his limo to whisk him off to a club in North Beach. Monica sat rubbing her feet and holding an empty champagne glass. She asked Sam to share the rest of the bottle as they discussed the opening.

"I'll go over the receipts and expenses tomorrow. I think tonight's take has us back in the black—big time. Probably our most successful exhibit to date."

They had decided to extend the exhibit, mostly due to Joi's absence. It would give them a breather and a chance to schedule other smaller events that could easily be handled with the four of them, and Phillip when possible.

Monica gave Sam a sleepy, boozy grin. "Sleep in tomorrow. Trev said he would open at eleven. I'm going to work from home and get my head around Monterey and what's left to do for the auction. I can tell you, I'm ready for some time off. Let's talk about that next week. I haven't had me-time in forever."

They locked up and Sam gave her a hug. "Yes, my dear, you do need some time off. Think about what you want to do. Where you want to go. We'll plan around that, and maybe Joi will be back by then. It will be fine."

"Okay. Give me a call tomorrow. I want some good financial news."

Jenny was on the sofa reading when Sam unlocked the door. She glanced at him over her reading glasses. "Hey, sweetie." Then at her watch. "It's nearly midnight. Must have been a successful opening." She got up and gave him a hug. "Tell me everything. Want some wine?"

"Good God, no. I've had enough champagne to warrant an arrest for impersonating a Frenchman. Whatever that means. And, yes, it was successful. Why are you still up and what are you reading?"

"I'm still up because I wanted to see you and hear about the exhibit. The one you've been working your ass off, for two weeks, in the absence of 'Princess Joi.'" She smiled and waved the book. "And this book is telling me all I need to know about scam artists, forgers, hucksters, and flimflam men. Remember the bar exam? The one I'm taking in less than a month?" She gave a dramatic roll of the eyes.

They looked at each other and burst out laughing. Sam grabbed her hand. "Let's go to bed. I'm too beat to think. Too beat to talk. But not to beat to . . ."

The next morning, Jenny woke to the sound of Sam humming an off-tune version of "Never Gonna Give You Up," a mid-'80s tune by Rick Astley. She groaned and pulled the covers over her head. *Sammy!*

Chapter 10

Joi awakened to thoughts of possibilities. Shopping first. Slacks, dresses, tops, shoes, boots, bags, and lingerie.

Her daydreaming was interrupted by her ringtone. Alex. He'd been with her all night—a very romantic night—but then told her he had some work to do and left early.

"Good morning. Are you dressed? Do you want breakfast? I have our day planned. Wear something stylish and meet me downstairs. And, please, hurry."

He was off the phone before she could tell him she had shopping plans. A little frustrated, she showered, piled her hair up in a loose bun, and put on the stylish green silk dress she'd worn at dinner and a pair of black pumps. Just as she checked her bag to make sure she had her phone, it rang again. "Yes, I'm hurrying. What? I'm on my way down right now."

Joi felt like she was being pulled in a million directions. Wake up. Get up. Eat. Hurry. Don't hurry. Be sexy. Sleep. Shower. Call me. And—dress stylish? *Who am I, Minnie Mouse?* Joi was grateful to be here in Paris and for Alex's generosity. She knew he bought and sold art, but not much else. He was moody at times but then extremely sweet and romantic. As she waited for the elevator, she fantasized about why he'd invited her. *What's his plan?* She laughed to herself and decided to make an adventure of her circumstances, recalling when, as a shy young girl, she would sometimes pretend to be a spy, collecting facts in a journal. Now she could jot down notes and take photos with her phone. Alex would think she was only being touristy.

He was waiting in the lobby and smiled as she approached. Looking her up and down, he asked, "Didn't you wear that dress the other night?"

Joi held back a snide remark and coyly said, "Well, yes, I did. Thank you for noticing. I remember telling you I didn't pack extra clothes and that I planned to shop the minute I got here. I would like to do that as soon as possible, if you can free up some time for me to do so." She smiled, playfully batting her eyelashes and giving him a quick kiss.

"Yes, of course. Later. Let's have something to eat first, and I'll tell you about our day."

They left the Hyatt and walked to one of Alex's favorite restaurants, Angelina. The decor and ambience were nothing short of seductive. Cream-colored walls, chandeliers, white linen—decadence at every turn. The hostess invited them to follow her to a table by the window with a view of rue de Rivoli. At a little after ten, the sidewalk was filling with the usual vendors displaying their paintings and wares, as well as visitors out for an early walk, starting what would be a long day of sightseeing, shopping, and consumption of fabulous food and wine.

Joi ordered quiche and a small fruit salad, and Alex his favorite, croque monsieur. "And two *cafés. Merci.*"

Still focused and businesslike, he said, "We're meeting a potential client this evening for dinner at the brasserie Bofinger. I've come across a small Chagall he may be interested in." He took her hand and kissed it. "I need for you to be charming. Give him your full attention."

Joi bristled, her cheeks flushing. Leaning in, she whispered. "What's going on? You asked me on this trip to . . . to charm other men? Explain, Alex. Now!"

"Joi. No. Of course not." He softened. "Listen. I'm in a world that attracts wealthy people looking for expensive art. I've been successful for many years. I know what I'm doing and how it works. You can be an integral part of the process simply by being here. Being your beautiful, sexy, and charming self. That's it. It's no different than what you do in your gallery with an art opening. You add pizzazz. Wine, music, hors d'oeuvres. Well, you're the pizzazz here. But if you would rather not, that's totally okay. I'm sorry for being so insensitive."

She calmed down and sighed. She knew he was right. Of course, he was right. He obviously knew how to work it. And of course, this would be the first thing she would write in her "spy notes." A little smile crossed her lips.

Chapter 11

Monica was waiting for David Waters to come by with paperwork concerning the restoration of the gallery building. A longtime friend, art collector, and historic preservation board member, his influence was key for the project. He was able to cut through red tape and get permission for them to proceed. The upcoming auction in Monterey was the final push for funding. David walked in just as she pulled up a spreadsheet on her computer.

"Good morning, David. Thanks for coming by. Here are the latest figures for the project. Take a look, I'll get you a coffee."

Monica returned and found David peering at a small painting on the wall.

"This is wonderful. Who's the artist?"

"Joi painted that for my birthday a couple of years ago. One of my favorite things."

"Your figures are spot on, by the way. I'm impressed with your organization."

"Well, organizing is *my* artistic talent." Monica paused then changed the subject. "David, in your many years of collecting art, have you heard of an art agent by the name of Alexander Marshal?"

He turned and looked at her with a start. "Have I heard of him? Yes, you could say that. I've been on his trail for a possible forgery scam. I can't prove anything yet. Why do you ask? Has he scammed you too?"

"Wait a minute. You're in publishing. What do you mean you're on his trail?" Monica nearly lost it, thinking of Joi and her involvement with Alex. "Forgery?!"

Surprised but not understanding her reaction, he continued. "Yes, I own a publishing company, but you know my time there is limited. My love of art is what I focus on now. Finding the obscure masterpiece to add to our collection." He nodded to the computer. "And helping with projects like this."

Monica wanted more information and fast. "Okay. You bought a forgery? How do you know? I'm confused."

"No, not me. An attorney friend of mine. We don't know for sure. Someone made a convincing comment about a small detail with the painting in question. He suggested that it be researched. My friend, who is not an expert or even interested in art, blew a gasket. I'm betting more for show than anything. This all took place at a dinner party he was hosting. Later, he asked if I would help. He hadn't bothered to inquire about the painting's authenticity papers. Actually, it was his wife who made the purchase on a trip to Paris a couple of years ago. Lots of money and pretense in that family, but not a lick of sense. It seems Alex is the ultimate pro. Covers his tracks."

"But why are you involved?"

"Oh, I don't know. Boredom. Time on my hands. Helping a friend."

Monica sat down, light-headed. Taking a deep breath, she explained, "Listen, David. Joi met this Alexander character at the recent auction in Seattle. She actually bought a painting from him. He apparently swept her off her feet—and into bed, I might add—then asked her to join him in Paris, along with his associate. I'm worried sick for her, and even more so now. Forgery?"

"And the plot thickens." David relaxed into a chair. "Let me add more. As I'm a known collector, Alex contacted me last week. Claims he recently discovered a small Chagall and asked if I would be interested. I said yes and told him I would be in Paris on business and could meet at his convenience."

"Do me a favor and call Joi when you arrive? Don't mention anything about the forgery. I'm not sure where her head is right now with Alex. I don't think she's actually using her head. She would think your calling was a social coincidence. Check in on her, please. Dinner, maybe?"

"Sounds good. In fact, this might make investigating the bastard easier. I'm curious though. You're pretty upset. What's going on?"

"Forgery is what's going on!" She took a breath and sat down, thinking back. "Something happened in our family several years ago. My uncle—my mom's brother—got in a mess concerning forgery. Our family bailed him out, and it nearly broke us financially. He ended up in jail for a while. I was young when it happened, but it made such an impression on me. My parents recovered, but they pretty much disowned my uncle. I have no idea where he is. And I don't care."

"I'm so sorry. I understand completely." He gave her a hug and assured her he would be sensitive to the situation, keeping this current information private.

"Here's Joi's new cell number." Shaking her head, she said, "David, my disgust, my abhorrence with forgery—it's every gallery's nightmare." She let out a sigh. "Call me anytime. Day or night."

David didn't tell Monica he had retained a private investigator. In fact, he had just gotten word that the man had successfully planted a bug in Alex's phone at the Paris airport. Now he'd wait and see what the bug would reveal.

Monica called Joi for a casual chat. "Hey. It's me. How are things in Paris?" Before Joi could reply, she continued enthusiastically, "Listen, David Waters was just here and mentioned he was on his way to Paris in a couple of days. Anyway, I took the liberty of giving him your phone number. Kat may join him in a week or so. I hope you don't mind. Maybe meet for dinner? Whatever."

"Monica. I've been here three days, and I've had maybe three hours to myself, not counting sleep. Alex has every second scheduled, and so far, none of it has included shopping or exploring the city. We did visit the Louvre yesterday afternoon and had a lovely dinner last night. But he just called, announcing I should dress up and meet him downstairs immediately."

"Well, what can I say? I still feel uneasy about him." Moving the topic away from Alex, the possible criminal, Monica continued. "Anyway, hope you get to see David. And I want to report that your exhibit was an absolute success. I'll text you a few pictures in a minute. Phillip really outdid himself. I would love to hire him full-time. We can discuss that when you come home. Have fun today. Keep me posted, sweetie."

Monica felt exhausted.

Joi was exhausted.

Monica's thoughts turned to Ben. She dialed his number. "Hey, Ben. I wanted to thank you for your generous contribution to the X6 opening. Fabulous! And the staff was top-notch. They kept the guests in good spirits—and in the spirits." She laughed at her little pun. "And the opening was a huge success for the artists as well."

"Great. Always happy to help out. Hey, I was thinking maybe we could meet for lunch soon. Someplace other than the Purple Puffin." He chuckled. "I need variety in my diet."

"Great. We can discuss your food plan for the auction. Also, I might have a problem with the venue. How about lunch tomorrow?" Ben agreed, and with that she hung up, feeling even more emotional than she'd expected. She knew she still loved him.

Chapter 12

Joi and Alex finished their meal at Angelina and strolled to the chocolate boutique area of the restaurant. Joi was captivated by the beautifully wrapped boxes with brown satin ribbons; the tin containers of cocoa; the most scrumptious bonbons, macarons, and *éclair chocolat*; and their specialty, the Mont-Blanc.

She absently fingered the ribbons on the boxes. Baiting Alex: "Are we meeting up with Pierre? I haven't seen him since we arrived. He's so quiet and reserved." She noticed Alex tensing a little.

"No," he said a little too abruptly but didn't elaborate, then caught himself and relaxed. "We have some time before meeting the client about the Chagall." Playfully, he turned to her and added, "Would you like to visit another museum? Or perhaps do a little . . . shopping?" He smiled at her, knowing that it was important to keep her happy. And he was beginning to love making her happy.

Her eyes widened. "Yes, please. Maybe the shops on Rambuteau or Les Halles?" The two places she had read about in her new travel book.

"We only have a few hours to shop and then back to the hotel to drop off packages and change if you want. Maybe you'll find the perfect outfit for this evening." He kissed her forehead and lingered a moment, inhaling her perfume—Shalimar—then flagged a cab. "Triangle d'Or."

The entire fashion district was right out of the pages of *Runway* and *Elle* magazines—beautiful flagship boutiques, clothing displays, and shoppers that looked like runway models.

Joi was savvy to fashion and high-end boutiques, but this was Paris, and a little daunting. She looked at her reflection in a shop window and tucked a strand of hair behind her ear, wanting to look tastefully appropriate.

Alex, obviously familiar with the area, said, "Let's start with Dior and Nina Ricci and then Prada. If you don't find what you want, we move on to Yves Saint Laurent, Hermès, and Chanel." He loved watching her reaction. Something wonderful was happening to him. Not his plan, but it was happening nonetheless. He took her hand and guided her to Dior.

The entrance was pale gray with white accents and double French doors. They were greeted and immediately offered champagne. The clerk asked Joi her dress size and what she was looking for, then retreated to the back room. Joi strolled around the shop, caressing satin sleeves, cashmere shawls, and lace-trimmed camisoles. The clerk returned and asked them to be seated for a showing of several outfits they had in Joi's size. Three models emerged and paraded a selection of nine altogether.

Alex loved watching Joi's reaction to the presentation. The Chagall, the client, and the dinner engagement were almost forgotten.

Chapter 13

Monica hadn't shared with Sam the extent of her concerns regarding Joi or the fact that David was now involved via his own personal connection to Alex and the forgery scam. At some point, she would need Sam's assistance.

Overwhelmed by the current revelation in Joi's "Paris Affair," she still had to focus on the Monterey event and the restoration project. She suspected it was like a movie producer in charge of three extravaganzas all at the same time.

She called Sam and told him there would be a slight deviation from the original plans but they could work it out Monday morning. "And Sam, we really need to hire Phillip full-time. The sooner the better. Let's make it happen."

Sam said, "Great!" He had no idea what was about to come down with the rest of Monica's concerns—specifically David's quest to expose Alex.

Chapter 14

After three hours of perusing the elegant shops, Joi announced her credit card was "on fire" and needed a break. She was floating on air, Alex right there with her.

They returned to the hotel, both carrying several bags and boxes containing items she would wear for a very long time. Classic and chic, to fit her ever-emerging style and persona in the art world. What better place than Paris to become that woman?

Alex looked at the bags, smiled, and shook his head. "Oh, what will you wear? Surprise me. I'll order champagne to be sent up to your room. I need to pick up some paperwork and change myself. Back in an hour." He kissed her cheek, lingered for a moment, and left her room.

The evening sky and the lights of Paris, once again, gave her room a golden glow. She turned on the fireplace and slipped into the bath, grateful for the break and some time alone. She knew love and romance were two different things, but this was worth pursuing. This felt like love.

Looking at several outfits arranged on the bed, she knew tonight was showtime. Sexy and charming. She chose a lace shift dress—the one with the dropped cap sleeves she'd purchased at Chanel. Alex liked the nude fabric against the bronze tone of her skin. She added open-toed leather pumps purchased at Prada. The treasure was the necklace Alex had given her that afternoon. A single strand of pink pearls with a rose gold clasp. She pulled her hair up off her neck in a casual French twist—simple and sophisticated. Just as she touched up her mascara, there was a knock on the door.

"Champagne, *mademoiselle*." The attendant wheeled in a beautifully displayed cart with champagne in an ice bucket, two crystal flutes, a small bowl of caviar with crème fraîche, and buttered baguette slices on the side.

She thanked him, wondering if she should offer a tip.

He saw her attempt to pull euros from her purse and politely responded, "*Non, mademoiselle.* The gentleman has taken care of everything."

Alex walked in as the waiter was leaving. He was about to say they had only a short time before they needed to leave, but seeing Joi, he stopped mid-thought . . .

"You like?" she said as she slowly turned in a seductive and playful twirl.

"*Tu es magnifique!*" he said, flushed as he gazed at her in awe.

She smiled and nodded toward the champagne. "Would you do the honors?"

He continued to stare, then said, "Oh. Yes." Composing himself, he turned to open the bottle.

"Tell me again about this evening and the man we're going to meet for dinner."

"He's a potential buyer from San Francisco. I believe he's in the publishing business. We'll find out more this evening."

Joi perked up. "What's his name?"

"David Waters." Alex turned away from her again to pour the champagne.

Joi was stunned. Her intuition told her not to say anything about knowing David. Odd. Confusing. Hopefully, she would have the chance to ask David not to reveal their acquaintance. Not until she knew what was going on. During their shopping spree, she had purchased a small leather-bound journal in which to jot down her spy notes. She slipped it into her bag just as her phone rang.

"Joi? Hi. It's David Waters. I hope I'm not disturbing you. I just arrived in Paris, and Monica asked that I contact you. Perhaps we could meet for a drink or dinner while I'm here. At your convenience, of course."

Joi pretended that Monica was on the phone and motioned to Alex that she would be out on the terrace with the call.

She whispered into the phone, "David, I can't talk. Just listen to me. I—we . . . I'm with Alex Marshal, and we're having dinner with you this evening. You must pretend not to know me when we're introduced. I can't explain now, but it's imperative that our meeting be viewed as the first time. My role in this meeting is to woo you. Just go along with it. I have a strong suspicion something is going on here. And it's not good. I have to go. See you soon." She composed herself and returned to a waiting Alex, who had champagne in one hand and toast with caviar in the other.

"Everything okay?" Alex came near and gently kissed her lips, then proceeded to take a bite of caviar before easing the rest into her mouth.

David slipped on his gray linen jacket and straightened the purple silk tie he'd purchased earlier that day. He smiled to himself. The anger he'd felt the last couple of years over the forgery scam was now beginning to be a caper—and a fun one at that. Odd. And he was delighted with Joi's innocence. She obviously didn't know why he was in Paris other than to look at a painting Alex had for sale. Okay. Let the show begin!

"Time to go, lovely lady. We don't want to be late," Alex said.

Mentally taking a deep breath, Joi gathered her bag and white silk shawl. "Let's go."

They arrived at Bofinger *en retarde*—a few minutes late. David was already seated at a table under the lavish stained-glass cupola. As they approached, he stood and smiled at the sight of Joi. She stood back a little from Alex, smiled, and shook her head with a finger to her lips in a silent *shh*.

"David. So nice to meet you. I'd like to introduce my friend and associate, Joi Pascale."

David took her hand and kissed it while playfully looking into her eyes.

Joi tensed. "Have you been waiting long, David?"

"I just arrived." He glanced around the room. "This is wonderful. I've been to Paris several times, but amazingly, I've never been here." David was enjoying the moment. Playacting with a dear friend and a suspected forger. He almost laughed out loud.

The waiter arrived at their table. "*Bonsoir*, and welcome to Bofinger. May I bring you something to drink?"

Familiar with the restaurant, Alex took charge. "*Oui, monsieur*, kir royales for the table. *Merci*."

Alex explained that Bofinger was something of an institution. "Originally a café for the working class, it was the first bar in Paris to offer beer on tap." He pointed to the cupola above them. "And the decor was influenced by the Belle Époque era."

The waiter returned. With a flourish, he served Joi first, placing a coupe filled with ice-cold champagne in front of her. A subtle garnet of *crème de cassis* settled at the bottom of the glass.

Alex ordered *foie gras de canard* for them to share. "*Et sauternes. Merci.*"

"Sadly, the sauternes has run out, but we have a lovely loupiac, not on the menu, that *monsieur* might enjoy." He smiled. "It is what the kitchen keeps for themselves, but I think I might persuade three glasses from them."

Amused, Alex accepted the offer. "*Merci.*"

David raised his glass. "Here's to new friends, fine art, and the magic of Paris." They clinked their glasses—"*Santé*"—and continued with small talk. "How was your trip? Which airline? Where are you staying? What are your plans?"

David turned to Joi and pretended to flirt a little, replying to their polite inquiries, "I'm staying at the Westin near rue de Rivoli. No definite plans other than one business meeting in a couple of days."

"That's quite close to our hotel," Alex said. "We can all meet at a café in the morning. Angelina is right next to you. They serve a delightful *petit déjeuner.*"

"Sounds good, as long as Joi is joining us." He gave her a sly smile. "And I'm so looking forward to seeing the Chagall." David didn't press for more information as to their plans. He wanted Alex to stay in charge.

The waiter soon returned with an artful presentation of foie gras, pinot noir jelly, dried figs, and toasted slices of brioche.

Joi felt uneasy playing her role in this scenario; too many unknowns were involved. After eating a small portion of food, she excused herself and found her way to the WC near the entrance. Tearing a page from her notebook, she wrote a message to David. *We need to talk. I'll call you later at your hotel.*

Both men stood as she returned to her seat. She slipped the note under the table, tapping David's knee. He casually slid it in his pocket.

Alex turned to her. "I apologize, but I took the liberty of ordering for you."

Joi was not surprised.

"*Choucroute Royale*, which is roasted lobster. I've had it here many times. One of my favorites." To accompany the dish, he ordered a *vin blanc de Mâcon* for Joi.

David chose roasted chicken and scanned the wine menu.

Alex ordered a grilled rib steak and suggested, "We can share a bottle of a good Rhône if you like, David."

"Good idea. Might I suggest a 2015 Beaucastel Hommage *à Jacques Perrin*?" David's eyes twinkled—he knew it cost around €400.

Alex glanced at him and laughed out loud. "Let's do it!"

David was amused by Alex's take-charge attitude; he saw for the first time what made him a successful art agent. Whether Alex was the criminal his friend believed him to be was yet to be revealed.

Wanting to keep the conversation going, Joi asked, "How long will you be in Paris, David? There's so much to see and do. The museums are wonderful."

"I'm not sure how long. My wife may join me next week. She's quite busy at our publishing company. We have a great staff, but she enjoys being directly involved. She's a great editor—and author, by the way. She recently wrote and published a book, *Unknown Impressionist Artists.* If she does come, we'll spend some time in the South of France visiting longtime friends. Otherwise, I'm here having a great time exploring on my own."

Joi, of course, knew David's wife, but not about the book. "I'll look for a copy and have her sign it for me."

Alex glanced up at David. "Hope we get to meet your wife." He took a sip of wine. "My mother is quite the authority on the Impressionists. Those two should meet."

The waiter returned and cleared the plates. Behind him, another waiter carried a large tray with their next course. The *promenade et service* was impressive, each waiter deftly doing his part in the production—pouring wine into fresh glasses, arranging the plates of food and side dishes of sauces and fresh baguette.

"*Mademoiselle*, I hope you enjoy the lobster. May I bring you anything else?"

Joi's eyes were wide as she stared at the delightfully arranged plate of food. Smiling up at him, she replied, "*Non. Merci.*"

David accepted his chicken, roasted with herbes de Provence, *haricot verts*, and roasted potatoes.

Alex smiled, knowing this would be an evening they would not soon forget. He wanted so much to take Joi's hand but needed to keep their relationship professional for David's benefit.

The waiter served Alex last. Steak, still crackling from the grill, crispy *frites*, and a side of *sauce d'hôtel.*

The sommelier appeared with the wine, presenting the bottle for their inspection with ceremony appropriate for such a special vintage. Alex sampled a taste and pronounced it, "*Parfait.*"

Conversation ceased for a moment while they proceeded to disassemble shells and bones and take that first delicious, perfect bite.

Joi looked down at the large lobster staring back at her. "Would anyone like a bite?"

Both men laughed. "Maybe later. Take your time. Enjoy." Alex teased, "We'll be eating *frites* and sardines the rest of the week."

The waiter returned once again, cleared the plates, passed out a *digestif* menu, and began to describe the desserts that had been prepared earlier that day.

They all looked at each other and declined the waiter's offer.

He added, "May I tempt you with a cognac? I happen to have a bottle of Paradis that is not listed on the menu." Alex politely ignored him as he slowly scanned the list, coming across Génépy des Alpes. He suddenly, and surprisingly, felt melancholy, as it reminded him of a friend—his first love—from when he'd lived in Paris as a young man. "We'll have the génépy."

"Very good, *monsieur*." He soon returned with three small glasses of the liqueur.

Alex explained the liqueur was a product of alpine botanicals, giving it a unique sweet and herbal flavor. They sipped in silence— Alex deep in thought and memory.

Joi couldn't hold back a yawn and apologized. "Excuse me. I think jet lag has finally caught up with me. This fabulous meal, and the attention of two handsome gentlemen. What can I say?" She smiled with a flirty little giggle at them both.

Alex motioned for the waiter. "*L'addition, s'il vous plaît.*" He paid the bill and helped Joi with her wrap. Once outside, he moved to hail David a cab.

David declined, saying, "It's a beautiful evening. I think I'll walk back to the hotel, especially after that incredible meal. Thank you so much, Alex."

The men shook hands, and David kissed Joi on the cheek.

"*Bonsoir*, David." She gave him a wink.

"*Bonsoir*. Call me in the morning, Alex. Looking forward to Angelina and Chagall!"

As Alex and Joi entered Joi's hotel room, he slipped his arm around her waist, bringing her close, then leaned down and gently kissed her. "You were perfect tonight. Just the right amount of charm to interest him. *Bonne nuit.* I'll see you in the morning, and we'll make our plan for the day with David. Rise early. I'll have a latte sent to your room."

Joi was relieved Alex didn't want to stay, having been prepared to feign an upset stomach or headache, just in case. She slipped out of her dress and ran a tub of water, sleepy but loving the soaking tub for the second time that day. While waiting for the tub to fill, she called the Westin and asked for "David Waters, *s'il vous plaît.*"

When David answered, she thanked him for playing along at dinner. "This is awkward. I think something shady may be going on. It's just a feeling, nothing specific. Alex is a complete gentleman, and I care for him. We've had a wonderful time these last few days. But I believe that he and his associate, Pierre, may not be exactly who they say they are. I've been taking notes in a journal I bought today. I know that sounds ridiculous."

David sighed. "Something is going on. That's why I'm here. A couple of years ago, a friend of mine purchased a piece of art from Alex. It turned out to be a forgery. Well, possibly a forgery. I've been trying to find evidence, but without success. No documentation to show authenticity or provenance." David poured a brandy. "Then, by chance, he contacted me regarding the Chagall painting and wondered if I would be interested. Well, I said 'absolutely.' To have him drop right in my lap like that—I was beside myself. Playing it cool, I told him that I was coming to Paris and would be delighted to meet with him."

Joi felt light-headed.

"Monica knows why I'm here and is, of course, concerned for you because of your romantic involvement. Since I don't have any real evidence, we need to take it slowly. You know, help each other. We need to see where this goes. Are you with me?"

"Of course. What should I do now?"

"Be yourself. Keep track of odd behavior. And don't worry. This could be nothing. Like I said, two years without substantial evidence. But, if it is real, I have a feeling his associate, Pierre, may be the actual forger."

"Pierre's never around. I haven't seen him once since we arrived. Alex says he has business to attend to." Sad and now exhausted, she said, "I'll follow your lead. See you in the morning. *Bonne nuit.*"

Joi called Monica, knowing she would be at the gallery. Trying to stay calm, she said, "Monica, David told me about his forgery investigation. I'm going to stay in Paris a little longer. I just canceled my return flight. I need to find out the truth about Alex." Her voice caught. "I can't talk now. I'll keep you posted." She hung up as tears filled her eyes and her heart.

Chapter 15

David woke early and had coffee sent to his room. Sitting on the terrace overlooking the city as it began to awaken gave him time to think about what might happen next. He hadn't found Alex to be the scoundrel his friend had claimed. In fact, quite the opposite. And now they were meeting for breakfast and to see the Chagall. After a quick shower, he decided to call Monica to fill her in on his plans but not about his doubts. She had told him earlier, "Call me day or night," and it was definitely night in San Francisco.

"Hello? Who is this? Do you know what time it is?" Monica's eyes blurred trying to focus on her alarm clock. One o'clock.

"It's David. Sorry to wake you. I have some news."

"David? What news?" She reached over to find the lamp switch and managed to knock over her water bottle and a half-eaten bowl of popcorn. "Dammit!"

"Monica?"

"Sorry. I just knocked over . . . never mind. Please continue."

"I had dinner with Joi and Alex last evening. I told her what's going on. She's upset but agreed to help me."

"I know. She called me and said she was staying a while longer. This forgery thing pisses me off more than you know. If I didn't have a business to run, I'd be in Paris right now ready to start *une révolution* of my own. You have to promise me we'll talk every day." She took a breath. "And speaking of calling. This time difference thing isn't working for me. Feel free to text anytime instead."

"Of course. Again, sorry for the late-night call. We're all meeting for breakfast in a half hour. Go back to sleep. I'll call you later."

Monica was now wide-awake. She found a notepad to outline the events up to this point and the players involved. Her life had always been mapped out in outlines and sticky notes—the only way she could project and plan. This scenario, however, was definitely the most bizarre—and probably the most exciting. She smiled to herself, actually enjoying the whole incredible drama that was unfolding. Someone should write a book, or a screenplay!

Joi woke early with plans to walk and do some artwork before meeting up with Alex and David at Angelina. She packed her art supplies along with her spy notebook and decided to call Alex.

"Good morning. Are you awake?"

"Well, I am now. What time is it?" He fumbled to look at his phone.

"Early. Eight o'clock. I'm going for a walk. What time do we meet David?"

"Not until ten thirty. Meet you in the lobby at ten fifteen." He hung up without saying goodbye and drifted back to sleep.

Amused by his sleepy abruptness, she felt free as she headed out the door.

After an inspired time drawing and painting Notre-Dame, boats on the Seine, street scenes, and early risers sipping lattes at a bistro, Joi returned to the hotel and noticed Alex in the lobby, quietly reading a copy of the *Paris News*.

He smiled. "Nice walk?"

Holding up her sketchbook, she said, "Lovely. Shall we go?"

Arriving a little early, Joi took the opportunity to peruse the display of confectionaries in the chocolate boutique by the front entrance. The young counter staff were delightful to watch as they playfully teased one another and boxed orders of delectables for their customers.

David approached. "Good morning."

"*Bonjour.*" Shaking his hand, Alex said, "I hope you slept well and that you're ready for another Paris favorite." He nodded toward the boutique. "And, of course, their chocolate has become Joi's latest passion."

"You've caught me drooling. We'll stop in here after we eat." She laughed and kissed his left cheek, then his right.

Alex smiled and greeted the hostess, "Three for breakfast. *Merci.*"

David was quite taken with the decor as they were led past displays of chocolate, large bouquets of fresh flowers, and gilded archways. The salon was almost full, with guests deep in conversation and beautiful food.

They were handed menus and asked for a drink order.

"This menu is overwhelming," Joi cooed.

The waitress brought mimosas and nodded to Joi. "*Mademoiselle?*"

"*Petit pain* and *salade de fruits. Merci.*"

David ordered, "Croque monsieur, *s'il vous plaît.*"

Alex chose *oeufs bénédicte* and added, "*Café* for three."

Conversation was casual, covering current art exhibits and possible excursions out of the city—Versailles, Épernay, and Giverny.

Alex explained, "After our meal, we'll go to my hotel room, to view the Chagall. I have the paperwork here if you'd like to take a look. The painting has been authenticated by experts at the Louvre and appraised by Sotheby's here in Paris. The artwork is a design rendered in watercolor for a tapestry. Chagall worked in many mediums: ceramics, stained glass, mosaics, and book illustration. An amazing Modernist artist. Have you seen his ceiling mural at Palais Garnier? Magnificent! He was seventy-seven years old when he painted it."

"I've seen it. Marvelous. My wife and I attended a Balanchine ballet there a few years ago. Champagne was served beforehand on the mezzanine overlooking the fabulous staircase. It was worth the visit just to see the staircase, and of course the ceiling."

Joi changed the subject. "The Chagall painting is exquisite, David. I think you'll be pleased."

Familiar with the authentication process, David perused the artwork's paperwork. The documentation looked genuine.

Alex announced, "We can't leave here without chocolate. I suggest the *chocolat chaud.*"

Joi sighed. "*Mais oui!*"

The whipped-cream-topped hot chocolate was so thick the spoon stood at attention, causing them to smile like children on holiday.

Back at the hotel and not wanting to join in with the business at hand, Joi excused herself to attend to some errands. "So nice to see you again, David. I'm sure we'll meet again soon. *Au revoir.*"

Alex took David up to his suite and offered him something to drink.

"No, thanks." He patted his stomach. "I'm quite content but anxious to see the Chagall."

Alex brought out an archival box and placed it on the desk near the north-facing window. "Natural light is good for viewing." He unwrapped the piece and offered David a pair of cotton gloves and a magnifying glass. "If you decide to purchase, I would be happy to pack it for secure transport as a carry-on. And I advise proper framing immediately once you arrive home." Alex was calm and remained quiet during David's inspection.

"This is incredible. And the papers and background information you've provided are impressive." He removed the gloves. "My wife left a message last night. She's decided to join me here in Paris. She's the real expert on artwork, and we make these decisions together. Let's make plans for a viewing and perhaps dinner." David shook Alex's hand. "Thank you, Alex. We'll talk soon."

"By the way—I'm involved with the Artcurial auction tomorrow. If you'd be interested, it might be fun." If David and his wife chose not to purchase the Chagall, Alex could keep him in the loop of art acquisition via the auction. "Give it some thought, and let me know later today."

"I can tell you right now—yes." He grinned. "I have nothing else to do." David was looking forward to seeing Alex in action.

"Great. Let's meet downstairs at eight. We can have a quick bite, then head over to the auction house."

As David returned to his hotel, he mused over how his investigation was playing out. They'd had a wonderful meal and conversation last night. Breakfast had been equally delightful. And now, seeing the Chagall painting with the authentic and appropriate paperwork . . . David couldn't see how Alex was involved in forgery.

Spending two years on a somewhat questionable quest for his friend was beginning to weigh on David. The question about whether the Derain was a forgery had been made at his friend's party by a guest with limited expertise. Authentication papers had not been supplied with the painting. His friend's wife had simply bought and paid for it. No questions asked. But that didn't make it fake.

Chapter 16

Arriving at the gallery early, Monica made herself an espresso and looked for something to snack on, before remembering her diet.

As she walked through the gallery, admiring the art from the X6 exhibit, she was surprised to see Phillip. "What are you doing here? Not that I'm not glad to see you."

"I don't know. Just feeling frumpy. I need a pedicure. And a manicure. Maybe a facial. Yes, definitely a facial. Brandon and I broke up." He fussed with the sweater around his shoulders and brushed at a phantom piece of lint, as if to say he was moving on. "Want to go have a spa day with me? I feel absolutely wretched."

"You and Brandon broke up? I didn't even know you were with Brandon."

"It was just the one night. But still. Oh, gawd. I need to be fawned over. My nails are a mess." Whining, he said, "Please come with me. We can do lunch after. I'm buying!"

Monica sighed, "Oh, sweetie. I don't know. I've got my head wrapped around a million things, and an important meeting this afternoon." She cocked her head and walked over to straighten one of the paintings.

"I'll take you to John's Grill," he said. His face lit up with a coy smile. He knew Monica couldn't resist the lamb chops. "And we can talk about the Monterey trip."

She grinned. "Let me see what I can do. I could use a little pampering myself. See if Isabelle can fit us both in for 'the works.' Funny, you using your day off to go the salon that you manage. Let me check in with Sam before we go."

Monica poked her head into Sam's office. "Got a minute? I need to update you on the Paris Affair."

"Sure. Come on in. I see you have coffee." Sam waved a fragrant paper sack enticingly. "I know you don't want one, but I brought in cherry scones and rugelach from the Noe Valley Bakery this morning."

She crossed her eyes at him. "Yes, I have coffee. And don't even think about not sharing some of that with me." She pointed to the rugelach, leaned over, and practically drooled on his sleeve.

Once Monica had filled Sam in on the Paris details and they had devoured most of the pastry—Monica's diet conveniently having slipped her mind—she said, "I feel much better knowing David is there and involved. He's savvy and the perfect protector for Joi. Good God, his size alone would deter anyone with the thought of bad behavior. And I think Joi is kind of enjoying the undercover spy thing—that's what I'm afraid of. She'll overplay it and get caught in the act." Monica's voice rose. "And who knows what kind of a guy Alex really is." Her eyes widened. "He could slit her throat in the night. Hide her body somewhere. No one would—"

"Stop! You're making this into something it's not. David's friend was stung two years ago. Maybe Alex isn't even in that game anymore. Maybe he never was. Give it time. David will figure it out."

Just then Phillip tapped on the door. "Our appointment is for eleven, and lunch after. You mentioned Dani and Trev might need help with the music gig they've got going next week. I'm going to go talk to them. Come get me when you're ready."

Sam gave him a thumbs-up. "Have some of this rugelach before Monica eats it all."

Monica found Phillip sitting in the main part of the gallery, looking like a man in crisis. Gloomy. He'd gained weight and was looking a little puffy. A little pasty. She knew he wanted a relationship, a life partner. A spa day was exactly what they both needed. They could talk things through. Make a plan. Dear Phillip.

"Ready to go?"

He perked up, grabbed her arm, and smiled like the Cheshire cat. "Dahling!"

At Maiden Lane Salon & Spa off Union Square, the two were warmly greeted by Isabelle. Phillip had been co-owner and manager of the salon since graduating from Pratt. Isabelle winked at Phillip and said, "Good to see you, Monica. Luckily, I was able to rearrange a couple of appointments." She led them to separate dressing rooms and handed them robes. "So, you both want a massage, facial, mani-pedi—basically the works?" They both chimed in together, "Yes, please!"

Phillip said, "Well, this is going to take us way past lunchtime. We'd better make our meal dinner—with lots of wine."

"We could do a little shopping after we're done here, then eat."

"I do adore you, Miss Monica! You can help me pick out a new outfit. Phillip needs a new look. Actually, Phillip needs a new life!"

Isabelle ushered them into the massage room. The tables were separated by a folding screen, so they could continue to talk.

After their treatments, they sat on the terrace and snacked on fresh fruit and ginger tea.

Monica glanced over at Phillip. "Everything okay? You look like a little boy who lost his new toy."

"I'm tired of my life. Tired of the bars and the parties, tired of being alone. I want to meet someone. I want a relationship. I feel so old."

Monica reached out and touched his arm. "I'm so sorry. My suggestion? Stop hanging out at those gay bars. It seems to me there isn't anyone over the age of twenty-five—with an IQ to match, I might add."

He glanced at her as if to protest, but then nodded in agreement.

"Here's what I think. First of all, you're a handsome, talented, and charming man. And you're one of the funniest people I know. I also know you're a gifted writer. Which begs the question: how's the book coming along?"

Phillip blushed slightly and sighed. "I haven't written a word in over a year. I don't feel inspired."

"I understand that, but writing could be a way out of this funk you're in. Go back to your manuscript and read it with fresh eyes. And then find yourself a group of writers to hang out with for inspiration and, who knows, maybe you'll find Mr. Right. At least you'd be with more interesting and intelligent people. And that's my sage advice for today."

Phillip perked up. "I was thinking about trying one of those online dating sites. Do you know—"

"Yeah, I was thinking about that for myself too—for about five minutes. I don't think so. It's such a cliché. Here we are in our late thirties. Is this what it's come to? Pathetic. We can do better, don't you think?"

Monica took another sip of tea and thought of Ben. "Let's get out of here and go shopping."

She took Phillip's arm. "Where should we go? Let's stop for a glass of wine and make a plan." She nodded. "There's the St. Francis." They strolled across the square and into the Clock Bar at the elegant landmark hotel.

Wanting to make their day special, she said, "We'll order champagne and I'll fill you in on Joi's adventure." Phillip hadn't been clued into the Paris drama.

"I thought she was on a romantic holiday with a Frenchman," Phillip said. "There's more? Ooooh. Tell me everything."

"I can tell you some basics, but at this point, things keep changing as fast as a Paris revue in Pigalle." She told Phillip a little about David's involvement regarding the forgery and let it go at that.

"Sounds a little contrived and confusing." Visions of Paris danced in his head. "I could go over and just hang out in the fashion district." Suddenly that sounded very alluring.

"Oh no you don't. We don't need another one of us joining the posse. Besides, I would miss you. And we need you at the gallery." She gave his hand a squeeze. "Where do you want to go shopping?"

"If my credit card was in better shape, I'd say Brooks Brothers or Wilkes Bashford. But it's not. The name and number are practically worn off from overuse. Let's wander over to Westfield Centre and take a gander at the shop windows. I could fall in love—with a handsome, well-dressed, and nonconfrontational mannequin."

"Okay, but let's order a little something to go with this champagne. How about oysters?"

After a good hour, Monica and Phillip were still at the St. Francis chatting and pouring the last of the champagne when Phillip saw Brandon out of the corner of his eye. He was in uniform and standing with two other chauffeurs by the entrance.

Phillip stood. "Time to go. Now!" They motioned to the waiter for their bill. Monica said, "My treat," and they were up and out before Brandon noticed them.

"What's the hurry?"

"It was Brandon. I don't want to talk to him. To tell you the truth, I'm embarrassed about our fling the other night. He's so young, and I'm so . . . not. Flings with young men are not what I want," he whimpered.

"Then focus on what you do want. That's the plan from now on." She slipped her arm through his as they left the hotel. "Let's find you some new clothes, mister."

Chapter 17

Sam arrived home at their apartment in Noe Valley, a quiet, "ahh" feeling neighborhood, and a relief after working in the downtown buzz all day. He wanted to share some aspects of the Paris Affair with Jenny, especially since she was researching forgery as part of her legal studies.

She sat cross-legged on the floor, sipping a cup of chai tea and poring over a stack of books while half watching a forgery documentary on her computer. A pencil was stuck in her bun hairdo while another was clenched in her teeth. Surprised to see Sam: "Hey, you. What brings you home so early?"

"Got a bunch of work done and wanted to come home. Do you have a minute?"

"Well, of course I do, big guy. Come over here and give me a smooch." She loved flirting with Sam but realized he had something on his mind. "Why the serious face?"

Sam went to the fridge for a beer. "I need your opinion and expertise on the subject of art forgery."

Jenny stood and walked over to him, wanting to lighten the mood. "Are you thinking of getting into forgery? Sweetie, you can barely draw stick figures." She smiled, knowing that he was far too ethical to ever consider a scheme like that, let alone execute it. Sam wasn't smiling. She toned down her playfulness.

"It's Joi and the two men she's with in Paris, Alex and Pierre. It seems that Alex, and perhaps Pierre as well, is involved in some kind of forgery scam. I'll fill you in with details later, but right now I need information on how the forgery business works. This whole thing is evolving quickly, and we're concerned for Joi."

Jenny stared at Sam in disbelief.

"You remember David Waters? He happens to be in Paris right now, meeting with Alex regarding a possible art purchase." Sam continued with the forgery situation, and Joi's innocent but romantic involvement with Alex. "David told Joi the reason he was there and asked that she play along until he could prove or disprove Alex's involvement. It's a touchy situation. We're concerned Alex will find out what David is up to."

They sat down on the sofa, Jenny facing Sam. "Well, what *is* he up to?"

Sam explained what he knew and asked again about how forgers conducted business.

Jenny stood and began to pace. "Look. People don't care. Everyone wants prestige and lots of money. This is how it works—the chain of command, so to speak—the cast of characters. You have the forger. You have the expert doing research on the piece of art. The art may go to an auction house or gallery. There are dealers and agents. And finally, you have the art collector. The bottom line is everyone wants the artwork to be authentic. Real. So, guess what? It *is* real! If you go to a private collector's home and see a well-known artist's work hanging on the wall, do you ask to see authentication papers? No, you don't. Now going back to the expert. If there is extensive testing done—paint samples, X-rays, et cetera—then there's a possibility for prosecution, *if* the forger is discovered. And prosecution of a forger or dealer is based on intent to deceive. It rarely happens, but if it does, then penalties are high and jail time is almost always certain."

Sam sat wide-eyed at Jenny's explanation and passion.

Jenny was intrigued to the point of wanting to go to Paris and join the fray. The more she thought about it, the more she was convinced she could help her friends. She suggested her idea to Sam, hoping he would agree.

He stared at her. "What are you talking about?"

"Don't give me that look. I know Paris. I went to school there, remember? I actually worked at the Artcurial auction house as an assistant one summer." The more she talked, the more passionate she became. "What I'm learning about forgery is mind-blowing. Forgers are still getting away with their scams, and I would like to be a part of this investigation. These are my friends, too, for God's sake." She tossed down the book she was holding but then softened.

"I think I could be of some help. Besides, you know I'm a good actress. You met me while I was in that college production of *Some Like It Hot*." She smiled to herself at the memory. Sam, all doe-eyed when he came to the cast party and introduced himself. "And this would give me real-world experience with art forgery. It's perfect!"

Sam wasn't entirely surprised by Jenny's interest in going to Paris. She had so much enthusiasm for adventure. She was clever, and he knew she could pull off whatever role she needed to play. But, because he was privy to her past wild lifestyle, going to Paris could mean disaster for their relationship. Could he trust her? He surprised himself by saying, "Okay. Let's talk to Monica." Sharing this new turn of events with Monica, however, would be a whole different story.

Sam took his time going to work the next morning. He wasn't looking forward to Monica's reaction to Jenny's proposal.

"Are you *crazy*? Are you both out of your minds?"

Sam had expected no less of a response. He sat down and casually put his feet up on the desk. Still trying to convince himself of Jenny's suggestion, he tried to remain calm and aloof. "Just think about it for a minute. Jenny has the forgery insight from her legal studies. She knows Paris. She's sharp. She—you know, works well with others. I don't know. It makes sense to me." Nervously, he grabbed a bottle of water and drank almost half before continuing. He shrugged. "She's my wife, and I trust her."

Monica stared at Sam, then walked to the window, quietly mulling over his proposal. She turned with arms crossed. "And in what capacity will she be joining this circus? Answer me that. I'm concerned about safety, not the more the merrier. Tell me, Sam. How will her going somehow make it all better?"

"I'm not sure yet, but Jenny is going. That's a given. We need to support her decision and make a plan that will work for her, for Joi, and for David."

Sam was light-headed just thinking about it. It was all happening too fast. Monica, on the other hand, was fuming as her feathers began to ruffle. She opened the bottom drawer of her desk and pulled out a bottle of Jameson.

"How about a drink?"

They both burst out laughing. Either out of relief or sheer terror at what would be unfolding in the next couple of days.

That afternoon, Monica arrived at Sam and Jenny's apartment, with the intention of taking charge of the situation. But somehow, she didn't feel in charge. It seemed like all of her chicks were chattering and scattering to the wind without a care in the world.

She was already talking when Jenny opened the door. "I guess there is no changing your mind, Jenny," she said as she walked in and flopped on the sofa. "What exactly do you think you can accomplish, and in what capacity? Who are you in this scenario? An outsider? A friend of the family? Chambermaid? What?"

Jenny took a breath, sat down, and put her arm around Monica. "I plan on being who I am. Not an attorney, because I'm not. Not yet. But a student researching forgery. Also, because I have friends in Paris, I can say I thought it was time for a visit. I know that the Artcurial is holding an auction in a couple of days. I looked online and have a good idea of the caliber of art and the patrons who will attend. I know how they conduct business, having worked as an aid one summer. This Alex guy will no doubt be there. This is a perfect opportunity."

Monica stood up and then sat back down. "May I have a glass of wine?"

"Yes, of course. Red okay?" Jenny grabbed a glass from the kitchen.

Monica took a sip, still deep in thought. Chewing on her thumbnail, she said, "Okay. I'm convinced. Get packed. I'll make your reservations and call David and Joi to let them know you're on your way. We're all crazy. You know that, don't you?"

Jenny smiled with excitement.

Sam stared into space, resigned his wife was jetting off.

Monica went home to sort out the next phase of this incredible turn of events. The Paris Team versus Mother Hen: 3 to 1. She was losing, and she knew it. But it was going to happen, so she'd best take charge of her brood. She had to smile. Chicks in Paris!

The trio arrived at the airport an hour early and sat at a bar close to the departure gate. Sam and Jenny sipped wine while Monica paced, half listening as she checked messages on her phone.

Jenny conjured possible scenarios and began to think out loud. "What I need to do is somehow be introduced to Alex—apart from Joi and David, of course. I would be coming in at another angle. Either as a patron of the auction house, or as a student, or—as a possible lover. Yes, that's it! I could be Alex's new love interest. Perfect. That way I don't have to be a long-lost friend of the other two. That would be too obvious and risky anyway. Yes. The lover." Jenny smiled as she thought of her new role.

Monica looked up from her phone. "What?"

Sam was stunned to the point of numbness. "Lover?"

Monica once again realized this was out of her hands, but had to admit that Jenny's scheme was right on. Luring Alex as a lover, if she was successful, would show what a lowlife he was. Cheating on Joi.

Jenny glanced at the arrival-departure screen and hopped off the stool. "Time to go." She beamed at the thought of returning to Paris. She gave Sam a long, lingering kiss and hugged Monica. "I'll call you when I arrive." She grabbed her one small bag, knowing she would be doing some shopping in Paris. *Mais bien sûr*—but of course!

Monica needed to talk to Joi fast and would call the minute she got home. She had a feeling Joi would feel like she was being manipulated by the growing cast of characters in this play.

Jenny had a mission, and she knew how to carry it out. Attracting the opposite sex had never been a problem for her. Beautiful, shrewd, and especially playful, she was the queen of diversion and seduction. Sam had no idea of her past, and he never would. Let him stay comfortable with his image of her now. She had changed since she met him, probably because of him. He was her rock, and he trusted her. She would never abuse that trust.

She found her seat in first class and was offered a glass of champagne. After her second glass, she asked not to be disturbed for the dinner service later. She desperately needed a break from her studies, and going back to the city she loved was the perfect elixir. Wrapped in the blanket and pillow provided, she fell fast asleep. After a short stop-over in Reykjavík, she retrieved her iPad and opened up her notes on forgery. Studying now had a different meaning for her. She was on assignment, so to speak, and it was thrilling.

Jenny smiled as she arrived at the Millésime Hôtel in the Latin Quarter, across the Seine with a view of Notre-Dame. She checked in and went up to her room. Small with modern decor. She quickly unpacked her few items, changed her shoes, and headed straight for the Seine. She had a ritual whenever visiting Paris: walk to the Seine and dip her fingers in the water, then to her lips. It was her way of saying, "I love you, Paris. I will always return." Jenny felt at home. Her wealthy parents had made sure she'd had the opportunity for time abroad while growing up. She would forever be grateful for that. Now, she could add adventure and intrigue to her curriculum vitae.

As Monica and Sam left the airport, she comforted him with a hug. "It will be okay. Really." She was feeling a little more confident now that David and Jenny were in Paris—two people who loved Joi. It was a team now.

"I'm really feeling fine about this, Sam. You know I fuss and fume about everything that feels out of my control. But this is going to work. All intelligent people taking care of each other. Some risk, but okay." She hoped she sounded convincing, even if she still had doubts.

She pulled up in front of his apartment. "Get some rest. See you tomorrow."

Sam entered his apartment in a daze. He knew he could trust Jenny. At least, he hoped he could. He knew about her wild past but had always kept it to himself. He felt helpless now. If she were in trouble, if she should need him . . . He grabbed a beer and sat in the dark. Falling into a restless sleep on the sofa, dreaming about *Some Like It Hot* and Jenny in an intrigue with two men in drag. He jolted awake. Eyes wide open.

Monica entered her apartment, now thinking of herself as a movie director. First, she'd been a producer of three extravaganzas—and now a director! Gather information to oversee the players and direct them in this art forgery caper. Not being in Paris gave her an advantage. Detached, she could calmly analyze the facts and make appropriate decisions. She smiled and said out loud, "Quiet on the set. And . . . action!"

Chapter 18

"David? It's Monica. One more cast member is headed your way. I'm so glad you're there, being the steady and intelligent man that you are." She tried to ease into the latest turn of events. "On my side of things—well, I tend to make people anxious."

David grinned and visualized her usual pacing with a clipboard, dotted with sticky notes, and a marker in her hand.

"Sam's wife, Jenny, offered to join in. You met her at the gallery Christmas party last year. Anyway, she arrives in Paris today. She's a law student, as you may remember, and just finished extensive studies on the legal aspects of forgery, specifically art forgery. She's smart and sassy and is looking forward to helping out."

Monica waited for a response from David. Hearing none, she continued. "She's not joining the group as an acquaintance. She's coming in as an outsider, with hopes of wooing Alex and perhaps getting him to reveal his art forgery plans."

"Continue."

Monica filled him in on Jenny's Paris background and auction house savvy. "She'll be a real asset to you. The trick is to be sure that

all communication is guarded. She will not become friends or socialize with any of you. Only Alex. Jenny may have a good chance of
becoming Alex's cohort with the forgery and maybe his lover. Not
actually his lover, but love interest—without the sex. Oh, never mind.
You know what I mean. Jenny is devoted to Sam, is all I'm saying."
Monica took a breath. "What do you think?"

"It actually sounds good. And I really do appreciate your involvement. After two years with no results, it's good to have a team. I'm
assuming Jenny will contact me soon and that she's staying in close
contact with you. Also, there's something I haven't told you. Back
when I made my plans to come to Paris, I hired a PI from the DuChat
Detective Agency here in Paris. I felt I needed some expertise and
backup. He managed to bug Alex's phone at the airport when they
all arrived in Paris." David shook his head. "How he did that, I don't
know. Anyway, the bug has produced only some business calls and
a lot of, shall we say, nighttime activity in the boudoir." He chuckled to himself at the thought.

"Well, keep me posted. I gave Jenny your number. Let me know
how she works out. I doubt she'll be calling me anytime soon."

Not happy with one more *chef en cuisine*, he didn't reveal his concerns.

David had not seen nor heard from Joi for two days. He decided to
call, hoping she would be alone.

"Joi, it's David. We need to talk. Are you alone?"

"David? It's Alex. Joi isn't here at the moment. She went shopping
and obviously left her phone. What's up?"

Taken aback, David had to think fast. "Hi, Alex. This is a little
embarrassing. I guess I ought to confess my need to speak with Joi.
Please don't tell her we talked. The other evening when we were all

out to dinner and you had stepped away for a moment, she asked if I would help plan a surprise for you as a thank-you for giving her the opportunity to be in Paris. I'm not good at that sort of thing but said I would help with whatever she decided."

Not at all fazed, Alex said, "Really? She doesn't need to do that." Wanting to keep his "associate" relationship with Joi evident with David, Alex said, "She hasn't worked with me for long. I wanted her to see how the auction houses work in Paris. That's why she's here."

Just then, Joi walked in, carrying several bags.

Alex held up her phone and said, "You left your phone here. David is on the line."

Joi turned away and felt her face flush.

Alex said to David, "Joi just walked in. Hold on."

"Hello, David. How are you?" she said, trying to appear aloof.

"I called because I was concerned—we haven't been in touch. When Alex answered your phone, and before I realized he was on the line, I said, 'We need to talk.' Then, when I heard his voice, I had to think fast. I told him that you and I needed to chat because we were planning a surprise for him. Play along with that story. We'll figure out something later. Call me the minute you are alone. It's important I talk to you! Hanging up now."

The call ended, but Joi continued to hold her phone for a moment and said, "Lovely to hear from you, David."

David dabbed his sweaty forehead and poured himself a scotch.

Alex smiled to himself, thinking about the two of them trying to be sneaky. He kissed Joi's cheek. "I have some work to do in my room. Do you mind?"

"Actually, I would love a hot bath and a little nap. Shopping takes so much out of a girl—especially in Paris." She gave him a hug and told him to be off.

"Okay, sweet lady. I'll be back in two hours. I need to call David to make dinner plans for when his wife arrives. And then I thought we could take a stroll over to Musée d'Orsay and Shakespeare and Company. There's a book I hope they have in stock. A book of poetry, *Classic French Love Poems.*" He smiled at her playfully and left her to relax and enjoy her bath.

Returning to his room, Alex checked his bag for the Artcurial catalog and felt something in the bottom. It was Joi's cell phone. He wondered why he'd ever pinched it. From past habits, he knew that any opportunity to garner personal information on potential clients and competitors was crucial, but he didn't want to scam Joi or hurt her in any way. He clicked on the screen and saw that she hadn't installed a security lock. He opened her text messages and saw the last message to Monica, describing *how wonderful Alex is*. He smiled and realized how much he really did care for her. He decided he would slip the phone in her luggage at some point.

Joi called David. "What's up? You sounded a little panicked on the phone."

"Monica called last night. We now have one more on our spy team. Jenny is in Paris now and will be in touch with me soon. This is important—we will not be seeing her socially. She is here in the capacity of a law student studying art forgery and also to woo Alex. She is never to be mentioned by name. We do not know her!"

Joi was stunned. The idea of beautiful Jenny coming on to Alex was unsettling.

Holding her emotions back, all she could say was, "This is getting rather complicated, isn't it? I'll talk to you soon."

On the verge of tears and with every emotion flooding her body like neon signs—Alex the Forger! David the Investigator! Jenny the

Seductress!—she wondered what kind of game they were playing and what her role was. Joi the Fool! She fell on the bed, exhausted, and into a hell-laced sleep, where Monica shook her finger and said, "I told you so."

Two hours later, still sleepy and wearing only satin boxer shorts and a tank top, hair piled up in a messy ponytail and no makeup on—Joi opened her room door.

"Look at you." Alex lifted her up, and she wrapped her legs around his waist as he pushed the door closed with his foot. Their passion was strong and urgent. He kissed her forehead, her earlobe, her neck, her mouth, and carried her to the unmade bed, still warm from her nap. "You're making me crazy." He slipped off his shirt and pants.

Their lovemaking was passionate and needy. Joi found herself making love in ways she had never known and didn't understand. Wild, yet tender. Despite her misgivings about his possible criminal activity, she knew she loved him. She moved beneath him and then hesitated. Holding his face in her hands, she saw a man in love. A man in love with her. She kissed him softly, then hard. They lay exhausted, questioning feelings neither had planned on.

Alex rolled over and smiled at her. He'd fallen hard. He loved her. He brushed a tendril of hair off her face. "Let's take a shower and then go in search of that book of love poems. We'll walk and do whatever you want."

She slipped out of bed, leaned over and brushed her lips against his, then playfully sauntered toward the shower, coyly looking back at him, teasing him to follow. Alex was soon standing behind her and once again exploring her body, lavender soapsuds running down their bodies like meringue.

Joi stood in front of the bathroom mirror with a towel wrapped around her body. She struggled with the tangles in her hair, thinking she should get her hair cut. Short, sexy, and French. She smoothed bergamot oil on her still-warm skin, then wrapped her arms around Alex's waist and purred, "What are we doing for dinner tonight? Could we do casual? I'm feeling relaxed and want nothing more than to walk and enjoy the city with you."

He looked down at her, eyes twinkling and feeling like a schoolboy. "Casual it is. We still have time to walk to Shakespeare and Company and go to one of the museums, if you'd like. Maybe a dinner cruise on the Seine later. Would you like that?"

"*Oui.* I would love it."

He watched as she slipped on a pair of tight jeans, a light sweater, short boots, and the burgundy scarf she'd purchased at Hermès on their shopping spree. She grabbed her tailored black jacket, umbrella, and bag, making sure her sketch pad was inside. They went back to his room so he could change. She hadn't seen him dressed in anything but tailored suits or sport coats and slacks. But now, watching him slip on jeans, a T-shirt, and a leather jacket was a sight she wanted to see again and again.

He wrapped a gray wool scarf around his neck, a corner of his mouth turned up, knowing she was watching his runway performance.

Joi swooned. "Oh my. *Regarde ce bout!*"

The bookshop was fairly close to their hotel. Alex took the opportunity to tell Joi a little history as they walked. "This shop, originally called Le Mistral, was opened in the early 1950s by George Whitman, an American. The building was originally a monastery, and George liked to playfully pretend to be the monk who lit the lamps at night, the *frère lampier*. He later renamed the shop Shakespeare and Company in honor of Sylvia Beach—the owner of the original Shakespeare and Company. Hemmingway, Fitzgerald, Stein, and the gang were frequent visitors then."

They stopped midpoint on the bridge crossing Île de la Cité. "That's what intrigued me as a student. To think of those writers hanging out, discussing their writing projects, and encouraging each other. George's daughter later took over the business, and he passed away a few years ago." Feeling a little melancholy. "Funny the details you remember. Sometimes I think I spent more quality time there than at home."

Joi kissed his cheek. "I love your stories and knowledge of Paris. My own personal tour guide."

They entered the shop just as it began to rain. "I'm going to look in the art section." Joi was interested in finding something about the painting she'd purchased from Alex in Seattle. She had purposefully not asked him about it since they'd arrived in Paris—not wanting to find it might be a forgery. She found a new edition of a book entitled *Unknown Impressionist Artists*. Joi couldn't believe it. *Kathryn's book!* She looked around, hoping Alex wasn't nearby. She continued to scan the shelves and settled on Hemingway's *A Moveable Feast*, a book she had begun reading in college but didn't finish. Purchasing the two books, she went looking for Alex and found him deep in thought as he scanned the book of poetry in his hand.

Alex made his purchase, along with a blue satin ribbon bookmark with a small silver heart attached. Still reminiscing, he said, "Another fact about George I love: he invited writers and artists to stay here." He pointed to the upstairs. "They could curl up on the benches and sleep among the stacks of books. He asked that they simply read one book a day, work in the shop for a couple of hours, and produce a one-page autobiography." Alex grinned at the thought. "He called them 'Tumbleweeds,' and he collected and saved their writings." Realizing he was rambling on, he stopped and guided her to the front. They looked out through the small-paned windows at the drizzling rain and decided to brave it and share her umbrella.

"Musée d'Orsay is too far away to walk in the rain, and I'm really hungry," Joi cooed. "What do you think?"

Alex said, "I think I'm in the mood for oysters and that I'm going to take you to the most amazing place."

Snuggled under the umbrella, they walked to their destination on a short street off Boulevard Saint-Germain—the very popular and very small oyster bar, Huitrerie Régis. Normally, a line of people would be waiting outside, but today, right now, in the rain, they were seated immediately. Régis, the owner, was shucking oysters as they entered the spotless bar. He nodded to them and continued to shuck as they found a corner table. The small room was painted white with French-blue accents; seven small tables were draped in white linen and accommodated only fourteen people. The white-and-blue porcelain plates and silverware transformed the bar from common to elegant. A large colorful painting hung on the back wall, and at the opposite end of the room were shelves of wine and a bar. The shucking counter was between the bar and the front door. Very tight but efficient.

Alex scanned the day's oyster selection. "Should I order for us?" He was eager to place the order before the place filled up. Already two couples had arrived and were seated.

"*Oui, s'il vous plaît.*" Joi loved how knowledgeable Alex was about, well, everything.

The menu revealed a selection of several types of oysters from various regions of France. Scallops, shrimp, clams, and sea urchins were also on the menu, along with dry sausage and the cheese of the day. Only one dessert was offered—*tarte aux pommes*, made daily by Régis himself.

Alex ordered a dozen each of two types of oysters, with a baguette and the cheese of the day, Saint Agur, a soft blue goat cheese made in the Auvergne region of southern France. "And a bottle of sancerre. *Merci.*"

As they waited for their food, Alex opened the book of poems and turned to one of his favorites, "More Strong Than Time." Joi snuggled close with her head next to his as he read:

"*. . . since it was given to me to hear one happy while, the words wherein your heart spoke all its mysteries, since I have seen you weep, and since I have seen you smile, your lips upon my lips, and your gaze upon my eyes . . .*" He glanced at her. "Victor Hugo."

Alex continued to scan the book as Joi did a quick sketch of the room with Alex as the featured subject.

The waiter appeared with their oysters, bread, and cheese. He opened the bottle of sancerre, filled their glasses, and wandered back to shuck more oysters.

Alex described the region where the oysters were harvested and explained why they were a particular taste, texture, and size. "The small flat ones are called Belons and come from Brittany. Meaty, almost crunchy, with a strong seaweed and mineral flavor." He offered her one and waited for her response.

"Yes, strong. I like it. Let me taste the other."

"This is a more delicate variety, Fines de Claire. Notice the body is small and elongated, with a salty and fruity flavor." Alex sipped the wine. "And the sancerre is basically a sauvignon blanc. Not too sweet, and perfect with the oysters."

Every table in the bar was now filled with low and intimate conversation. At that moment, nothing in the world existed for Alex. No David. No Chagall. No auction house business. Only Joi. Pure joy!

They left Huitrerie Régis sated, happy, and ready to walk. Alex suggested the Palais and Jardin du Luxembourg a few blocks away. The rain had stopped, the sun was out, and the neighborhood glistened as they splashed through rain puddles, playfully bumping hips and laughing. Joi was in awe of the immaculate gardens and terraces of the sixty-acre estate. Statues of French queens lined the walkways. The octagonal pool, the bandstand—all swept down from the Florentine-style royal palace. She squeezed Alex's hand. "*C'est magnifique.*"

"*Et toi aussi*—and so are you."

After a leisurely one-hour walk through the gardens and back through the Saint-Germain quarter, Joi said she wanted to buy a gift for Monica. "She's like a sister and has put up with a lot lately, with my being gone."

Stopping at Longchamp, a high-end handbag and luggage shop, Joi found handbags ranging from barely affordable to outrageously expensive. She chose a Le Foulonné, soft black leather hobo bag, and arranged shipment to the gallery.

Alex put his arm around Joi. "Time to head down to the Seine and decide which barge we want to spend the next couple of hours on. You're going to love it. The view of the city from the river is quite amazing, especially at night."

They reached the banks of the Seine and found several barges, each promoting their bill of fare. Some diners waited in line while others continued to study the various menus. Alex chose one that advertised live music with a small dance floor. *Bateaux Parisiens.*

"*Bonsoir.* May we have a table toward the back, *s'il vous plaît? Merci.*"

They were guided to a window table, away from the noise of the kitchen and serving area. The waiter appeared just as the last guests had boarded and the boat was preparing to pull away from the dock near the Eiffel Tower. Alex requested champagne, scanned the menu, then said, "You choose for us."

Joi glanced at Alex, surprised he was abandoning his usual take-charge manner. "Mmm. Should we start with poultry terrine and then shrimp for the main course? And I think we should share." She patted her stomach, indicating she was still a little full.

"Excellent choice. May I choose the wine?"

She winked at him. "*Mais oui, s'il vous plaît.*"

There was a playful buzz as other guests were seated, excited as the cruise began. The large domed windows allowed for a stunning view of the city as the boat began its slow journey, headed for the far tip of Île Saint-Louis. Orange remnants of the setting sun gave way to a dark blue-and-purple sky.

Joi was mesmerized by the view of the city at the level of the Seine. Every building was alive with glittering lights. The Louvre, Notre-Dame, Musée d'Orsay, the Grand Palais—all glowing and magical—bringing images of Paris from a different time.

Alex was mesmerized as well. Only it was the lovely view across the table from him.

"*Monsieur.*" The waiter had arrived with their entrée—chicken terrine, accompanied with foie gras and pistachio, and an onion and raspberry sauce. Perfect with champagne.

"I can't believe I'm hungry after the oysters we had earlier. But suddenly I am." Joi shook her head. "This is delicious."

They sipped their wine and discussed places Joi could visit tomorrow while Alex was busy with the auction. "You could spend the afternoon in the Marais. Lots of small shops, the Picasso Museum, Centre Pompidou."

Two waiters returned. One removed their plates while the other brought the main course. "*Mademoiselle.*" He placed the shrimp in front of Joi and then Alex. "*Monsieur.*"

Their plates were piled with bright pink shrimp swimming in lemon and cream of leek.

"Have you chosen a wine, *monsieur*?"

"*Oui.* Domaine des Echardières Rosé. *Merci.*"

"This has been a wonderful and beautiful day, Alex. Thank you."

He raised his glass to her and said, "To a wonderful and beautiful lady."

A jazz combo began softly playing near the front of the boat as the Eiffel Tower lit up against the now blue-black sky. A perfectly orchestrated performance between the band and the tower inspired oohs and aahs as guests pressed close to the windows to see the light show. Everyone except Alex and Joi, who were pressed against each other, the only ones on the dance floor in their own sensuous world. Joi's hotel room was on both their minds.

As they walked, conversation came around to plans for the next day. "You'll have fun exploring. Has the guide book been helpful?"

"Yes. I love that little black book. I feel quite confident being on my own. I think Centre Pompidou will be my first stop."

"Good. The place is alive with contemporary art, gift shops, and a wonderful restaurant. And the Stravinsky Fountain is a whimsical delight."

Alex was beginning to feel slightly indifferent about the auction. His whole career, in fact, suddenly seemed meaningless.

I don't want to be that person any longer. And I don't want to lose Joi. I need to talk with Pierre.

Chapter 19

Travel always knocked Jenny out for a day or two, but now she was awake and eager to walk the streets of her beloved Paris. As she was about to leave her room, her phone rang.

"Jenny? It's Monica. I wanted to give you a quick update."

"What's up?"

"David and Joi know you're in Paris and why. David is the point person. You and Joi will contact him but not each other. Do you understand?" She took a deep breath. "It's important you keep David posted on all activity concerning Alex, unusual or not. And it seems Pierre has made himself scarce. Find out as much as possible about him." She sat down, practically hyperventilating.

"Glad you called, Monica. But you need to relax." Jenny looked at herself in the mirror and adjusted her scarf. "I'm on my way out for a bite to eat and a walk. The Artcurial auction is coming up, and it was easy getting a clearance pass. Since I don't know what this Alexander character looks like, I'll find someone who knows him, then I'll casually introduce myself. We'll see what happens after that. And please do me a favor. Give Sam a hug for me. I'll call him later." She ended the call promising to stay in touch, to be careful, not to take chances, to stay clear of the team . . . and to call David.

Outside, Jenny soaked in the sun and the bustle of the city. She walked to L'Écritoire café and found a table outside with a lovely view of the fountain and the entrance to the Sorbonne. Sitting there brought back a flood of memories of school, old friends, and the experience of simply living in Paris. One of her favorite memories was an art class assignment requiring the students to choose a famous artist and one of their paintings, write a report, and take the class to the museum and the painting. The student would then give a presentation as a gallery docent would do. Jenny had chosen the Édouard Manet painting *Le Déjeuner sur l'herbe* at the Musée d'Orsay. The well-known scandal at the time the painting was created was that a naked woman was nonchalantly sharing a picnic with two men dressed in suits and ties.

The waiter approached. She gave him a flirty smile and said, "*Rosé, fromage, et tartine, s'il vous plaît.*" She took out a notepad and began jotting down must-have items for her wardrobe. Items to lure Mr. Alexander Marshal. She hoped he would be young and handsome, or else she'd need to up her acting skills to get through this.

Joi had a leisurely breakfast in her room while glancing at an article in a travel magazine about the artists and writers Alex had spoken of the day before. The article recommended a book about Gertrude Stein and the neighborhood where she'd lived. Curiosity piqued by the colorful stories, she decided she would visit the Latin Quarter and Saint-Germain instead of the Marais and Centre Pompidou. Her plan: Shakespeare and Company, a museum or two, a light lunch, then stroll and find the haunts of writers past.

Walking toward the Left Bank, she thought about Jenny's role as seductress. It was unnerving. She had feelings for Alex. Strong feelings. And with Jenny involved, she could hardly breathe thinking about Alex and Jenny together intimately.

Joi realized she was standing on the bridge where only a few months ago, the railing had been completely covered in padlocks, placed there by couples professing their love and visitors promising to return as they flung the lock's key into the Seine. The locks were now being removed because of the weight and stress they caused on the bridge. That was how she felt now. Like a dead weight. Like part of her had been flung into the Seine.

Joi purchased two books at Shakespeare and Company—*Le Petit Prince* in the original French and *Walks in Gertrude Stein's Paris.* Outside, she sat on a bench that encircled a hawthorne tree, pulled out her pad, and began to sketch the old shop and surrounding buildings. Then something caught her eye. A group of students came out of the shop, and Jenny was with them, laughing and teasing one of the boys. She looked up and saw Joi and approached. They stared at each other and instinctively looked around to see if anyone was watching.

Jenny said, "I can't believe I'm standing here looking at you. Especially with Monica's strict orders."

They hugged and laughed and said at the same time, "Well, what Monica doesn't know!"

"I'm whipped, jet-lagged. Want to go for a drink? There is no way in hell anyone would see us."

Joi hesitated. "Yes. But first I want to get my hair cut." She pointed to her mass of hair. "Short. Help me find a place that—"

"I know the perfect place. It's close by."

They entered the Jean Philippe Audebert Salon—modern, white walls, spotless, with white leather furniture. Jenny explained to the girl at the counter, in perfect French, what they wanted. A cut and style for Joi, and a manicure for herself. They sat scanning hairstyle magazines while they waited. "Here it is. This is the cut I want."

One hour later, Jenny had trendy pink lacquered nails, and Joi looked like a tall version of Juliette Binoche, with a short, straight, wispy bob.

Jenny said, "I'm going to take you to Brasserie Lipp for a drink—one of my favorite haunts when I lived here." They walked arm in arm, laughing and talking about the escapade they found themselves in now. Joi, however, avoided specific talk about Jenny's role as seductress.

They entered "the Lipp" and found a corner table away from the other patrons. Jenny explained that this had been one of Hemingway's favorite places to sit and write. It had a wonderful ambience: crisp and clean, with polished wood and brass and painted tropical murals around the room. They both ordered scotch on the rocks.

Joi, warmed and relaxed from the whiskey, tentatively asked Jenny about her role in this ever-evolving saga. She referred to her own involvement as simply a detached bystander helping David on his quest. She was in love but couldn't tell Jenny, or anyone else, right now.

"My role is to seduce him to the point where he trusts me—a flat-out love affair."

Joi, feeling stronger from the drink, exploded internally but kept her voice low. "But you're married to Sam. How can you do that?"

Jenny sat back. "I'm an actress. That's what I was doing when Sam met me. Remember? This is a role. And it's a role that will hopefully bring these forgery bastards to their knees! Besides. I won't actually go to bed with him. It will be a tease. I'm after information, not sex."

She shook the ice in her drink, took the last sip, and smiled, thinking about her new role.

Joi felt deflated, angry, sad. "I need to get back, Jenny. Dinner plans. With David, I think." They left the iconic bar and walked toward the Seine, casually talking about nothing in particular.

Jenny, in a reverie of her own, was oblivious to Joi's sullen mood. "You look great. We should probably walk separately now." She hugged Joi and pointed her in the direction of the Pont Neuf. "Have fun tonight."

Alex went to Joi's room to wait for her. He studied the program for the auction, making notes in the margin. This was always a tense time, no matter how many times he had participated. Working the room, meeting old and new patrons, charming the many widows with old money and new couples with new money, eager to invest. He would also be advising David.

Taking the opportunity to return Joi's "lost phone," he opened the closet, found her travel case, and slipped the phone in a small inside pocket. He heard the key card click and quickly returned to the sofa and his papers.

Joi opened the door, startled to see Alex. "What are you doing here?"

He looked at her and smiled. "Your hair! You look fantastic. Come here."

She walked over to him, confused and suddenly with mixed feelings.

He kissed her and turned her around for a full scan of her hair. "I love it. And actually, I just walked in, thinking you might be taking a nap since there was no answer when I knocked. Thought I would have a glass of wine and read the auction catalog here instead of my room."

"Okay." She smiled and looked at him slyly as she set her purse and packages down and took off her jacket. She preferred more privacy than this. "I've been out walking and decided against Centre Pompidou today. I spent some time at Shakespeare and Company and bought these." She showed him the two books and kissed him on the cheek. "What are the plans for this evening? Dress up? Dress down?"

Alex rubbed his chin, contemplating a dinner plan. "I talked to David, and we'll meet him tomorrow for breakfast instead of dinner tonight. Let's make it casual. We'll go to a club. Some of the best jazz in the world is here in Paris. I have a couple of things to do first, so I'll be back in an hour."

Joi slumped in the chair by the window, wondering what she was doing in the middle of the "Paris Affair," as Monica called it.

Alex returned, looking his casual best in jeans, a black shirt, and a dark blue sport coat. He was smiling and happy and every bit a man in love.

Joi melted inside and hoped their romance would last. But then Jenny's image began to haunt her. Once Alex turned around to open the door, Joi's smile disappeared.

Alex knew of several jazz clubs, mostly in Saint-Germain, but wanted to eat dinner in a quiet place first. The city slowly became a light show as the sky turned from orange to lavender to inky blue. Les Deux Magots was a popular café and always busy—not quiet and intimate like he'd planned—but he wanted to take Joi there at least once.

They arrived and were lucky to find a table outside. A waiter, dressed in a black three-piece suit with a short jacket and long white apron, arrived within minutes, offered menus, and asked for a choice of wine. Alex ordered a bottle of rosé and still water while they perused the menu. They agreed on a light meal and chose items they would share.

The wine was brought, opened, and poured. Joi immediately picked up her glass and drank half before the waiter left the table.

Alex glanced at her, amused. "Rough day?"

Unable to tell him the truth, she said, "No, just long. It's nice to sit here with you and relax. This is a great café." She looked around at the other diners. Couples in close conversation. Couples in love.

The waiter soon returned with two plates: grilled vegetables in a puff pastry and smoked salmon.

"You know this café is famous. It was once a rendezvous for the literary and intellectual elite. The likes of Picasso, Hemmingway, Jean-Paul Sartre, James Joyce—" Alex took a sip of wine. "Hey. You're a million miles away. Is everything okay?"

She mentally pulled herself together. "I'm just so happy. I think this trip and all we've done in such a short time has simply overwhelmed me." She kissed his cheek and held her wineglass up for a refill.

The waiter returned with one salad they shared, a beautiful mix of lettuce, chicken breast, green beans, raisins, hard-boiled egg, and curry dressing.

"Shall we share a dessert? Maybe crème brûlée or cheesecake?"

"Ooh. Crème brûlée, please." Joi was feeling no pain.

Walking was exactly what Joi needed. Alex put his arm around her, and they strolled toward Chez Papa Jazz Club on rue Saint-Benoît. They heard the music long before they arrived. The place was packed, so they stood outside and listened to a couple of sets.

Alex recognized one of the musicians. "See that piano player? He once played with Romane, the famous French guitar maestro. Amazing!"

Joi hung on to Alex's arm. She leaned over so he could hear her. "Let's try another club so we can hopefully sit down."

"Absolutely. Caveau de la Huchette is close by." He turned her around and hugged her, and they began dancing in the street. "I do love your hair. You. I love you!" Alex shook his head and laughed out loud as he swung her around. "I'm in love!"

Chapter 20

Sam hadn't heard from Jenny since she'd arrived in Paris. Near as he could tell, Monica controlled all communication and strategy.

Weird situation. Everyone had been working on gallery and auction events, doing their job, a normal existence. Now, all of a sudden, they'd been thrown into international intrigue.

Monica walked in with a bag of carrots. "Hey, Sam. You okay? You look a little disheveled."

"Truthfully, I'm feeling a little uneasy. What have you heard from Paris, more specifically from my wife? Because I haven't heard a thing from her!"

She gave him a sideways glance. "What I know, at this point, is that everyone is doing their part. The Artcurial auction is coming up, and then the action begins. I did speak with Jenny for just a minute. She sends her love and said she would call you later. It's *fine*, Sam."

He let out a sigh and shook his head. "Okay. Sorry. Let's not talk about anything Paris-related right now or my brain will explode. I've been looking at what we have for Monterey." He handed her the latest budget figures.

Staff was in place, and they'd been able to secure their favorite auctioneer. A man who could sell eggs to chickens, fried with a side of bacon. Phillip's plan for the event was tastefully subdued. She saw Ben listed for food and drinks from the Purple Puffin. She had asked him herself. "I'm so glad Ben was available for the food for this particular event." She squinted at Sam. "But just out of curiosity, how does it happen that Ben gets a contract for almost all of our events?"

"We all love working with Ben and his staff. He's practically family. And besides, his bids come in the lowest. Is there a problem?" He smiled to himself. He loved opportunities when he could get Monica and Ben together, as much as Ben did himself. Ben also knew pressuring Monica to rekindle their relationship could backfire. For now, working events with her would have to do.

Sam stood and stretched. "Let's get out of here and get a beer. I'm tired. I'm stressed. And you, my friend, are going to join me for dinner."

Monica grinned. "You're on! Where shall we go? I've been munching these friggin' carrots for a week. I want pizza!"

"Well, then," he said, holding out his arm, "Pizzelle di North Beach, of course!"

Paris was not spoken of for the rest of the evening. They focused on Monterey and the ambience that Phillip, Dani, and Trev had designed.

When they'd acquired the building that now housed their gallery and Chic, they were told it was listed on the National Register of Historic Places. It was important for them to consider this when renovating the space for their two businesses. They'd contacted a local preservation foundation, a non-profit whose mission was to help with that process. David Waters, being on the board of directors, had offered to help them file the necessary paperwork for restoration. The auction was simply a means to raise money for that effort. And now David was involved with yet another project—art forgery in Paris! Dear David.

Auction items had been coming in for the last three to four months, through generous contributions from gallery patrons, friends, and word of mouth. Promotion had been going on for a year, with information available at all of their events. This was a labor of love. Love for historic preservation and love for the arts.

"The old photo panels and the simple statements to draw interest are perfect." Sam was relaxed now and focused. "I'm really glad we changed the venue to the Hyatt. It's smaller and more intimate than the convention center. Now we pray the attendance is high, with lots of plastic."

"I agree. And there's also a golf course. Not that I play much anymore, but it makes for a beautiful setting. I talked to Ben about his plan for food and drinks. He's great with this type of event. All materials are ready from the printers, and movers are lined up to transfer auction items. Thank God our auctioneer has a team to set up and organize that part." They clinked their beer mugs. "We have less than a week, and we are ready!"

After a moment, Sam said with a smirk, "Hey, not to change the subject too much, but how's that internet dating thing going?"

Monica took a sip of beer. "Well, let me tell you about that. I actually found someone I thought would be fun to meet. Nice-looking, great sense of humor, confident, and in love with his career as curator at the Maritime Museum. But when it came time to meet him for a drink, I couldn't do it." She shook her head. "No reason. Just couldn't do it. So that's my dating experience."

Sam nodded. "Hey, I forgot to tell you—Dani and Trev's gig at the Chapel the other night was amazing. Not only were Phillip's lighting effects phenomenal, but there were two A&Rs in the audience. I saw one of them talking to the bartender and a few other people about Dani and Trev. Checking on their background. If there was ever trouble with the law, that sort of thing. And if they have a fan following—which they obviously do. The place was packed. The reps were impressed with their talent and stage presence and made a point to talk with them after the show. I think they may have a good chance of a recording contract."

Monica stared at Sam. "Our Dani and Trev? I thought all they did was open for other bands. You know, country strummin' ditties. And what's A&R?"

"Oh my God. How can you not know about your own staff? There isn't a lick of country in their music. They do a cross between jazz and rock. Both incredible singers, both play guitar and keyboard. They trade off during performances. The audience loves them. And A&Rs are music recording scouts."

"Sorry. I had no idea."

"Monica, you need to talk to them tomorrow. They are so excited. But I'm thinking a little apprehensive about talking with you. They want to do their music full-time. And they should. Find out when their next gig is. We could all go. And we'll worry about replacing them later. It shouldn't be too hard to find a couple of artsy techy geeks. They're everywhere in this city."

Monica's head was spinning. Partly because of sharing a pitcher of beer with Sam, but also with the possibility—no, probability—of losing two incredibly talented and much-needed staff at the gallery.

Sam dropped Monica off at her apartment and headed home. Paris and Jenny returned to his thoughts like a slap in the face.

Chapter 21

Alex hadn't seen or spoken with Pierre since they'd landed in Paris. He gave him a call. "Pierre. I'm coming over in about an hour. We need to make plans for the auction. And we need to talk."

He arrived at Pierre's apartment, just off rue Rambuteau in the Marais. Alex had rented the flat for several years before Pierre moved back to Paris. The brothers shared the space for two years, then Alex moved out and Pierre purchased the apartment with Alex's help. With two bedrooms, a separate kitchen, and a large, open living and dining area, the space was perfect for his studio.

Pierre opened the door after one knock. He had just poured a glass of wine and offered one to Alex.

"*Oui, merci.*" Alex entered the tidy studio, glancing at canvases stacked against the wall and on several easels. "Is the painting ready?"

From the kitchen Pierre called, "The aging process is complete. I think it's good. We need to choose a frame." He brought out a glass of Beaujolais for Alex.

Uncovering the painting, Alex took a closer look. "The color. The detail. *C'est magnifique,* Pierre. *Extraordinaire.*" He patted him on the back. "Maybe your best."

They proceeded to look through Pierre's impressive collection of old frames and decided on one he had recently purchased at the flea market in Clignancourt.

"I'll put this together and have it ready for you to pick up later."

Alex sighed. "You know what I want to talk to you about."

Here they were having "the conversation" again. Alex wanted out—now more than ever. A couple of years ago, he had confided to Pierre how trapped he felt in his own profession. Sure, the money was good, providing a luxurious lifestyle, but the travel was stressful, and the documentation required for the artwork could be an arduous process.

Two years ago, they had schemed to produce and sell a forgery as sort of a test to see if they could get away with it. And they had. They'd agreed that would be the end. But then it wasn't. Alex had talked Pierre into producing ten more over the next couple of years.

"I'm in love, Pierre. She's the most beautiful, intelligent woman, and an artist like you. I want to build a life with her. Settle down. Maybe have a family." Alex was smiling like a schoolboy. "You have to meet—no, actually you have met her. It's Joi!"

Pierre was amused seeing his brother relaxed and genuinely happy and wanting a new life. With the stress of the last two years, he knew he wanted out as well.

Alex became serious. "Now is my chance at a new life." Pointing to the painting, he continued. "This is the last one, then we're done."

Chapter 22

Monica arrived at the gallery early, needing to put the Paris Affair aside and focus on business and the auction. Everyone would be arriving soon to pack up equipment and supplies in the company vehicle—an old, beat-up van they'd acquired when they first opened the gallery. It ran like a charm but looked like something out of the '70s, with gold shag carpet lining the entire inside and a history of who knows what. They'd appropriately christened it the Shaggin' Wagon.

With a fresh espresso in one hand and nibbling on a blueberry muffin, she called Ben. "I'm at the gallery waiting for the crew. Just checking when you'll arrive in Monterey."

"There's been a slight change of plans. Since the venue was moved from the convention center to the Hyatt, I was basically banned from catering from the Purple Puffin. I did make arrangements, however, with the staff at the hotel's TusCA Ristorante to be a guest chef for the event. This just happened, so I didn't have time to tell you sooner. I've worked with the head chef before. Actually attended a few classes with him at Le Cordon Bleu years ago. Anyway, we recently connected again, and I told him about your auction and how important it was to you. He's the one who suggested I guest chef for the event." Ben added some chopped spinach to the blender along with orange juice and fresh mint. "I should arrive around ten o'clock to go over details with him and then maybe hit the golf course for a quick round. Unless you need me for anything."

Monica beamed. What a team they made—when it came to events. "We'll be there around ten as well. And I love the idea of you as guest chef. This is all coming together better than I ever thought. Phillip has a fabulous plan for decor. Simple but amazing, as always, and it won't take us long to set up."

"What about the auction itself? Did you hire the same company you've used before?"

"Yes. A dynamite team. They pick up and deliver auction items and even provide bid cards, paddles, a photographer, and a red carpet. I passed on the carpet but love the idea of photos. This is a wonderful project and cause, and since the rental fee was donated by one of our supporters, we shouldn't have much overhead. By the way, what will it cost for food and your culinary skills, now that the plan has changed?"

Ben hesitated. "We'll talk about that later. Glad you called. See you later this morning." He ended the call. The food and his expenses would, of course, be donated. And spending the next couple of days with Monica would be nice. Out of town, on the coast, relaxed—he hoped there would be an opportunity to be alone.

Phillip was first to arrive. Monica heard him whistling before she saw his face.

Phillip said, "Fabulous morning. Fabulous. Where are you?"

Monica yelled, "Back here. Did you bring your bag? We don't have time to stop by your place."

Phillip walked in with his bag slung over his shoulder, looking like a model out of *GQ*. He walked over and kissed the top of her head.

"Look at you, handsome! Go get yourself an espresso."

Phillip had already walked away—Monica still talking, and no one listening. He returned and nodded his head in agreement as she was saying, "—and as soon as everyone gets here, we can start packing up the van, and we're off. It's about a two-hour drive. We'll check in at the Hyatt first, then meet up with the events manager in the ballroom."

She heard Dani and Trev kibitzing, obviously excited about the trip. Continuing in her director mode, she called, "Okay, you two. Let's get going." She tossed Trev the keys. "Back up the van. Dani, help Phillip load the boxes of brochures." Then her phone rang. "Sam? Where are you?"

"I'm home, where else would I be?" Sam slurred. "Lil' hungover . . . or drunk. Alive. Not so well."

"We're all here packing up the van. We leave in less than an hour."

Silence.

"Sam! Snap out of it. Get your ass over here." Then she considered the situation. "No. Wait there. Don't move. Eat something. I'm coming over." By then Monica's voice had reached another octave.

"Yeah. Okay. Eat." Sam said weakly into the dead phone and tossed it on the table. He was doubtful about eating.

"Phillip, Sam's having a crisis. I'm going over to pick him up. You're in charge here. The auction guys should be here shortly. Be back soon."

She arrived at Sam's apartment in Noe Valley in less than ten minutes. She knocked. No answer. She tried the door, and it swung open. *What the hell?*

"Sam?" she said tentatively. "Where are you?"

She walked to the back of the apartment, peeking around corners as she went. Sam was sitting at a table on the small patio that opened off the kitchen, looking like he'd been sleeping in the street all night with stray cats. A half cup of coffee in his hand, while a piece of dry toast still sat in the toaster.

"Oh, sweetie. What's wrong? What happened?" Monica felt bad about yelling at him earlier.

Sam looked up at her with puffy, bloodshot eyes. "Jenny called last night. All excited. Told me about Paris—and her plans to seduce Alex. She was giggling. Then she hung up. Just like that. Hung up." Sam let out a sigh. "What should I do? I love her. So much. The thought of her with someone else—I can't stand it. I can't do this."

Monica began rubbing his shoulders. "She's only going to tease him, not actually follow through. It's a trick. Not unlike what Alex is doing with his art scams. She's an actress. You know that. She can accomplish what needs to be done without going to bed with him. Don't you see that?"

Sam stared, not comprehending her words. "I lost it last night. Walked to the Dubiner . . . Dubliner. Had a beer. A few. Watched some stupid game on TV. Saw a buddy of mine. We drank whiskey . . ."

Monica found some aspirin in the corner cupboard and poured a tall glass of water. "Here. Take these." Finding nothing else to combat a hangover, she held a cold cloth on his neck while he drank. He looked and smelled like hell, but they'd deal with that later.

"Okay, buddy. Time to go." She led him to the front door and noticed his overnight bag. She threw it over her shoulder as she steadied him down the steps and to her car. This was going to be a very long day, especially for Sam.

Leaving the gallery later than planned, Monica was distraught, sweaty and anxious. Not in control. She took off her jacket and put the top down on the Miata. Phillip joined her, while Sam and the others rode in the van.

"Phillip, how about a coffee or something? I'll swing by Starbucks. Do you want anything else besides your usual double-shot vanilla latte with a single pump of chocolate, extra whipped cream, and a splash of caramel?"

"No thanks. Unless you want to share a bistro box. Maybe the cheese and fruit one? I can feed you bites." He looked lovingly at her and winked.

She knew Phillip would make the ride to Monterey fun.

"Sam and I went out for pizza the other night. He chastised me for not knowing the extent of Dani and Trev's music world. I had no idea they were anything but openers for other bands. I feel really bad."

"Oh my God. They are so amazing. Why don't you go next time? After the performance at the Chapel, they landed another gig next month *and* a possible recording contract."

"Sam said the same thing. A group of us could go and cheer them on. Groupies. I could ask Ben to come too."

They arrived at the Hyatt a little past ten. Monica told Sam, for obvious reasons, to stay in the van while she checked in at the front desk. Four rooms had been reserved. Dani and Trev would share one while the others had their own. She was directed to unload the van near the restaurant service entrance.

"Okay, Sam. Wake up. Here's your room key. Go take a shower and come down as soon as you can. The rest of us will unload but will need help setting up." She patted his back while giving directions.

Just then, Ben walked up and asked if he could help. "Looks like Sammy here had a rough night."

Monica grabbed a box from the van and handed it to Ben. "We'll talk about Sam later. In fact, I have so much to tell you. Once we're set up, want to go for a glass of wine?"

"Absolutely. Let me see if the Hyatt can spare some staff to help unload. The auction team arrived earlier. They've got that part under control. And your staff is great. So, let's make it wine and lunch."

"Love it. You do know I'm trying to lose weight? Make it a green lunch and white wine. No bread. No dessert."

Ben beamed. "Anything for you, my dear. Hey, how about a round of golf? I know you haven't had much time to play lately, but it would be fun. I could coach you on your stance and swing. What do you say?"

"Are you kidding?" She giggled, ready for the challenge. "Bring it on, Mr. Graham."

Monica gazed at the auction setup. "It looks great. You okay, Sam? Ben and I are going for a quick round of golf and lunch."

"Be on your way, madam. We're set. I told Dani and Trev to take a break too. I think they went down to the beach. Not sure where Phillip is. Maybe the shops. I'm going back to my room for a long nap."

"Sounds good. Let's meet back here at five, ready to rock and roll and showtime!"

Ben watched Monica get in position at the tee. "Concentrate. Relax and focus on the ball. Swing back and follow through while keeping your eye on the ball."

"Geez, Ben. Stop. I really do know what I'm doing." Monica swung and nailed it. The ball flew in a perfect arc toward the first green and landed a short two feet from the hole.

"Holy shit." Ben was in awe. Then grinned. "Ah, pure luck!"

"Not luck. I've been golfing since I was fourteen. You never lose the magic of the swing." She did a mock, slow-motion swing. "You're up, big boy."

Ben approached the ball, surveyed the distance, and focused. Doing a practice swing, he stood back, surveyed again, and swung. Slice to the left.

Monica whooped. "Oh, don't worry. We've got eight more holes to go. Relax, Ben. Relax." Monica was ready to whip his ass.

The club restaurant was a typical golf course eatery with a limited menu. After being seated on the patio overlooking the putting green and driving range, Ben ordered a bottle of Rombauer chardonnay while they glanced at the menu.

"You were amazing. I'd forgotten what a good golfer you are."

"I may be short, but I'm deadly fierce." Monica grinned and realized she hadn't felt this relaxed in a very long time.

The waiter returned with the wine and regaled them with the day's lunch options. They both ordered a mixed green salad with grilled chicken.

"This is nice, but I have to say I'm surprised you're actually taking some time for yourself. I thought you'd be fussing and running around setting up for tonight."

"I have a really great team, even if one of them is a little hungover today. With Phillip on board, I feel confident. Even relaxed. And it's perfect for him to have the opportunity to take charge. I want to hire him full-time. Partly because I need to take some time off.

I'm exhausted, and I'm missing out on doing things—like today, for instance. Playing golf."

"I understand, and I'm proud of you. So, you said you had a bunch of stuff to tell me. What's up?"

Monica sat back and sipped her wine. "A situation has developed in the last couple of weeks. Hard to believe, but it's taking place in Paris right now." Monica filled Ben in on the art forgery, Alex, Joi, David, and now Jenny.

"That's crazy! I'm surprised you're not over there with them."

"Well, someone has to stay home and keep the gallery afloat. Besides, I'm kind of enjoying it from afar. Like reading a really good novel. Sam and I are making it work. Darling Phillip helps out when he can. We'll keep the X6 exhibit up an extra month to buy us time until Joi returns. If she returns. It really does sound crazy."

Their salads came with a small loaf of warm bread. Monica hesitated, then broke off a piece as she glanced at a smiling Ben.

"And another thing. I recently found out that we're probably going to lose Dani and Trev. Did you know they play music gigs? Well, apparently, they blew it out of the water the other night at the Chapel." She regaled him with the details of a possible recording contract. "I had no idea they were so good. Sam suggested we all go to their next gig and support the hell out of them. Want to go?"

"I'm stunned by everything you've told me. Paris. Forgery. Music contract." He shook his head. "And, yes, I'd love to see them perform. There might be an opportunity for them to play at the Purple Puffin. I'd need to hear their music first, but wouldn't that be a hoot? Let me know when you're all going."

After lunch, Monica and Ben went their separate ways. She took another quick scan of the ballroom. Walking through, she straightened a couple of napkins and rearranged one of the table decorations. Other than that, it was all perfect and ready to go. The auction was less than three hours away. Returning to her room, she took a shower and fell into the most restful nap in a very long time.

Monica stood in front of the gallery and auction staff like a drill sergeant, everyone dressed to the nines. "I couldn't be happier or prouder. You have all done a phenomenal job with design and execution. This is going to be one hell of an event. Thank you! Thank you!" Monica bowed to each one of them. "And by the way, you all look fabulous!" She drifted away to speak with the auctioneer. She felt relaxed, happy, and renewed.

They all looked at her and each other. "Wow. She's not strutting or futzing," Sam said. "Or basically being unpleasant." They all said in unison, "What's happened to Mother Hen?"

The next morning, Monica stretched and rolled over in bed. The sun and soft ocean breeze poured through the slightly ajar sliding glass door. Soft jazz meandered from the other room as she snuggled under the covers. She could smell coffee brewing and, all of a sudden, wanted breakfast more than anything. Something wonderful wafted from the kitchen. Bacon. Sitting up, she suddenly became aware of a throbbing headache. She stumbled to the bathroom in search of aspirin, then splashed water on her face, slipped on her robe, and tentatively peeked around the bedroom door.

"Ben! What are you doing here?"

"Good morning, sleepyhead. Breakfast is almost ready." He slathered butter on a slice of toasted baguette and expertly flipped an omelet, then handed her a cup of coffee. "Go sit outside."

"Ben, why are you here?" She took a sip of coffee. "Thank you. Sorry. I do believe I'm a little hungover. What time is it?" This was not a normal situation for Monica. She was always conscious of alcohol consumption and always in control!

Ben smiled at her, knowing what she was probably thinking.

"It's eleven. Last night was amazing. And you, my dear, had a very successful auction. You should be proud."

He plated their breakfast and brought it out to the balcony, letting the moment linger. "After the event was over, you and your staff joined me for a champagne toast. I think between the event and your highly successful golf game, you may have had a little too much to drink. I brought you back here and tucked you in."

"And?"

"And I went to my room and came here this morning to fix you breakfast. That's it."

Monica felt relief, but then didn't. It would have been nice if they had spent the evening together.

They ate in silence, relaxed and refreshed by the sea air.

"I need to call Sam. What time is it? We've got to pack up."

Ben looked at his watch. "It's now eleven ten. And everything has been taken care of. I met with the events manager early this morning. The hotel staff helped with packing the van and everyone headed back to the city. The auctioneer settled up with his paperwork and gave it to Sam before they left. All you need to do, my dear, is shower and dress."

"Thank you, Ben. What would I do without you?"

"I'm more than happy to help out. Listen, you need a break. Between your two businesses and now the situation in Paris, it's time to rethink what's going on. Do you need more staff? Are you still planning on expanding to accommodate a bistro in the gallery?"

"I don't know. I seriously don't know. It's easy to sit in my apartment and visualize all kinds of wonderful things. But now that Dani and Trev are leaving, even if Phillip joins us, it's not enough."

Ben cleared the table, and Monica followed him to the kitchen. He turned and wrapped his arms around her and slowly rubbed her back. He looked in her eyes and kissed her forehead.

"Go take your shower. I was thinking it might be nice to stay one more night. Sam was totally in agreement when I mentioned it. There's nothing pending at the gallery. Take some time for yourself. Stop and smell the flowers." He pointed to the ocean. "Or the sea air. I'm here for you, if you want. We could hit the links again—if you're up to it."

She closed her eyes and let out a sigh. "Let me get myself together, and I'll call you. Staying another night sounds wonderful."

Ben returned to his room and called the front desk. "This is Mr. Graham in room 405. Please extend my stay one more night. And the same for Ms. Graham in room 407. Thank you."

Chapter 23

Alex was happy with David's response to the Chagall and that his wife would be joining him soon. A showing of the painting and dinner afterward might seal the deal.

He almost called Joi to join him for lunch but then changed his mind. He needed to be alone for a while and mentally prepare for the auction. Leaving the hotel, he walked a couple of blocks, making notes on his phone when he accidentally bumped into someone coming out of the boutique he was passing.

"*Excusez-moi*," he said without looking up.

"Alex?"

He turned and saw an attractive woman with long blonde hair smiling at him. He stared at her in a daze and blinked. "Jenny?"

"Alex Marchand. You have not changed a bit. Not one bit." She hugged him, then stood back shaking her head. "I can't believe I'm standing here looking at you."

"Jenny, what are you doing here? How are you?" He was at a loss for words.

"I'm here for a few weeks doing research for my studies. I'm going for a law degree. Are you busy? Can we go someplace and catch up?"

"I would love to, but I have to be somewhere in about ten minutes and won't be free until day after tomorrow. Can we meet then?"

"Yes. Perfect." She dictated her number as he punched it into his phone under Jenny Cole.

"You look great. I'll call you in a couple of days." He smiled then kissed her on each cheek. He shook his head. "Amazing."

Alex went back toward the hotel in absolute shock. He had been reminded of her only a couple of evenings ago when he saw Génépy des Alpes on the menu at Bofinger.

Chapter 24

The day of the Artcurial auction, David sipped an espresso as he dressed. Being a large man, he'd paid close attention to his wardrobe. The suit had been tailor-made a short week ago with superior fabric and craftsmanship.

He reminisced about the last auction he'd attended in Paris a few years ago. He had won the bid on a small Renoir, which now resided in their study, along with their extensive collection of old manuscripts, limited and signed first editions, and of course art.

"*Bonjour*, David." Alex was in the dining room with a *café*, reading the morning paper when David approached. He stood and they shook hands. Alex was dressed strikingly in a dark charcoal-gray suit, black shirt, and no tie. He would be serving as agent for three clients, all via his cell phone, as well as informally advising David.

"*Bonjour*." David was visibly delighted to be spending the day with Alex—an opportunity to watch him in action and also see what treasures the auction had to offer.

They ordered a simple *petit déjeuner* of orange juice, croissants, marmalade, fresh berries, and a soft-boiled egg. Alex explained they could have a late lunch after the auction or plan on dinner if David liked, and maybe invite Joi.

"Let's see how the day goes. I may need a stiff drink and a nap if I get carried away with bidding."

The venue began to fill with patrons scrutinizing items up for auction. Alex excused himself to sign in and speak with the auctioneer, while David perused the jewelry selection, hoping to find an anniversary gift for his wife, Kat.

The house coordinator announced the auction would begin in five minutes and asked for everyone to please be seated. Two aides passed out programs and assisted the last of the attendees to their seats.

Alex found David toward the back and explained he needed to be at the side of the room, where cell phone reception was best. They agreed to meet up later.

As the auction began, David watched how Alex drew attention from regular bidders who at one time or another had secured him as their agent. He could see the respect Alex received from these people and found it hard to believe he was involved in forgery.

After several paintings had been bid on and sold, the auctioneer announced the collection of jewelry would be up next. David knew exactly the piece he would bid on. A Cartier platinum wristwatch bracelet, set with diamonds, circa 1940–1950.

Jenny arrived late, just as the bidding for jewelry began. Showing her pass to the attendant, she asked if he could point out Alexander Marshal. He nodded and directed her gaze to the side of the room and the man in the dark gray suit. Jenny thanked him and moved further into the room, peeking around a tall gentleman in front of her. She searched the farthest wall and saw Alex. Stepping back, she asked the attendant again. "No. Alexander Marshal."

"Yes, *mademoiselle*. Alexander Marshal. Talking on his cell phone."

She was stunned. Alex? *Alexander Marshal is Alexander March-and?* She quickly turned and left before being noticed.

Jenny needed to think, to plan—she needed a drink. Sitting at a window table at the Lipp, she retrieved a notebook from her bag, ordered a chardonnay, and began jotting down memories from their past. She thought about the Alex she'd known and loved. Alex Marchand wasn't a forger. She didn't know Alex Marshal. She decided to spend as much time as possible with him. Get in his head. Talk about their history together and where his life had taken him after leaving Paris. She took a sip of wine and jotted in her book: *Who are you, Alex Marshal?*

She also needed to call Monica and David. But—not quite yet.

David was ecstatic about winning the bid for the Cartier watch. He knew Kat would love it. He scanned the room for Alex, who was engaged with a small group of bidders and regular clients.

Alex excused himself and met David at the checkout station. "I see you won the bid for the watch. Excellent!"

"This was fun, Alex. Thank you for inviting me. I'm going to pay up and head back to the hotel. I want to secure this treasure in the hotel safe. Kat arrives tomorrow. Dinner and the Chagall in the next couple of days?" He shook Alex's hand and turned to the cashier.

Alex was happy. He'd placed the winning bids for all three of his clients, which meant a nice profit for himself. He gave his regards to the auction staff and left. Walking back to the hotel, he pondered his life and profession. It had always been easy, exciting even, but now it was all simply rote, tiresome.

Chapter 25

David arrived at Charles de Gaulle airport an hour earlier than Kat's scheduled two o'clock arrival. Seated in the airport lounge, he ordered a scotch neat, thumbed through a *Saveur* magazine, adjusted his tie, glanced at the flight information screen, checked his watch, and finally began to pace the now-crowded arrival area, feeling like a schoolboy.

He looked forward to their time alone. Being around Alex and Joi had stirred something in David that he hadn't felt for a long time. He missed the intimacy he and his wife used to share. He was proud of her success as a writer and editor, but now, in Paris, they could relax and revisit favorite places, new restaurants—and perhaps each other.

Kat spent most days at their publishing company, and with the recent release of her book, her time also included promotional book-signing events. Their individual schedules, plus trying to stay connected with their two grown children, had been challenging lately. But now, here in Paris, David felt relaxed, alive, and was contemplating a slower lifestyle for their future. Maybe that future would include more time in Paris or perhaps a move. They would be celebrating their thirtieth anniversary at Le Taillevent, one of their favorite restaurants. It would be an exquisite dining experience for him and his darling wife.

He spotted Kat among other stylish travelers, alongside exhausted-looking people in need of a restroom or a smoking area. She smiled and waved, happy to finally be on the ground.

"*Bonjour, mon chéri.*"

They embraced and shared a lingering kiss. Kat stood back surprised, then leaned back in for another kiss. "Goodness. Paris has had a wonderful effect on my husband."

David was already showered and dressed when Kat woke to a sun-filled room and a bouquet of flowers he'd had delivered to their suite first thing that morning.

"Happy anniversary, my darling," he said.

"Mmm, and happy anniversary to you." She smiled and blew him a kiss.

There was a knock on the door. "Breakfast has arrived," David said, encouraging Kat to get up and into the shower.

The waiter entered and set the food on the table in front of the window overlooking the courtyard and carefully tended gardens below. He took care to arrange the napkins and cutlery, nodded, and left the room.

David placed a small wrapped package beside Kat's plate. Five minutes later, she emerged from the bathroom dressed in a blue floral kimono, fluffing her short damp hair with her fingers. Smelling of orange and mint and wearing no makeup, she was strikingly beautiful. David wrapped his arms around her, kissed her forehead, and led her to the table.

Kat saw the gift. *"Pour moi?"* She quickly pulled the blue satin ribbon from the box. "You'll receive your gift tomorrow, darling." *Something I need to purchase on the sly.*

"Oh, David!" The watch lay glistening in the blue velvet case with diamonds twinkling around the minuscule watch face. She thought she might need reading glasses to check the time.

"I bought it at the auction I attended with Alex yesterday. It's Cartier, 1940s."

"So unusual. I love it." She leaned over and kissed him. "And I love you."

After a leisurely breakfast and catching up on business and family news, they planned their day of walking around the city.

"I made dinner reservations at Le Taillevent for this evening. Remember when we went there a couple of years ago?"

"I do. It was our anniversary then too." Kat let out a hearty laugh. "Looks like we're setting a pattern here, darling. What time?"

"Nine. I thought we could try to see the Edward Hopper exhibit at the Grand Palais first thing this morning. It's been incredibly popular, with waiting lines around the block. Want to give it a try?"

"Love to. I'll be ready in ten minutes."

But Edward Hopper would have to wait. Instead, they decided on Kat's favorite museum, the Musée d'Orsay, home to the largest collection of Impressionist art in the world. The museum building, once a railway station, had been built in the Beaux-Arts style in 1900. The high, vaulted glass ceiling, extending the length of the building, gave the main space perfect lighting for the sculptures displayed.

"Ah, home." Kat was delighted to be back among art that was as familiar to her as her husband's handsome face. They entered a series of smaller galleries devoted to Monet, Van Gogh, Degas, Cézanne,

Seurat, and Gauguin. "Thank you, sweetheart." She took his hand as they strolled through the familiar halls and salons.

Back at the hotel and after a long nap, they began to dress for dinner. David selected a superbly tailored charcoal-gray suit, faint-blue silk shirt, narrow bottle-green challis tie, and softly polished, chestnut-colored calfskin shoes.

Kat looked at the array of outfits on the bed, then at David, and whistled. "Look at you. Hmm." She rearranged a few items and finally chose a dark blue fitted dress with cap sleeves and a square neckline and a fitted bolero jacket. She asked David to fasten the watch to her wrist while choosing simple drop earrings with single diamonds.

"Lovely as always," David cooed. He leaned down and kissed her neck, inhaling her favorite perfume, J'adore by Dior, then called down to the concierge and arranged for an Uber to take them to Le Taillevent.

They were met by the maître d' and shown to their table by a window showcasing a splendid view of the Arc de Triomphe, brightly lit against the indigo-blue sky. The room was breathtaking, with cream-colored walls, satin drapes, a winding staircase, and huge bouquets of white roses, orchids, and camellias placed on pedestals around the room.

The *chef d'étage* approached with menus and a leather-bound wine list the size of an atlas. Amused, David ordered champagne as they perused the extensive menu.

"We could do the tasting menu or à la carte. What do you think?" asked David.

Kat scanned the menu again. "À la carte. I'd like the crab and *petit farcis* to start."

David nodded. "I'll do the scallops. We can share bites."

Two waiters approached, dressed elegantly in black suits, with the champagne and a delightful amuse-bouche—tiny cheese puff pastries, *gougères*.

David surveyed their entrée choices, raised his glass to Kat, and smiled. "Happy anniversary, darling."

Her eyes smiled. "Happy anniversary, sweet prince."

Kat broached the subject of Alex and the possible forgery. "Have you spent much time with him, and have you learned anything new? What is your gut feeling about this situation?" Kat was always straightforward, and David appreciated that about her. He trusted her judgment and knew her presence here would be invaluable.

"To be honest, I don't know. I like him. He's extremely professional and knowledgeable and has been more than generous, inviting me to breakfast and dinner on a few occasions. And Joi is a darling. She's quite taken with him, which could pose a problem. We'll see."

The first course was served, again by the two waiters. The sommelier ceremoniously poured the Château Simone Rosé. David nodded his approval. They gazed at the food, so beautifully presented. The crab, rémoulade sauce, and dill with *crème fleurette* and lemon. And the *petit farcis*, a variation on a traditional Niçoise dish, was a visual delight, an edible still life of perfectly cooked vegetables, each with its own delicate stuffing.

David's beef tartare was served with caviar and a raw egg yolk. The ground rib-eye steak was surrounded by small amounts of condiments—aioli sauce, capers, parsley, red onion, and pickle. A small baguette and *frites* were placed to the side.

With a smile, they raised their glasses and recited, *"Bon appétit. Amen."*

The toast was a memory they shared with their children from the summer they'd spent in Provence. Abby, then five, had announced she wanted to say grace as they all sat down to dinner. Kat and David were surprised but lovingly nodded their assent. Abby had closed her eyes and very seriously asked blessings upon her favorite things: her cat Felix, her teddy bear with one button eye missing, the chain bracelet she'd found at the park, and the frog she'd captured and put in a jar that morning. She'd finished with "*Bon appétit.* Amen." From then on, the family tradition was to raise their glass of chosen beverage and make the toast before beginning a meal.

Kat looked around at their opulent surroundings and smiled at David. "I can't believe we're actually sitting here. With so much going on." She sipped her wine. "But here we are. In Paris. Sharing a fabulous meal." She realized she was getting a little tipsy as she leaned over and kissed his cheek.

The waiters arrived with the main course. Kat had ordered duck, roasted to perfection with cherries, lemon verbena, and fresh almonds. David's Brittany lobster glistened on the plate, surrounded by artichokes, basil, and dried tomatoes.

David noticed the sommelier standing close by and nodded for him to come to their table.

"*Monsieur?*" He looked down at the dishes that had been placed before them. "Ah. With this," he said, gesturing to the food, "I highly recommend a Givry—a nice red burgundy."

David nodded in agreement. The wine was brought to the table and presented to David for approval.

"Excellent!"

David turned to Kat. "We'll be meeting Alex at his hotel tomorrow evening to view the Chagall. I think it's stunning, and quite authentic. I'm anxious for your opinion."

Kat nodded in a distracted sort of way. "This duck is quite delicious." She wiped her fingers on her napkin, then reached over and took David's hand. "Okay. Let's talk about this tomorrow. I want to focus on this meal and the charming man I'm sharing it with. I love you, darling."

David smiled and let out a sigh. He hadn't been aware he was practically holding his breath as he talked about the intrigue they were in now. Over the last two years, he had been consumed on and off with the forgery scam. But now, after meeting Alex and seeing the respect he had garnered in the art world, the game seemed to be changing, and time would tell.

"Did you see the kids before you left?"

"Yes. Actually, they took me to the airport. And, of course, they were both trying to figure out how they could come along. Those two! Fun, but this isn't the situation to involve more people. They adore Joi, but it would have been tricky trying to keep everything under wraps." She took a sip of wine. "Okay. More family news. Max was just offered a contract at a huge company to design their ad campaign. He is beside himself. And Abby might have a chance working as sous-chef at the Purple Puffin. Could our cadre of friends and family get any more connected?" She laughed, shaking her head.

David hesitated to bring up Alex again, but then said, "I think we need to spend a day with Alex and Joi. I was thinking of a day trip to Épernay. We could rent a car and take our time getting there. Remember when we went? Such a lovely village. I think it would be good to get the two of them out of the city. People tend to open up in a neutral environment when given the opportunity to relax. What do you think?"

"I think you're a genius. Let's ask Alex tomorrow night."

Playfully, David leaned toward her and said, "May I have a bite?"

Kat stabbed a piece of duck with a bit of cherry and offered it to him.

David did the same and gave her a bite of lobster. She closed her eyes and purred, "The dinner is wonderful. And you, my darling, are wonderful."

Having a long and relaxing meal was exactly what David and Kat needed. Coming down from a chaotic schedule, one tends to absorb and appreciate life, especially in Paris.

They reminisced about their last trip to France. David said, "What would you think of buying a place in Paris? Or maybe Provence? Would you consider living here?"

Kat was taken aback. Her whole existence in San Francisco revolved around their publishing company and the literary world. Friends, family, and colleagues.

"Darling. Are you serious?" She put her fork down. "Well, I won't say yes or no. This is quite a proposition." Kat felt overwhelmed all of a sudden. She changed the subject. "I am utterly stuffed to the gills. And as much as I love cheese, I do believe I'm sated." She hesitated. "However, it wouldn't take much convincing to share the wild strawberry and basil sorbet. It's such a small amount. We can do it, right?"

David chuckled and motioned for the waiter.

Back in their suite, Kat kicked off her shoes, grabbed the small blanket on the bed, and went out on the balcony. "Come sit with me."

David removed his jacket and shoes, poured two small glasses of cognac, and followed his wife. He kissed the top of her head and handed her the glass. They sipped their drinks and reviewed their splendid day and evening. He took her hand and playfully said, "Come to bed with me, *ma chérie*."

Chapter 26

Monica hadn't heard from David, Joi, or Jenny. Her mind wandered, wondering if they were either all dead in an alley in Montmartre or having the time of their lives in the Latin Quarter.

She called David. No answer.

She called Joi. No answer.

She called Sam. "Have you heard from your wife? I haven't heard from her, Joi, or David." She was practically screaming into the phone.

"Only short, cryptic messages that tell me nothing. Why did I agree to her going?" Sam had been in a funk the entire time since Jenny left. "I've been contemplating a trip to Paris myself. She's my wife, for God's sake. I didn't expect this. Not even close." He grabbed a bottle of water from his refrigerator and tripped over a pizza box and a pair of sneakers. Their apartment looked like his bachelor pad before he had gotten together with Jenny. Dirty dishes and underwear among wrappers and empty bottles. She had straightened him out, given him confidence, and made a lovely, well-organized home for them. Now the place looked like a cheap set from a bad movie.

Monica took a deep breath. "Okay. Slow down, partner. We're bound to hear something soon. Besides, there are too many clowns in the tent already. And it seems no one is in charge." Monica secretly agreed with Sam. She felt like catching the next flight out to Paris herself.

"Yeah. Clowns. We're the clowns! They're in Paris having the time of their lives."

Monica continued. "On another note, we need to start planning the next exhibit for the gallery. The X6 has only two more weeks before we take it down. I've been thinking of maybe student art. No specific theme, but simply focusing on students and their individual vision reflected in their work. And I think Dani and Trev should do the music for opening night. The whole event would be hip and cool."

Sam said, "Hip and cool?"

"I know, I know. Anyway, let's try to focus on business."

As they talked details, they could both hear music and singing downstairs—Dani and Trev laughing and working out riffs and chord changes.

"I'll call Phillip and ask him to come in tomorrow, and we can brainstorm." Monica felt a little better by focusing on responsibilities she could control.

"Hey, Phillip. Can you come by the gallery tomorrow? I have something to pass by you. Actually, I need your help planning the next exhibit. We only have a couple of weeks to get it together." Monica was off and running, not giving Phillip a chance to respond.

Phillip, used to Monica in her hyper mode, was in the middle of getting dressed for work and fretting over whether to wear a tie or not. "Okay, I'll wear a tie. But which one?" he whispered to himself. He pushed the speaker button on his phone so he could talk and continue to choose a tie. "Lavender with pink dots or coral with black stripes? I can't come by the gallery, but I could do lunch, if we chose a place close to the salon. Yes. Coral with black stripes. It's going to be a busy day. Sushi sounds good. Want to do ANZU?"

Monica loved sushi. "Perfect. Who are you talking to?"

"Myself."

"I'll come by the salon and pick you up at what, eleven thirty?"

"Better make it eleven forty-five."

Parking was always insane downtown, but Monica was able to find a spot fairly close to the salon. The stress of being shorthanded at the gallery and trying to keep up with what seemed to be a fiasco in Paris had caused her to lose almost ten pounds. She was happy about the weight loss, but the stress was giving her migraines. That alone stressed her. "Mother hens don't have time for migraines!" she said out loud.

Phillip was talking to Isabelle when Monica walked in. "Okay, I'll try to be back by one." He waved and grabbed his Italian over-the-shoulder leather bag.

They walked the few short blocks to ANZU and were lucky to find a table by the window. Phillip scanned the menu even though he knew exactly what he wanted. "So, what's the new exhibit?"

"Nothing in place yet, but I have an idea about contacting the Art Institute to see if we could pull together student art to display and promote at the gallery. And I was also thinking it would be a perfect opportunity for Dani and Trev to play for the opening. Young and edgy art and music. What do you think?"

Monica also knew what she wanted to order. She nodded at the waitress, who was busing a table nearby. "May we order, please?"

"I'll have the north duck and an iced tea."

Phillip smiled up at her. "The usual."

"Titus roll?"

"Yes. And an iced tea for me too. Thank you."

Phillip had been mulling over Monica's idea for the exhibit. "I like your idea. But I think instead of the entire class, you should hand-pick seven or eight top artists—all with their own definite style. Each artist could prepare a short statement about their work. We print them up in large format to be displayed with the art. The students would, of course, attend the opening, giving them the opportunity to discuss their personal art journey. What do you think?"

"I think you're a genius. Would you be willing to help choose the artists? I can't do this alone. Sam is beyond helping right now. He's of no help at all, in fact."

"Love to." Phillip hesitated. "I need to talk to you about something too. Maybe this isn't the best time, but I want—need—to get out of the salon. As much as I love Isabelle and the other girls, it was never meant to be a career for me. It was simply an available place to work when I got out of college. That was over six years ago. Six! So, here's the pitch. I want to work in your gallery. I have always wanted to be a part of what the three of you have created. Every time you ask me to help out with an exhibit or event, I'm in heaven. I'm at my best." Phillip was breathless and somewhat drained. "I don't need a large salary. We could work something out. Maybe someday I could actually buy in as a partner. I just know I belong with all of you."

Monica was both happily surprised and relieved. She had always wanted Phillip to be a part of their business. In the beginning, it hadn't been possible; they were all struggling just to open the doors. Success had come slowly, but now they were actually pretty solid, thanks to Sam and his financial-genius oversight. The situation in Paris was leaving them shorthanded, but financially they were okay.

"Phillip, I've been thinking about this too. We all have. It will be tight, but let's talk to Sam and try to make it happen. And besides, with Dani and Trev leaving, that would free up salary for you. Can you get out of the salon easily?"

Phillip was red in the face and ready to cry when the waitress arrived with their orders. He pulled himself together. "You, my dear, have made my day. My year. My life. I'll talk to Isabelle this afternoon. In all fairness to her, I will stay on and help find a replacement."

They sat grinning at each other, both of them relieved for different reasons. They began role-playing, pretending they were doing a TV ad for ANZU.

Monica leaned forward with her hand on her chest. "I *love* the north duck roll. It's made with duck, chestnuts, honey, cranberries, and . . . brussels sprouts!"

Phillip threw his hands up in the air and closed his eyes. "And I *love* the Titus roll. A blend of tuna, salmon, cucumber, and . . . avocado!"

They burst out laughing, while other diners were either amused at their antics or shaking their heads in disbelief.

They parted company at exactly one o'clock. "Good luck with Isabelle. Call me later."

"Whew." He fluttered his hand in front of his face. "Yes. And thank you for lunch." He blew her a kiss and sauntered into the salon like a man who had just won the lottery.

Monica was ecstatic. Help with the next exhibit was a go, and with the most amazing designer, good friend, and, hopefully, future partner. She could hardly wait to get back to the gallery to tell Sam.

Once back at the gallery, she tried David one more time. He answered after one ring.

"David, we haven't connected for several days. What's going on?"

"I apologize for not calling. So much has happened, one thing after another. Kat arrived two days ago, and we're going to Alex's suite to view the Chagall tonight and dinner after. I can't talk right now, but be assured that all is well. I'll call you tomorrow and fill you in on everything. Again, I'm sorry, but I have to go. Talk to you soon."

Monica was both frustrated with David's lack of information and relieved to hear his voice. As to all being well, she doubted it. Joi was romantically involved with a criminal.

Chapter 27

Alex arranged for David and his wife to come to his suite to view the Chagall before dinner. Joi was nervous about seeing Kat, even though David had assured her that Kat wouldn't reveal their knowing each other. She straightened pillows and fussed with the flower arrangement on the coffee table, then turned on the gas fireplace for a bit of atmosphere and partially opened the balcony doors to let in a soft, cool breeze.

Alex came out of the bedroom, straightened his tie, and tucked in the back of his shirt. "The room looks great. Like you." He smiled. "A small gin and tonic? I'm going to have one."

"Yes, that would be nice." She sat on the sofa and twisted the chain of her necklace, reflecting on her choice of a plain black sheath and black pumps for the evening. It seemed a subtle indication of wanting to blend into the background. She didn't want to be here.

Alex sensed her nervousness, thinking it had to do with the pending sale. He handed her the drink and sat down. "You know you haven't told me much about how you came to pursue a fine arts degree and a related career. Or anything about your family, for that matter."

She looked at him, somewhat surprised but glad to engage in conversation other than the evening's activities. "My parents are wealthy, but very frugal and extremely religious, in a quiet sort of way. I could have gone to school here in Paris, traveled the world, but they didn't see that as a necessity when Stanford offered perfectly good education opportunities. I rebelled and insisted on joining my friends for an education that appealed to me. The art world was like the Emerald City. A quest not only to become a good artist but also to be on my own. Make my own decisions." She shook her head. "Oh my gosh. My life changed in ways I can't even explain." Joi suddenly smiled at the memories of a very young, innocent girl going to New York City for the first time.

Alex kissed her cheek. "Good for you. You have a wonderful sense of style that attracts people. I can see that. But I also see a future in a more global way. Maybe we can discuss that at some time." Alex had no clue why he'd just said that.

A knock on the door brought Joi back to reality.

"Right now, my sweet, it's time to welcome David and his wife— and hopefully entice them to purchase this most amazing piece of art." He slipped on his suit jacket and adjusted his shirt cuffs as he walked to the door.

Alex greeted his guests with his usual suave demeanor, shaking David's hand and slightly bowing when introduced to Kathryn. Both had dressed in simple but tasteful elegance. Kathryn's scarf, a painterly splash of color, draped over her shoulders and seemed to announce her playful personality.

Joi thought Kat looked like Anne Bancroft. Classy, with salt-and-pepper hair and a mischievous glint in her eye. Somehow that had a calming effect. "Kathryn, it's wonderful to meet you. I'm so glad you decided to join David here in Paris. Come sit down. I think he's missed you." She smiled to herself, thinking about how often David lovingly referred to his wife, with an almost boyish grin.

"Please, call me Kat."

Another knock on the door, and champagne was rolled in. "Perfect timing!" Alex opened and poured the wine and handed everyone a glass.

"To good friends, art, love, and beauty," David said.

They all raised their glasses in unison. "*Santé!*"

Joi said she needed to go back to her suite for her purse and wrap. Kat said, "I'll go with you."

Making casual conversation, Alex complimented the perfect cut and fit of David's suit. "Did you have it made here in Paris?"

David glanced at his sleeve, amused at the question. "No. I have a tailor in San Francisco I've gone to for years. With my large build . . ."

As they talked, Alex set the archival box with the Chagall, two pairs of cotton gloves, and a magnifying glass on the table.

In Joi's suite, Kat asked if she was romantically involved with Alex, causing Joi to blush. Not wanting to discuss her feelings, she said, "He's very charming, isn't he?" To change the subject, she busied herself with choosing a wrap and held up two for Kat's opinion.

She pointed to one. "You know me, the more color the better." She walked over to a stack of books by the window. "My book!"

"Yes, and I haven't had a minute to myself to sit down and read it yet. I'm looking forward to it so much."

Kat remarked what a labor of love it had been to research and write. "Beautiful works of art attributed to no one in particular. Very sad, but my joy has been to bring them to light. If you have a pen handy, I'll sign it, if you like."

"Yes, please. And thank you for your discretion regarding Alex. I don't know what's going on. Actually, a lot is going on." Joi was visibly distraught.

Kat put her arms around Joi. "This will all play itself out, sweetie, believe me. And I'm a pretty good judge of character. Let's relax tonight. Have a good time. Tomorrow is another day."

Returning to Alex's suite, Kat gave her husband a peck on the cheek. "Shall we?"

Alex opened the box, pulled out the folder, and laid it open to reveal the painting.

Kat took the magnifying glass and carefully scanned every inch and brushstroke. "This is fantastic. I'm fairly certain I've seen the completed tapestry at the Musée Marc Chagall in Nice. Chagall worked closely with Yvette Cauquil-Prince, who transferred his masterpieces into woven works of her own. The tapestries hang in museums all over the world." She glanced at David and grinned. "We just may make an excursion to Nice and find out."

David was visibly impressed with his wife's knowledge and her certainty regarding the authenticity of the painting. He was also aware of Alex's nonchalant attitude. It was as though he didn't care one way or the other if he sold the artwork.

"May I please see the paperwork, Alex?"

He passed her the folder of documents, feeling confident the sale would be made.

Kat scanned the paperwork, looked at Alex, then David, and back at Alex. "I do believe we have a deal, Mr. Marshal." She turned to her husband, kissed him, and said, "Happy anniversary darling."

"Excellent. I'll prepare it for travel."

With that, the evening of celebration commenced.

Alex had made reservations at Le Meurice, a short distance from the hotel. Walking there now, he felt relieved the sale had been made. He looked over at Joi and his heart soared. He wanted a life with her.

They arrived at the restaurant twenty minutes early. Alex suggested they have a drink in the hotel's Bar 228.

Kat put her arm around Joi as they walked to an antique cream-colored leather settee in a quiet part of the room. They chatted about shopping, what museums Joi had seen, and any suggestions she might have for a good oyster bar.

"Alex took me to Huitrerie Régis a few days ago. It was wonderful. A tiny place in Saint- Germain. I've never in my life had oysters so fresh and delicious. We should all go." Joi felt close to Kat, like the relationship she had always wanted with her own mother, but had failed to achieve.

David and Alex approached, with the waiter close behind. He carried a tray with four glasses of Volnay Premier Cru pinot noir. The men chatted about a possible trip to Épernay in the next few days. "We could rent a car and enjoy the countryside."

David was intent on spending as much time with Alex as possible. He wanted to discover who this man was, fake or genuine. Right now, he hoped genuine.

Alex announced that he'd made reservations at the Chef's Table. "The main dining area of Le Meurice is elegant. An extravagant decor mix, between the Salon de la Paix at Versailles and playful modern touches, including iconic Eero Saarinen Tulip chairs. The Chef's Table, however, can only accommodate up to eight diners. It's basically a glassed-in room in the middle of the kitchen, showcasing the chefs at work. It affords a private, intimate dining experience and an insider's view of those preparing the meal."

David was, once again, impressed with Alex's style and knowledge. He patted him on the back. "Well done, sir. What a treat this will be."

The maître d' ushered the four of them into the private dining room and discreetly revealed they would be sharing the room with four other guests. Unlike the main dining area, this room had a sleek modern decor, with a long dark wood table and plush leather bucket chairs. They were handed menus and asked if they would like a champagne aperitif as they decided on their meal.

Alex responded, "*Oui, merci.*"

The menu boasted delectables from sea and land, intermixed with surprising ingredients, mingled in sauces and paired with wine from an impressive cellar inventory. As they perused the menu choices, the *chef de cuisine* appeared and introduced himself.

"I'm so happy you are joining us. The menu in your hands represents dishes we can prepare this evening. All of the ingredients are fresh today, including the crayfish, sea bass, and eel. I personally go to market early for all the fresh vegetables, fruits, and seafood. Today the girolles and artichokes are perfection. I will prepare a meal for you according to your tastes and preferences. I guarantee you will be surprised and entertained." With that, he returned to the kitchen, visibly in cooking mode, inspecting and tasting sauces, speaking with his sous-chef, and checking each station for cleanliness and prepped ingredients.

Alex spoke first. "If we can all decide on a meal theme we can share, that would be great. If you want to choose your meal individually, that's great too. Personally, I like the idea of agreeing on seafood or meat, and letting the chef go with it."

They glanced at the menu, then each other, and said practically in unison, "Yes. Let's do that."

Waiters appeared with their champagne aperitif, including nuts, olives, and sliced radishes with butter and red salt. The *chef d'étage* stood by, ready to take their orders.

Kat spoke up first. "David and I had an amazing anniversary dinner last night at Le Taillevent. Our meals consisted of both seafood and beef. So, I'm up for anything this evening."

David agreed, nodding for Joi and Alex to make the decision.

Alex asked Joi if she had a preference. She smiled and shook her head no. Alex took a moment with the menu again and suggested a seafood dish of the chef's choosing, with foie gras as a first course. Everyone nodded in agreement.

They discussed Épernay and decided to make the trip two days later. Alex would secure a comfortable sedan, in consideration of David's size and comfort.

The door opened, and the maître d' ushered in the four diners who would be sharing the room. Alex and David stood, shook hands with the two men, and nodded to the women. The new arrivals were seated and given menus. Everyone smiled politely and went back to their conversations.

David recognized one of the men, but couldn't place where he had seen him.

The *chef de cuisine* returned and introduced himself to the final four guests. He gave a quick explanation of the menu and the option to allow him to surprise them.

He turned to Alex and David and asked if they had made a decision.

Alex said, "We have indeed. Seafood it is. Do your magic."

David sat quietly, thinking about the man at the table. He subtly nodded at David with a slight smile. *Bingo.* The PI from DuChat Detective Agency, looking suave and impeccably dressed in a dark suit, white shirt, and burgundy tie, his demeanor elegant and self-assured. The woman beside him was equally elegant and didn't seem privy to the connection between the two men. David excused himself and left the room. Within minutes, the investigator stood up, holding his phone and faking that he had an urgent call, and stepped out of the room. The two men met off to the side of the restaurant entrance.

Amused, David asked, "What are you doing here, Michel? I almost didn't recognize you. Alex certainly didn't. Do you have anything to report?"

"I needed to talk to you. I knew from the bug in Alex's phone that you would all be here for dinner this evening. I was able to secure the other four seats at the table due to a last-minute cancellation and because a friend of mine works here." He gave David a grin. "My fiancée was delighted and, of course, knows nothing about this situation. I have information that Alex will be putting a forgery in the auction next week at Artcurial. He was talking to someone named Pierre, who apparently is the forgery artist."

David nodded, his heart sinking. "Do you have anything else, other than romantic interludes?"

"Yes. On a walk, Alex ran into a friend he apparently knew in school, here at the Sorbonne, years ago. They hadn't seen each other in several years. They agreed to meet for lunch in a few days to catch up. Other than the meeting with Pierre and the forgery piece, it's been pretty normal behavior."

Feeling disappointed with the update, David forced a smile and thanked him. "Keep me posted, and have fun this evening—on me!" He found the maître d' and handed him his credit card, explaining he would pay for the other four guests at the table. He knew Alex would be paying for their party.

"*Très bon, monsieur.*"

David returned to the dining room and slipped into the middle of a conversation about octopuses and their extreme intelligence. He cringed, thinking about how much he loved eating them.

Michel returned a few minutes later, faking that he was still on the phone. He smiled and nodded at his dining party, then hung up.

Alex said, "Look."

They all turned to watch the *spectacle de talents culinaires.* Kitchen staff were chopping, sautéing, and arranging the most beautiful and intricate food onto plates.

"This is quite a show. I'm surprised they're not juggling knives." David chuckled.

He looked over at Kat, knowing he would share what he had just learned from Michel. But for now, they were about to enjoy the most amazing meal.

The food was served, consumed, and then they were done. David, now quiet, desperate to stay calm and gracious, thanked Alex and shook his hand.

"A lovely evening. Thank you so much," Kat said and kissed his cheek. She turned to Joi. "Shopping tomorrow?"

"Yes. That would be nice. And lunch. *Bonne nuit.*"

David and Kat strolled back toward their hotel. Ever observant, she asked him what was going on.

"The man sitting at our table was someone I know. He's the PI I hired before coming to Paris. I didn't recognize him at first. I had arranged for him to be at the Paris airport when Alex and Joi arrived. He managed to install a bug app on Alex's cell phone and has been monitoring his activity and reporting to me with significant information." David explained the rest to Kat, shaking his head, feeling incredibly disappointed and sad.

"Oh no. This is not good." Kat took his hand and led him to a nearby bench.

"He also mentioned that Alex had run into a friend he knew from his school days at the Sorbonne and that they were planning to meet for lunch. Other than that, nothing out of the ordinary."

"Well, we've already made plans for Épernay. It may feel awkward, but maybe it's not an appropriate time to bring up the forgery with Alex. It's your call."

Chapter 28

Joi woke to the sound of the shower. Not wanting to get up, she turned over and faced away from the light streaming through the open window.

Alex came out of the bathroom with a towel wrapped around his waist, rubbing his hair with a small hand towel. He slipped back into bed beside Joi, asked what her plans were for the day, and said he was exhausted and didn't want to do anything in particular.

"Mmm. What? Oh, good morning." She stretched out, turned, and wrapped one leg around Alex and snuggled close. "Kat asked if I wanted to go shopping and have a late lunch today. We really hit it off," she cooed. "I like her a lot. A very smart lady."

Alex kissed her cheek. "It's almost eleven now. I'll have *café* sent up for you and wait until it's delivered. Go ahead and shower."

Joi responded in a daze, "That sounds nice." She kissed Alex gently on the cheek and drifted to the bathroom. A lavender-infused soak in the tub was what she wanted. Not a shower.

"My day will consist of arranging for the rental car and hotel in Épernay. I don't know from there." He smiled to himself, knowing she hadn't heard a word. As he waited for the coffee, he reminisced about the evening with David and Kat and the sale of the Chagall, as well as the reality of withdrawing from his career as an art agent. Something he would do gradually. The last painting had been created for the upcoming auction, and that would be it. Pierre would be free to create his own art with his own signature.

The coffee was delivered. Alex tapped on the bathroom door and took it to her. "I'm going now." He bent down and kissed the top of her head. The lavender scent embracing Joi's body caused him to linger for a moment. "Have a wonderful day with Kat. Call me later."

Once back in his room, he changed into jeans and a white shirt. He called the car rental company and arranged for a sedan for the next morning. They had all agreed on an overnight trip, so he made reservations at the Hôtel Jean Moët, a delightful little hotel situated on the gardens of the town square and within walking distance of the Moët & Chandon champagne cellars.

Alex decided to call Jenny. As amazing as it had been running into her, it was also slightly unsettling. "Jenny. Hi, it's Alex. If you're not busy, I would love to take you to lunch. We have so much to catch up on."

"Sounds wonderful. I'm staying at the Millésime Hôtel on rue Jacob. Meet me in the lobby, and we can decide where to go for lunch?"

"Sounds great. Shall we say one thirty?"

"Perfect. Can't wait." Jenny switched her plan from jeans and a T-shirt to something more playful and seductive.

Joi finished her toilette and called Kat to make their afternoon plans. "Good morning, or is it afternoon?"

"Slightly into the afternoon. Do you still want to go shopping?"

"Of course. It's become one of my favorite things to do here, along with occasions of divine food and wine. I'm almost dressed." She slipped on a pale pink linen sleeveless dress, low black heels, and a simple pendant necklace. "Where do you want to meet? I know—Angelina. It's right next door to your hotel and close for me too. See you in fifteen minutes." Joi looked forward to an afternoon with Kat, especially without the men around. She trusted Kat's frank and honest advice, especially since she was in on all the facts of the situation with Alex.

Alex arrived at Jenny's hotel and found her waiting in the lobby. She looked radiant in a pale yellow off-the-shoulder top, black slacks, and black low-heeled shoes. A splashy colored scarf—à la Kandinsky—draped around her neck, and large hoop earrings peeked out from her long blonde hair. They stood smiling at each other, shaking their heads, and finally hugging. Feelings flooded both of them—teenage memories, but no longer romantic ones.

"It's wonderful being in Paris, Alex. Familiar and always enchanting. And now, seeing you."

"You look lovely, Jenny. Let's get a bite to eat, then take a walk. How about Angelina?"

"Perfect. I love Angelina."

Just as they were about to enter the restaurant, Jenny said, "No, wait. Let's go to the old neighborhood. How about La Palette?"

The Seine shimmered with the afternoon sun as they strolled across Pont Neuf. The familiar streets and neighborhoods brought back memories from school.

"There it is. I swear it hasn't changed. And I wouldn't be surprised if Luc still works there. Remember we would laugh over his full name, Luc Antoine Renard Dubois, making his initials LARD. And he was short and stocky too. He should never have told us his full name." Jenny's eyes twinkled at the memory. "We should ask if he's here."

They chose an outside table and were approached immediately by a tall, handsome waiter.

"I'm really hungry. What do you think of a charcuterie and *frites*?"

"That's almost the equivalent of burgers and fries in the states," Jenny said.

"Yes, it is. And the house salad. Chardonnay?"

"*Oui*. Alex, do you remember the last time we saw each other? You were getting ready to move. It was such a sad time."

"Yes, sad. Leaving Paris, my home and friends, and having to give away my dog. At that age, it was devastating. I resented my father, for more reasons than the move." Alex tensed and began thumping the table with his thumb. "He was an insensitive bastard." It was still a painful memory, so Alex changed the subject. "Ah, our waiter."

He relayed their order and asked if Luc still worked there.

"*Non, monsieur*. Luc moved to the country with his wife and eight children two years ago." He nodded and left their table.

Jenny's eyes got big as she mouthed, "Eight children!"

"What brings you to Paris, Jenny? You said the other day you're going for a law degree?"

"Yes. Actually, I'm here doing research on art forgery. You remember when I worked at Artcurial that summer? I thought I could hang out there and talk to some of the staff and maybe pick up some inside information, if they're willing to share with me."

Alex tensed and went quiet for a minute. "Interesting. Have you been there yet?"

"No," she lied, "I've been settling into the city and taking a short break before getting back to the research." Jenny knew she was making Alex nervous. "What I've read so far on the subject is mind-boggling. Do you know that art forgers are still at work, making lots of money and scamming the public? Even with the current technology to authenticate artwork, they're still getting away with it."

Alex shifted in his seat and glanced to see if the waiter was on his way back with the bottle of wine. He took a deep breath to calm himself. "All I've heard about forgery is that collectors aren't always so vigilant about acquiring authentication papers. They're more interested in status. And if they can purchase a painting, they believe to be authentic, simply because of where they bought it or if the seller is thought to be reputable, then they don't question the paperwork. The deal is made. Everyone is happy."

"Yes, I understand that. But it still doesn't make it right. I don't care one way or the other, personally, but as a lawyer, I may be in a position to fight that battle for a client. Oh, here comes our food."

Alex let out a sigh of relief. He thanked the waiter and asked for a bottle of still water.

"So, tell me why you're in Paris, Alex." Jenny coyly popped an olive in her mouth, anxious to hear his reply.

"Actually, I'm in the art field. I'm an agent and work on behalf of clients looking to add to their collections. When my family left Paris and moved to Washington DC, I became interested in art. Not as an artist but as a businessman. I received my business degree from Georgetown University, started mingling with the social set—friends of my family—and from there, it opened up for me. I worked for an auction house for a while, a couple of well-known art galleries, then decided to go it alone as an agent. My mother was completely ensconced in the art world. She was the one who taught me at a young age to love the Impressionists."

"So, are you working here in Paris?"

"Actually, I live in Paris most of the time and spend a little time in New York. I have a small apartment there. I sold a nice piece of art to a client just last night. A wonderful Chagall watercolor."

"Nice. Congratulations." Jenny changed the subject. "And I must ask. Are you married? Children?"

"No. Not married. I've managed to stay a bachelor. But I recently met someone. I've fallen in love with her." He grinned and shook his head. "She's beautiful, smart, and sexy as hell. We met at an auction in Seattle. I asked her to come to Paris with me—and she did."

"That's amazing. What does she do? Other than the beautiful and sexy part. Is she interested in the art world as well?"

Alex loved the conversation, being able to finally talk about Joi to someone. "She is part owner of an art gallery and events planning business in San Francisco. She's also an accomplished artist." Alex took a sip of wine. "And I can't believe I'm saying this, but I think this is the first time in my life I can say I'm truly in love. I've met many women, but none of them was Joi. She's the one."

"San Francisco? I live in San Francisco! Where is she now? I would love to meet her." Concerned she was taking the subject too far, she switched gears. "Well, I'm sure we can work that out before I leave." She began eating her salad and took a large sip of wine.

"What about you, Jenny? Are you married?"

"Yes. I'm married to Sam, a darling man. He's a financial wizard and works for a small business. He totally saved me from myself when we met. I was pretty much a wild child, going to college, involved in the theater group. I was studying journalism, with the dream of working at a prestigious magazine or newspaper. After meeting Sam, I needed to take a break. I left school and eventually took a job with a law firm. The work has been interesting and pays well, but it also piqued my interest in a law career. So here I am, almost ready to take the bar exam."

"Impressive. You've obviously found your passion in the legal realm. Do you and Sam have children?"

"No. Not yet. School and getting established is upmost. Sam is supportive and making his own way in finance. He would love to own his own business," she lied. "We have time for family later."

They finished their lunch and passed on dessert. As they walked back toward the hotel, Alex's phone rang. He saw that it was Joi and let it go to message.

"I'm pretty exhausted. Can we plan on another visit soon? I would love to meet your girlfriend."

"Absolutely. We'll be out of town for a couple of days. I'll call you when we get back, and we can plan on dinner."

Alex kissed both her cheeks. "So good to spend time with you. Talk to you soon."

Alex had always held a love memory of Jenny from when they'd attended the Sorbonne many years ago. But seeing her and spending the afternoon together, there was absolutely no feeling at all. People grow up. Life goes on.

Jenny was relieved to be back in her room. She called David. "Hope you're sitting down. Here's my report. You may want to take notes. Think of yourself as Monica for a moment, you know, sticky notes and all." She took a breath. "Okay. This has all happened since I arrived four days ago. First, I was out for a walk in the Latin Quarter and ran into Joi at Shakespeare and Company. We were both so surprised but immediately decided to sneak off for a drink and a visit. We agreed not to tell you or anyone at that point."

David listened and asked Jenny to continue.

Jenny took a breath. "Second, a day after that, I ran into Alex while out on another walk. But this is the Alex I knew when I lived in Paris as a teenager. I didn't think anything of it. Why would I? I didn't know who the 'forgery Alex' was. I had never seen him before. So, my friend Alex and I exchanged phone numbers and agreed to get together for lunch so we could catch up. All very sweet and normal."

David's head began to swim. He picked up a pen and began jotting down notes.

Jenny continued. "And third, I acquired a pass to Artcurial so I could go to the auction the next day to see who Alexander Marshal was. You know, scope out the love interest I would be pursuing. The attendant pointed him out, and it turned out to be Alexander Marchand, my boyfriend from the Sorbonne. Needless to say, I left before he could see me."

David finally spoke up. "Jenny, you need to—"

She interrupted. "I tried to figure things out. I decided not to call Monica or you just yet. I had to plan the next step without everyone freaking out."

David said, a little frustrated, "And? Is there more?"

"Yes. He called me this morning and asked me to lunch so we could catch up. We had a great visit. He told me about his love for Joi. And that she was part owner of an art gallery in San Francisco. I told him about Sam and that we lived in San Francisco too. Probably shouldn't have done that. Anyway, I asked about his career. He said art agent. I told him about my forgery studies and the bar exam. It was so weird, talking to him as an old friend and then coming back to the realization that he's the one involved in forgery. Where it stands now, he wants me to meet Joi."

"Take it easy. This will work itself out. Not how we initially planned, but it will be okay. Don't agree to see him again just yet. I'm going to call Monica with an update. I'll call you later."

David poured himself a scotch, then asked Kat if she would like one.

"Who was that on the phone? You look pale. What's going on?" Kat knew her husband and also knew that whatever it was, they would work it out together. "Yes. A scotch would be great." She got up from her computer and went to the sofa so they could be comfortable.

"That was Jenny on the phone. I guess you figured that much out. You are not going to believe this story." David explained the details of Jenny's phone call and took a sip of his scotch. "Are you with me?"

Kat nodded, completely mesmerized with David's account.

"This morning, Alex called and invited her to lunch. She accepted. They visited and asked all the normal questions two old friends would ask. Are you married? What do you do? Why are you in Paris?"

David stood and walked to the window. "Alex said he wanted Jenny to meet Joi. That they would plan a dinner when Joi and he got back from their trip out of town."

Kat sat quietly for a moment. "And this was never the plan, right? Wasn't Jenny supposed to be an outsider? No social connection to all of us?"

"Yes. But she found herself in a situation and had to play it by ear."

Kat was in deep thought. "Okay. Maybe it's time to move this forward. We're going to Épernay. We'll all be relaxed and open to conversation. Maybe it's time for you and Alex to go off by yourselves and have a little chat. He obviously admires you. Actually, there's a good rapport going on with all four of us. Be honest with him about all of it: your friend Geoffrey and the forgery quest, the whole cadre of friends trying to help. Maybe there's more there to consider. You need the whole story, darling. And he's the only one that can tell it."

"Your insight is impeccable." He hesitated. "To tell you the truth, I don't care about the forgery any longer. What I do care about is Alex and Joi. I'll call to see if we're set with the car and hotel."

173

Chapter 29

David was apprehensive about speaking with Alex. Things had changed. It was no longer a *maybe* forgery, it was now *another* forgery. He wanted to hear Alex tell his story. He wanted to help and advise him both morally and legally, but only if he was open and honest about the whole business. The Derain could possibly be taken care of with a financial payback, but there was no way he could stand by Alex if a new piece was put up for auction.

Alex beamed as they pulled up in front of the Westin in a slate-gray 2017 Citroën C-Elysée. "*Bonjour.* Your carriage awaits."

Joi moved to the back seat and invited Kat to join her while David gladly stretched out in the front passenger seat.

"The drive is about two hours. We could stop for lunch in Hautvillers, where Dom Pérignon learned the craft of making champagne," Alex said.

David countered, "Or we could wait until we arrive in Épernay. Either way."

Kat whispered, "Men! The technical details of everything. Personally, all I want is a delightful lunch that will accompany the champagne." Both women piped up from the back seat: "Épernay."

Jenny called Sam, feeling bad she'd neglected him these past few days. "Hi, sweetie. I'm sorry I haven't called you sooner. How are you? What are you doing?"

Sam was half-asleep and half-drunk when the phone rang. "Jenny? You . . . okay? Jenny, I've missed you so much."

"Sam, you sound like shit." Then she realized the time. "Oh, sorry. I guess it's early at your end. I miss you. I wanted to let you know that there's been an interesting turn of events. But it will be okay."

"What do you mean? What in the hell is going on? No one tells me anything. When are you coming home?"

"I have a feeling it will be soon. I'll let you know. Tell Monica I'll call her later. Sorry about the time difference and calling you so early. I love you." She hung up, not wanting to talk to Sam in his condition. She worried her trip to Paris may have harmed more than it helped.

Monica arrived at the gallery early, anxious to start planning the student exhibit with Phillip. Having him on board, soon permanently, had been the best turn of events since Monterey. She fell into a reverie, thinking about Ben and their romantic interlude that weekend.

"Good morning, sweet pea." Phillip burst in carrying a small sack from the Andersen Bakery on Market Street.

"You darling man! What's in the sack?"

"What I have here is a choice between a raspberry cream cheese Danish or a saffron raisin twist." Phillip held the sack up high, enticing Monica like a pet shih tzu.

"How about we open that sack and cut the pastries in half. Share. How's that?" Monica was starving, as usual. Losing weight. Starving. Tired. Starving.

Phillip found a plate and cut the pastry into bite-size pieces. "May I fix you an espresso? Yes? No?"

"I think tea sounds better. There's English Breakfast in the blue canister."

Phillip returned and placed the treats on Monica's desk.

She dunked the tea bag a few times and removed it from the cup. "I called the Art Institute yesterday. They were delighted with the idea of an exhibit here and said to come by this morning. I'm impressed with the caliber of art the younger generation is producing—edgy and fresh. Will you have time to go with me at nine?"

"Oddly, yes. It's a slow day at the salon, but I do need to be back by eleven thirty. As far as the exhibit, I'm thinking seven artists and a title like *The Magnificent Seven*. No, maybe that's too dated for a young crowd." Phillip grinned. "Or nine artists, with the title *Nine and Waiting.*"

Monica put her feet up on the desk and took a bite of the Danish. "What does that mean? Nine and waiting? I don't get it."

Phillip cocked his head with a sweet smile. "Just a little hint of things to come. Sweetie, I'm pretty sure someone in this room is pregnant, and it isn't me."

Monica stared at him. "What in the hell are you talking about? I'm not pregnant. Sure, I've lost weight. I'm tired all the time. I feel like crap first thing in the morn—Uh oh. No. I can't . . . oh my God. I can't be pregnant. Not now. I have no time. I have responsibilities. Events, exhibits. Oh my God. Ben." Light-headed and wanting to throw up, she rushed to the bathroom and did just that.

Returning to a sympathetic Phillip, she said, "You know what's weird? I've been dreaming about kangaroos lately. Lots of them hopping around the streets of San Francisco. Pouches with baby roos."

Phillip stared at her. "My point exactly!"

Chapter 30

Monica hadn't seen Ben for the last few days. With his new restaurant opening soon, he was spending extensive time in Monterey, overseeing details of the remodel of a small restaurant space that had gone under two years before. She also didn't want to tell him over the phone that she was pregnant. In fact, she wavered back and forth about telling him at all. An internal battle went on in her head. *Will he be angry? Will he be happy? Is this the right time for a baby?*

She told her head to shut up and proceeded to call Ben. "Want to come by for dinner tonight—or are you still in Monterey?"

"Still in Monterey. Can't do dinner, but I'm heading back to town this evening. How about nine?"

"Perfect. See you then."

Monica began to fuss. She fluffed pillows, trimmed dead leaves off her ficus plant, and changed her outfit twice. She fixed a snack of sliced cold chicken breast, almonds, olives, and a baguette. Gruyère and Camembert were at room temperature, and a bottle of rosé was chilling along with a bowl of red grapes. Turning on the gas fireplace, she worried about Ben's reaction. Just then, there was a knock on the door.

"Hey, you." Ben smiled and gave her a hug and a soft kiss. "Mmm, feels good to be here. It's been an incredibly long day." He walked over to the fireplace, grateful for the warmth and ambience of the room. "Crazy traffic. Doing a project like this looks great on paper, and you'd think with such a small space and the fact that it was already set up as a restaurant, it would go smoother. But no. We're finding wiring and plumbing that should have been replaced years ago."

Monica stayed calm and let him rant. Ben was Mr. Hyper when he worked on a new plan or project. "Would you like a drink or glass of wine? I fixed a little snack in case you didn't have a chance to eat."

"Wine would be great." He kicked off his shoes and sat in the teal-colored leather chair close to the fireplace. "How was your day?"

Monica placed the snacks and a glass of wine on a tray and returned to the living room. Also on the tray was a pair of baby booties, strategically placed next to the wine. She set the tray down on the coffee table and curled up on the sofa next to his chair.

"That looks great. Thank you." He reached for the wine then glanced at her. "You're not having any?" Then, seeing the booties, he glanced at her again. "Wha . . . ?"

Monica could hardly contain herself. Hormones at their peak, she wanted to cry, but began giggling at the look on Ben's face. "So? What are you thinking?"

"I'm shocked. I'm blown away." Grinning, he stood and pulled Monica to her feet. "Ah, Monterey."

"Yes, Monterey. Golfing, fresh air, and one magic night. I love you, Mr. Graham."

"And I love you." Tears filled his eyes. He looked down at her stomach, expecting to see a round tummy.

"Sweetie, the baby is only this big." She pinched two fingertips together, indicating the approximate size of a pea.

"Let's make it official. Will you marry me . . . again?"

Monica's eyes glistened as she turned off the lamp by the sofa, the room illuminated only by the twinkle of lights reflected on the bay below and the glow from the fireplace. She threw a few pillows on the floor and said, "Join me?"

Chapter 31

Alex pulled the Citroën up to the entrance of the Hôtel Jean Moët, a beautiful old building with a modern glassed-in entryway and lush greenery on both sides.

The young valet welcomed them, nodding at the car. *"Bon."* Obviously anxious to drive the short distance to the parking area, the valet gladly helped the porter unload the few pieces of luggage, then took the keys from Alex.

After checking in and unpacking, they made their way back down to the hotel lobby and were greeted with a complimentary glass of champagne. The space was intimate and lovely, with bouquets of wildflowers intermixed with roses and the fireplace set and ready to go.

They decided to have lunch at Café le Progrés a short two blocks away. Entering the main entrance, they were seated in the garden at the last available table. The waiters seemed to know every local patron, making comments and playfully engaging guests to sing along with the two guitar players in the corner.

As they feasted on *salade niçoise* and a charcuterie, conversation moved to the wine houses, most notably Moët & Chandon. Alex described the acres of underground tunnels and rooms. "Touring the caves is a must. Each bottle aging to perfection. Workers meticulously turning the bottles at the exact degree and scheduled times. Fascinating."

Joi was enthralled. "I love it here. I wouldn't be surprised to see a young Leslie Caron dancing in the streets."

"That's how I felt the first time David and I visited Épernay," Kat said. "We were driving the countryside and stopped here for lunch. We didn't visit any of the wineries, so this is a first for us also."

They passed on dessert, wanting to save room for wine tasting. The waiter appeared with their bill, and David quickly retrieved it from Alex. "My treat."

Making their way to Moët & Chandon, David and Alex walked ahead on Avenue de Champagne and casually talked about art and Alex's next auction.

David said, "You mentioned Artcurial in a couple of days. Will you be involved?"

"Yes. I have a piece that will go up for bid. It's quite lovely. An unknown work by Camille Pissarro."

"Really? I think I told you Kat recently published her own book, *Unknown Impressionist Artists*. It's beautiful and has done quite well on the market. A labor of love for her. And, of course, the Impressionist collection at Musée d'Orsay is one of her favorite places to visit when we're in Paris." David kept the conversation casual, seeing where Alex would take it.

"You mentioned the book when we had dinner at Bofinger. That's wonderful. I'll buy a copy and have Kat sign it. By the way, I haven't told you this—I ran into a friend of mine from when I attended the Sorbonne. So amazing. We had lunch the other day and had a great visit. She's studying law in San Francisco and came here to research art forgery. I told her about Joi and that I've fallen in love for the first time in my life. She wants us to meet for dinner." Alex shook his head at the memory.

David carefully eased into this piece of news, information he already knew but couldn't reveal. He decided to comment and then change the subject.

"That is amazing. Life is funny. How things are revealed to us at just the right moment in time. Things that are meant to happen, whether we think so or not."

Alex glanced at David, not quite getting his drift.

"Here we are. I think you'll enjoy this tour." They walked through the gates, glancing back to see Kat and Joi close behind.

The courtyard featured an impressive statue of Dom Pérignon by the entrance to the main building. They entered, paid the fee for a short tour, and were instructed by a guide to wait for the other guests. The tour would begin promptly at two o'clock. Alex explained they could peel away from the crowd if they wanted to shorten their tour. They all agreed, preferring to actually drink the wine rather than stare at old bottles.

A half hour later, they climbed the stone stairway back to the entrance hall and the tasting room. A beautiful, modern, and thankfully, warm room with a long, sleek wooden bar. Two attendants poured champagne and offered information about the history of the winery.

Kat spied the boutique through the glass doors of the tasting room and playfully told David, "We should pick up a few bottles. What do you think?"

David purchased the wine and took the bottles back to the hotel, not too far away. He rejoined the others as they slowly walked Avenue de Champagne, lined with old and new gated, château-style buildings with attractively manicured gardens. After visiting several wine houses, they jointly declared, "Enough!"

"I'm so ready for a bath and a nap," Kat said.

Alex agreed. "Meet up at seven for dinner?"

David suggested they dine at La Grillade Gourmande. "Kat and I ate there a few years ago. I'll check what time they can accommodate us."

Alex was delighted with dining suggestions other than his own. He took Joi's hand and headed upstairs. "Let us know what time."

Kat returned to their room and ran a bath, happy to kick off her shoes and have a moment to herself.

David walked to the nearby restaurant and was told they could be seated at seven thirty. Needing time alone to think, he stayed to have a drink in the bar. "Scotch, neat, *s'il vous plaît*." He stared at the glass in his hand, then finally gulped the drink and made his decision. He would confront Alex tomorrow. Alone.

Alex and Joi woke from their nap, curled around each other like grapevines.

Joi said, "I'm going to have a bath. We have time, right?"

"Yes. David left a message saying our reservation is for seven thirty. I'm going downstairs for a bit."

Alex felt anxious. He needed to pick up the painting at Pierre's apartment tomorrow and deliver it to Artcurial. Finally, he could put this whole business to rest. He went to the bar and ordered a glass of burgundy, then found a comfortable chair by the fire, grateful to have the room to himself to think. But not for long.

"I thought you'd still be napping." David walked in and joined Alex. He sat down in an overstuffed chair across from him. "I took a short walk after making the reservations." He motioned to the waiter and pointed to Alex's glass and to himself. The waiter nodded and brought a glass of burgundy.

"This has been a nice break, David. The countryside is rejuvenating, fresh. But now I need to get back and prepare for the auction. We can have a leisurely *petit déjeuner* in the morning and be back to Paris before noon."

"I agree. Spending time with you and Joi has been a delight."

They raised their glasses in a toast. David set his glass down. "Now I'm off to check on my beautiful wife. Meet you down here at seven fifteen."

David found Kat sitting in the chair by the window. A cool breeze wafted into their dimly lit room. "It's so beautiful here. Quiet." She reached for his hand. "Where have you been?"

"I took a little walk, then ran into Alex in the bar downstairs." He sat down. "I have something to tell you. When we were walking to the various wineries earlier, Alex told me he had run into an old school friend. Well, we know it was Jenny. I decided then and there I would not confront Alex about the forgeries on this trip. I'll meet with him alone tomorrow. I've got to convince him not to put that forgery up for bid."

"Well, this changes things, doesn't it? What can I do to help?"

"I think staying close to Joi, for one. At this point she knows nothing about this last painting. She'll need your support. When Alex finds out we all know his past misdeeds, he is going to lash out. I guarantee it. Jenny may be our only hope. He believes her to be simply an old school pal and not part of this mess. He'll probably confide in her if he speaks to anyone at all. I don't know. I told Jenny to stay neutral and not be available to see Alex for a while."

Kat stood and went to David, brushed his cheek, and rested her head on his chest.

He held her. "I'm dreading this, Kat. Knowing what the outcome could be."

"Okay, darling. I'm with you. But right now, we need to get ready for dinner. Let's make this a wonderful evening—with two people we adore. Tomorrow is tomorrow."

"And I'm dreading tomorrow. You should spend the afternoon with Joi and tell her what's going on. I'll be with Alex. That's all we can do."

David and Kat waited quietly in the lounge by the crackling fire, where David had solemnly sat a short time ago. Suddenly the room felt festive as they heard giggling and footsteps—Joi was radiant in a flowery summer shift and wearing the pearls Alex had given her on their shopping spree, and Alex, dressed semi-casual, was beaming, obviously a man in love.

The modern entrance to La Grillade Gourmande restaurant was painted white with a thin black iron railing surrounding a small garden. A simple white sign with scrolled black lettering hung above the windows. They entered to the exact opposite: bright orange walls with white trim, high-backed orange-and-black leather chairs, and bright abstract art on the walls.

"*Monsieur Waters? Bonsoir.* Please follow me." The waiter led them to a corner table with a view of the patio and garden and the now purple-and-black streaked sky.

"What may I bring you to drink?"

David spoke up. "I think champagne is in order. *Merci.*"

The waiter returned with a tray of four flutes, while another waiter brought an ice bucket with a bottle of Moët & Chandon. The bottle was expertly opened, and the flutes filled.

"Let the celebration begin. I make a toast to two very special friends and to my beautiful wife. *Santé.*"

They all raised their glasses. "*Santé.*"

"This menu is overwhelming, in a good way. May we have a bite of everything, please?" Kat wanted tonight to be fun, even though she knew tomorrow could possibly be a disaster. "Darling, what looks good to you?"

"I'm thinking foie gras to start. And the sea bass for the main."

Kat nodded. "I think I'll have the smoked salmon to start and the chicken stuffed with morels and foie gras."

Joi continued to study the menu.

Alex said, "I'm going to start with a dozen escargots that we can share. And I think the grilled turbot."

Joi wasn't paying attention to the others. Finally, she looked up and saw them all smiling at her. She giggled. "I think I'll have the lobster slices to start and the same as Kat, the chicken."

The attentive waiter returned immediately to take their orders. He nodded and conveyed they had chosen well and poured them more champagne.

Alex spoke up. "You know what I love? I love being out in the wine country and away from the shops that sell it in the city. Being here, seeing the vines that are meticulously trimmed, the workers, the vintners who study the earth and weather and determine the exact time to harvest." He took a sip of wine. "What I'm trying to say is we all enjoy a nice wine, but do we give credit to the ones who make it happen? I heard this somewhere, and I apologize to the person who wrote it, but it goes something like this: 'Wine is not a substance to be analyzed or studied or ranked. It's a story—geology, weather, wars, and domestic strife. A form of communication—conversation across the table and through the ages.'"

Joi reached over and touched his hand. "That's beautiful, Alex."

David and Kat agreed and raised their glasses. "A wonderful tribute to wine."

The waiter brought their entrée, serving the ladies first. Alex passed the escargot to Joi.

She laughed and shook her head no. "Remember our first meal at Verjus?" She turned to David and Kat. "I washed down that one tiny bite of escargot with a lot of wine."

He passed the tray to David and Kat, encouraging them to take as many as they wanted.

Kat's smoked salmon was served beautifully with a small bowl of gazpacho on the side, and Joi's grilled lobster slices were layered with duck liver and a dollop of carrot cream.

"This is superb." David's foie gras terrine was served with a strong herb and spice ratafia and red wine jam. "I could go home right now and be incredibly happy."

"Oh no you don't. We have another course and another wine choice to make. I'm thinking a pinot noir. It would go well with all of our dishes," Alex said.

They chatted about their return to Paris tomorrow. Alex commented on the auction but then changed the subject to the Edward Hopper exhibit. "Have you seen it yet? I've heard the lines are insane."

David said he had tried a couple of times but to no avail. "We might try the Picasso Museum in the Marais in a couple of days."

Conversation seemed to slow to a pedestrian saunter, everyone absorbed with their own thoughts. Alex, with the auction and wanting a new life with Joi; Kat and David, with the confrontation tomorrow; and Joi, with being stuck in the middle of it all.

Kat realized what was happening and jumped into action. "I need to powder my nose. Come with me, Joi." They made their way to the WC through what was now a full house of diners. "We need to get this party going. It's way too serious. I'm going to propose a question that we all have to answer, so play along. It'll be fun. We do this all the time at home when conversations begin to lag at parties. Just follow my lead."

The two men stood as the women approached. The next course had been served, and the bottle of wine uncorked and poured. "Oh good. More food." Kat grinned as she settled in her chair. She took a generous sip of wine and winked at David. "Okay. I'm going to ask a question, and we all have to answer. Who's the one person that's influenced you the most? Joi, you go first."

"Hmm. I'd have to say my best friend and business partner, Monica. She's extremely smart and organized and has encouraged me to be confident and go after the things I want in life. Not what everyone else wants for my life. My parents are very conservative and tended to hold me back from my dreams and ambitions. It wasn't until I was college age that I finally broke away with the help of Monica's prodding. She's also shown me, and those we work with, that honesty and integrity in all things is the key to success and a happy life."

Kat turned to Alex. "Who was your greatest influence, Alex?"

"Without a doubt, my mother. A strong, confident woman. Very bright—an accomplished artist and art historian. In fact, my parents, through my mother's insistence, formed a foundation to support the arts in Washington DC. I grew up meeting some remarkable people in the art world."

Kat made a mental note. She wanted to meet this woman.

"David? I know your story, but the others don't." She smiled lovingly at her husband.

He took a sip of wine and cleared his throat. "I would also say my mother. Our family came from old money. Actually, on both sides of the family. But it was my mom who refused to let that fact interfere with a normal upbringing. My siblings and I worked hard all our lives. Paper routes, mowing grass, saving for things we wanted. College was no different. We all contributed toward our education. Of course, the family was there with financial support, but it was never to be assumed. We were encouraged to love reading, to explore and have opinions and discussions, to always look out for each other and those in need. She has shared her wealth for the good of mankind, and chosen the best way to serve."

Kat never tired of hearing David speak of his family, especially his mother. They had shaped him into the honorable man she loved.

"How about you, Kat? Who's your hero?" Alex prodded.

"I would have to say both my parents. Seriously. They are like two peas in a pod. They have their own opinions, but they complement each other. So, growing up was fascinating. They gave good advice and then left it up to me to decide. I loved learning from their encouragement to try things on for size. To have my own opinions. And to keep a sense of humor. Humans are a funny lot. We're all scrambling around, trying to make our way in life."

Kat felt satisfied. Sharing thoughts on the same subject brought uplifting results. A little glimpse into what makes us tick. She looked over at Alex. An intelligent man—savvy, handsome, confident. What had drawn him to this craziness with forgery?

"Does anyone want dessert? I'm looking at the strawberries with black pepper and champagne sorbet. Really, I must try it." Joi looked around the table, waiting for a response.

"I'm in."

"Me too."

"Me three."

They walked back to the hotel, Kat and Joi lagging behind.

Joi said, "What's going on? Something is. I can feel it."

Kat sighed. "Maybe. David needs to talk to Alex tomorrow when we get back. Let's you and me go out to lunch and maybe shopping." She put her arm around Joi as they walked in silence.

Back at the hotel, everyone expressed contentment after an amazing meal and conversation. They wished each other *bonne nuit* and sleep well.

No one slept well.

Alex nudged Joi in the direction of the shower at eight o'clock the next morning. He called David. "We'll meet you downstairs for *petit déjeuner*. Then we hit the road back to Paris. Are you packed?"

David chuckled. "Well, good morning. And yes, we're packed. See you shortly."

Chapter 32

They arrived in Paris just before noon. After dropping David and Kat at their hotel, Alex arranged with the concierge to have the rental car picked up. He kissed Joi, and explained he would be gone for a while.

"Okay. I'm going to change and maybe take a walk."

"You okay with the bags?"

"Yes. I'll see you later." She kissed him, holding him in limbo for a moment, then grabbed both bags and walked to the elevator, barely keeping her emotions under control.

A half hour later, Kat called Joi. "I need food, wine, and shopping. Let's stroll over to Angelina because I also need chocolate! David is about to call Alex."

"Okay. Give me ten minutes." Terrified by what was about to take place, but not really knowing the details, Joi could only whisper "Alex," tears streaming down her cheeks.

David paced the room, stared down at his phone, cleared his throat and made the call. "Sorry to bother you, Alex. I know you're occupied with auction prep. I need to talk to you about something of great importance. Can you come to my hotel? Kat is out shopping, I think, and won't be back for a while."

"I can't be for long. As you've probably noticed, I get a little tense before an auction. I need to stay focused."

Kat was waiting in the lobby of Angelina, checking her phone messages, when Joi arrived. It was obvious she'd been crying. Kat hugged her. "Hi, sweetie. You, okay? Do you want to walk instead?"

Joi shook her head no and nodded to the hostess. They were led to a small table at the side of the room under a large mural of the Côte d'Azur.

"Chocolate is a must, but right now I want a glass of wine," Kat said. "And you know what they say about chocolate: a day without chocolate is a pretty damn sad day."

"I've never heard that."

"Well, I just now made it up. But it's true, don't you think?" She smiled at Joi with a tacit it-will-be-okay look.

When the waitress returned, Joi said, "We would both like *la salade verte* and rosé. Please bring the wine immediately. *Merci.*"

Kat leaned toward Joi so their conversation would be more private. "There's no easy way to say this. We all knew this day was coming, but now it's more complicated."

The waitress brought two glasses of rosé and left without a word. Joi took a long gulp from her wineglass.

"Partly because the two of you have fallen in love, and partly because David and I have become close to Alex. Everything has turned completely upside down from the original plan of confrontation." She took her own gulp of wine.

Joi retrieved a tissue from her purse.

Kat lowered her voice to a whisper. "It would be one thing to ignore the quest David has been on for the past two years for his friend—you know, just drop it. But now, through information David received last night, we know Alex is planning to put a forgery in the auction tomorrow. If he goes through with it, we can't stand by Alex. It's dangerous, and it's illegal."

Joi's face flushed, as if slapped. "What? Kat, I don't understand. Of course, I . . . I agree. He can't . . ." She finished her wine and scanned the room for the waitress. "But . . . I love him. He's the most important person in my life. What should I . . . ?" She looked down at her salad. "I'm not so hungry."

Kat patted Joi's hand. "This is no time to go on a hunger strike. Let's eat our meal and purchase some chocolate on our way out. We'll walk, breathe the fresh air, and wait. We can't do a thing until we hear from David. Hopefully, he will have some influence on Alex."

Joi motioned the waitress over and asked for more wine.

They left Angelina and found a bench by the fountain in the Jardin des Tuileries. Closing their eyes and soaking in the warmth of the sun, they both sat deep in thought.

Wanting desperately to change the subject, Joi turned to Kat. "I know we're waiting for this to play out. But I have something to tell you. I was looking through your beautiful book earlier and found the painting I purchased at the auction in Seattle. When I met Alex. I couldn't believe it."

Joi thought about her first impression of Alex: straightforward, professional, handsome, generous, and sexy as hell. She desperately needed to keep that memory and their current relationship alive.

"That's incredible. I would love to see which one it is. Do you mind telling me what you paid?"

"Eight thousand. I felt it was a reasonable price. What do you think?"

"I'll tell you when I see it. Some of the artists I studied were not completely unknown. They were part of the new movement. And some were recognized on a smaller scale—students of some of the masters, giving them credibility." She stood and reached for Joi's hand. "Let's go shopping. After that wine, I need to walk, or I'll fall asleep. Shakespeare and Company first, then a few boutiques."

"I should call Monica first. Give her a general update. Do you mind?"

"Not at all. David will be calling her, too, after speaking with Alex." Saying it out loud again made Kat sad.

Monica answered after four rings, her voice weak. "Hello."

"Monica? Hey, are you okay? You sound terrible."

"Really?" Standing up, she groaned. "Well, I'm pregnant! That could account for it."

"What? Oh my God. That's wonderful! I can't believe it. Who's the father?"

"Who's the father? Well, it's not Phillip! Who do you think it is? Who have I loved my entire adult life?"

"Ben! I'm so happy for you. Have you seen a doctor? Due date? Tell me everything."

"Yes, and, oh, I don't know, nine months? Uh, gotta go." Monica ended the call and rushed to the bathroom.

Joi turned to Kat. "Pregnant, and I'm guessing morning sickness."

Kat laughed out loud, shaking her head. "Monica pregnant! The drama going on here and back home. What's next, running naked through the streets? Oh, but that wouldn't necessarily cause alarm in Paris." She grabbed Joi's hand. "Let's go look at books."

They arrived at the iconic bookstore just as it started to sprinkle. Kat immediately noticed the shop had changed since her last visit; the space was more open.

"They made a doorway leading to the space next door and added a children's book section. On the other side of that is a café. Also, this is where I bought your book. Let me see if they still have a copy. We can look up my painting." Joi wandered over to the art section.

Kat slowly followed, browsing as she went. Reverently touching books.

"Here it is." They flipped the pages and landed on the painting. "Beautiful, isn't it? Would you tell me more about the research you did?"

"Lovely. The colors are so pure and vibrant. In the style of Degas but with less refined brushstrokes. We can talk later about that. Let's have coffee."

Entering the café, Kat added, "And chocolate croissants."

Joi's phone rang, giving her a start, as she thought for a second it might be David.

"Sorry about that," Monica said. "I seem to be spending more time in the bathroom than at my desk. So, what's up? How's the Paris adventure? By the way, I received your package. Thank you so much. The bag is perfect."

"You're welcome." Joi took a sip of coffee. "The reason I called was to let you know that David is speaking to Alex right now. Confronting him about the possible forgery."

"Yes, well, David called me earlier. He said he'd learned about another forgery being put up for auction tomorrow. The game is over, Joi. I hope he nails the bastard!"

Joi felt like she had been hit in the stomach. "Monica, no!" A mix of anger and sadness overcame her. Motherly instincts, like a cat protecting her suffering kit. "I can't talk now." She hung up and envisioned Alex as a small boy being abused. Alex needing her.

Alex climbed the hotel steps two at a time, not wanting to wait for the elevator.

David answered the door immediately. "Thank you for coming. Have a seat. Would you like a drink?"

"No, thanks. I have some errands to run before meeting with the staff at Artcurial." Alex remained standing by the door. "What's up?"

David set his drink down and nodded toward the sofa. "Please, sit." He gripped his hands together, nervously massaging his fingers. "There is no easy way to tell you. What I'm about to say is very hard. I want you to know how much I've come to admire and respect you, as a lover of art and as a friend." David shifted to face Alex and hesitated.

Alex stared at David intently, wishing he would speak his mind. He nodded. "I admire you, too, David. And Kat is wonderful. I'm so glad to spend time with both of you."

"Alex, my reasons for coming to Paris weren't solely for a business trip or to see the Chagall painting. I'm here on behalf of a friend in San Francisco. He purchased a painting two years ago and later found out, quite by accident, that it was most likely a forgery. I offered to do some investigation and found that you were involved with the sale."

Alex stood and stepped back, suddenly feeling like a trapped animal. His face flushed; sweat appeared on his brow.

"Then I learned that Joi had come to Paris with you. She is part owner of the gallery in San Francisco, of which I am a strong supporter. Kat and I have known her for years. I came to Paris because of you and also to make sure Joi was okay. She knew nothing about any of this when she came here with you."

"Does she know now?" His head started to throb; his ears filled with ringing.

"Yes. She found out the night of our dinner at Bofinger. She wasn't emotionally involved then. And it became kind of a game for her, taking notes, playing coy. But that's all changed. She's very much in love with you. Her heart is breaking over all of this. She's with Kat right now."

Alex was stunned, his emotions a mix of rage and embarrassment. "So, this is all about getting Alex? Making a fool of me? What are you going to do, David? Turn me over to the Paris *préfecture de police*? What proof do you have?" Alex started toward the door.

"Alex, wait. I know about the piece you're planning to put in the auction tomorrow. I beg you not to do it. It's not worth any amount of money to take that kind of risk. I can try to help you regarding the Derain painting my friend bought, but I can't help you with this."

David reached for Alex. Like a father to a son, desperate to protect him.

Alex pushed his hand away. He ran out the door and stumbled down the stairs. Finding it hard to breathe, he stopped and leaned over with hands on his knees, wanting to disappear. He entered Harry's New York Bar on rue Daunou and chose a table toward the back. He wanted to disappear into the crowd. He ordered a whiskey.

David called Kat. "Well, it's done. But I'm afraid we've lost him. All we can do is wait and see. I'll be here when you get back. I love you."

Kat held her phone tightly as she listened. "Okay, darling. I'm so very sorry. I'll tell Joi. I'm on my way." Kat turned to Joi. "They talked. Apparently, Alex didn't take the news well and ran out. David is devastated. Grieving. We're all grieving. Time to go back."

As they walked along the Seine toward Pont Neuf and the hotel, Kat said, "Do you want to stay with us for a while?"

"No, I have some things to figure out." They sat on a bench nearby. "I love him so much, Kat. I didn't think how this would play out. In the beginning, it was a crazy spy game, thinking he was a bad guy. But he's not. He's wonderful. I don't know what to do." Resting her head on Kat's shoulder like a child. "Maybe it's time I go back to San Francisco. Monica is having a rough time, and I've ignored my responsibilities long enough."

Kat took Joi's hand and pulled her to her feet. "Come back with me. Let's see what David says."

After two double scotches, Alex had calmed a bit. Not sure what to do next, he paid the bill and stood out on the street, squinting into the sun. He called Jenny. "Hey, it's Alex. I need to talk to you about something. Can you meet me? I just left Harry's Bar. Too many damn tourists. Choose a place. I'll be there."

"Sure. Since you're not far from my hotel, why don't you come here. I guarantee there are no tourists in my room. Suite 302." She tried to make light of what she was sure had just happened.

Ten minutes later, Alex arrived.

"Are you okay?" She put her arm around his shoulder.

He shook his head. "No. I have some things to figure out. I think you're the only person I can trust." He stared down at the floor then looked up at her, slurring his words. "I can trust you, can't I?"

"Of course, you can. Sit down, and I'll call down for *café*. Want something to eat?"

"No. Yes. *Frites* and . . . whatever."

Jenny ordered *café, frites,* Perrier, and a croque monsieur.

"Okay. What's up?"

"It's a long, long story. Something happened two years ago. You remember my brother, Pierre? Incredible artist. Incredible." Now deep in thought, thinking of his strong and silent brother. "Well, a situation fell in my lap. A joke, really. I asked Pierre to do a painting in the style of André Derain. Not a copy, but an 'unpublished' and 'unknown' piece. You know, with no paperwork available." Alex took a breath, trying to get his thoughts together. "And the reason he painted . . ."

Jenny could see he was having trouble speaking. She handed him a bottle of water. "Here. Take your time."

Alex laid his head back on the sofa, closed his eyes, then turned and looked at Jenny. He told her about meeting the woman from San Francisco who was looking to purchase a piece of art. "It was obvious. She only wanted to impress her friends. And colleagues of her attorney husband. I gave her my card . . ." Flipping his hand, he continued. ". . . and said I would be happy to help."

Jenny's ears perked up. She recalled her boss talking about a Derain when she first started working at the law firm.

"I asked Pierre to do the painting. For a few thousand dollars, it was a done deal. No questions asked. She didn't have a clue." Alex shook his head, disgusted with the memory and with himself.

"Hold that thought. Our snack has arrived." A tray of food was brought in and placed on the coffee table next to Alex. *"Merci."*

"Continue." Jenny opened the Perrier and took a bite of *frites*.

"Fast-forward. A few days ago, I met some people, also from San Francisco. I sold them an original, and authenticated, Chagall. The real deal. All fine and dandy." Alex took a bite of the croque monsieur. "Fast-forward again to about an hour ago. This same man who bought the real deal invited me to his hotel for a little talk. Turns out he has been on my trail. The Derain painting was sold to friends of his. Jenny, I could hardly breathe. I felt trapped."

"That's quite a story. What's this person going to do? Turn you in? Can he actually prove anything?"

"I don't know. Have no idea. But there's more." He raised his finger for emphasis. "I asked Pierre to do another painting. And that would be it. No more. He could go about his business. I could go about my business. Everyone happy as friggin' clams." Alex swept his arm out dramatically, and awkwardly, while holding a *frite* in his hand.

Jenny watched Alex and almost snorted at his theatrics.

"So, Pierre painted a . . . painting. An 'unknown' floral by Camille Pissarro. Same situation, no paperwork available. Stunning piece of work. Stunning. It's ready for the auction tomorrow. But now, the man, the real deal guy, somehow found out about this new painting. And honest to God, how did he know?" Alex shook his head. "No one, only Pierre and I knew about it." Sitting in a daze, he said, "I need to use your bathroom."

"Yeah, sure. Through the bedroom."

Jenny found her phone and quickly called David. "David, Alex is here spilling his guts about meeting with you. What should I do?"

"Just listen to him. Keep him calm. Reassure him."

"Okay. Call you later."

Alex returned and sat back down on the sofa next to Jenny, still talking like he hadn't left the room. ". . . He said he would do whatever. You know, help me figure something out. And said not to put the new painting up for auction." Looking down, he shook his head. "I was angry. Couldn't think. I ran out. Got drunk. And here I am."

Feeling a little more compassionate now, but still trying not to laugh, Jenny furrowed her brow, nodded, and tried to look serious. "Yes. Here you are." She patted his shoulder. "I'm blown away by

what you've told me. Actually impressed, in an odd sort of way."
Jenny hesitated. "What did you say the name of the San Francisco
lawyer was?"

"I didn't. Umm. Geoffrey something. Geoffrey Reid. Why?"

Jenny could hardly believe it. Her boss. "Oh, no reason. I have to
tell you I'm in agreement with this man, whoever he is. Please don't
put the painting in the auction, Alex. Let it go. You're successful as
a legitimate agent. Don't take the chance. Please."

Turning his attention from the plate of food before him, Alex
stared at Jenny. A mix of emotions, mostly anger, flared up. He
couldn't talk. He simply stood, gave her a dismissive wave, and stumbled out.

Alex called Pierre. "I'm coming over. Wrap the damn painting. I
need to deliver it to the auction house. Now."

Alex began to panic, thoughts darting like a pinball machine. He
returned to his hotel room to shower and change, hoping not to run
into Joi. He slipped on a pair of jeans, an old Paris tourist T-shirt
that had once belonged to Pierre, and a sport coat.

He arrived at Pierre's apartment, punched in the security code,
and slowly climbed the four flights of stairs. The door was open, and
he saw the painting sitting on the floor, propped against the sofa.
Exhausted, he shouted, "Pierre!"

Pierre walked out of the kitchen. "*Café?*"

"Yes." He rubbed his hand through his hair. "Dammit. Why isn't
the painting ready? I only have half an hour to get it delivered." He
slumped into a chair. "I have something to tell you. I met a man who
knows about the Derain." He pointed at the latest painting. "He also
knows about this one. Told me not to put it up for auction." Frus-

trated, he stood up and began to pace. "I don't agree. I'll sell it, and then we're done."

Pierre shook his head and thought for a minute. "*Non*. I don't agree with you."

"Why in the hell do you care? No one can prove you had anything to do with it. You're living in the Marais, free to paint and live your life." Alex walked around, looking for a blanket or cloth to wrap the painting in.

Pierre stepped toward him and demanded, "This must *stop*! This is not about getting back at our father any longer. His abusive ways. Alex. *Mon frère*. We can start over right now."

They struggled. Pierre, taller, stronger, and sober, pushed Alex to the side. He grabbed the painting and put his fist through it, ripping the canvas to shreds. "*Fini*. End of story. And another thing—I'm done painting forgeries." He began to pace the room. "Figure out what to do about the Derain. We must face up to it. You will always be my brother, and I will always love you, but all of this ends now!"

Stunned, Alex struggled to his feet with Pierre's help. Exhaustion consumed him like a cloud, holding him in limbo. He considered the last couple of hours. People pretending to be his friend. Even Joi. Now his brother was turning on him.

Alex began to sob, dizzy from drink and confrontation.

Pierre held him until he relaxed. Until he no longer struggled.

"Sit down. Why are you wearing my old T-shirt?"

"What?" Alex looked down, stunned and unaware he had put the shirt on. "I-I don't know."

"Let me tell you a story. When we were young, that T-shirt became a kind of a security blanket for you. Every time you felt scared or worried, you would snuggle with this shirt. Whenever I saw our father yelling or hurting someone, I would wrap you in the shirt and quickly carry you to a room to play Nain Jaune or Felix le Chat. To distract you. The fact that you still have, and actually wear it, is quite telling." Pierre continued. "It doesn't matter now. He's dead. He can't hurt any of us again."

Staring at the floor, then at Pierre, Alex slowly began to weep. Softly at first, then with loud sobs he couldn't control. "I'm so sorry, Pierre. For everything. For getting you involved. So sorry for doing all of this."

Pierre said, "Go wash up. I'll make you a *café*."

They sat quietly for a while, then Alex said, "I need to make a call."

"*Bonjour*. This is . . . Alex Marshal. I'm calling to . . . to let you know . . . I will not be putting the Pissarro up for auction tomorrow. Yes. *Merci*."

Chapter 33

Alex had a lot to think about. People he had thought were his friends had turned on him. The first woman he'd truly loved had joined in the quest to bring him down. And then there was Jenny, the only person he could trust right now. Feeling beaten and ashamed, he called her. No answer. He left a message. "Jenny, it's Alex. I need to see you. Please call me back."

It was late afternoon. Jenny didn't answer her phone or call Alex back—she called David. "When I saw Alex earlier today, he was drunk and completely out of control, emotionally distraught. He told me about his visit with you. That you knew about the new forgery and had discouraged him from putting it up for auction. I told him I thought that was good advice but didn't reveal that I knew you or the rest of the group. He stormed out. He just now called me, sounding sad and desperate. I didn't answer the phone. What now, David? What should I do?"

"It's all good. The fact that he trusts you may be what saves him. Call him back and spend some time with him. Don't be too quick to give advice; just let him talk."

"I'll call him now and let you know what happens. By the way, this saga is getting even crazier. When he told me about the Derain, I casually asked the name of the person who bought it. He was so drunk he didn't think it was an odd question. But get this—it's my boss."

David shook his head. "Seems to fit in perfectly with everything else. Can this get any stranger?"

Jenny called Alex. "Hi, Alex. Sorry I missed your call. I was napping and had my phone turned off. Do you want to come over?"

"Actually, could you meet me tomorrow? I'm beat. It's been a long day, and I've had way too much to drink. I need to sleep it off and figure out some things. Thanks for being my friend. *Bonne nuit.*"

David called Monica with an update. "How are things in San Francisco? And how are you? Doing the same amount of work with one less partner must be getting old."

"You have no idea. And it sounds like you haven't heard the news. On top of everything else, I just found out I'm pregnant. Only a couple of weeks, and heaving my guts out. But I won't elaborate." She sipped her tea. "Phillip is helping here in Joi's absence. What a blessing he's been."

David let out a hoot. "Monica, that's great news. And you're sick at only two weeks? I thought that came later."

"Apparently, I'm one of the odd ones in experiencing morning sickness practically at conception."

He regaled her with recent Paris events. "I told Alex everything, except about Jenny. Right now, their relationship is probably what will save him."

A scowl washed over Monica, both of worry and rage. "What do you mean save him? I thought you were out to nail his ass. This is forgery, David. Illegal! And what about Joi?"

"It's all completely upside down. I'm not so sure I want to pursue this quest. I'm seeing Alex in a different light, and so does Joi. She has fallen in love with him. Since Kat arrived, the four of us have spent some quality time together."

"I understand, David. I know this has been your quest—a somewhat half-hearted one. But I have three concerns: One, my naive best friend and her involvement with a criminal. Two, I work with talented artists, doing amazing original work. They struggle to make a legit living. And three, the forger. Talented, yes, but making thousands of dollars duping the world. It's dishonest. It's a damn mockery. And it's illegal!" Monica's voice had reached an octave capable of stripping paint.

David hesitated. "I know that, of course. But I need more information. There's a story here, and Alex is the only one who can tell it." He continued with the latest revelations, including the new painting and auction tomorrow. "I just talked to Jenny, and she said he came to see her. Right after he left here. She's keeping her ruse as his school friend. She also expressed her advice to him about not putting the painting up for auction. Apparently, he stormed out of her place as well. That's all I know at this point."

Monica's head was reeling, and her stomach as well. "That's quite an update, David. I don't understand your change of heart. It's extremely troubling to me. One thing I do know is that Joi better start making plans to return to San Francisco. I'm overwhelmed here. Phillip and I are putting together the next exhibit, but we've cut back on Chic events. It's hurting our bottom line."

Phillip arrived at the gallery with the list of students chosen for the next exhibit. He took a moment to study the signage on the outside of the building.

MUSE FINE ARTS GALLERY
and
CHIC **EVENTS**

Graham . Pascale . Robson

He realized he had never really looked at it before, but now, the sign took on a new importance. Edwards could be added.

"We've got the students for our next exhibit. I spent the morning at the Art Institute." Phillip rambled on as he entered Monica's office. "Dani and Trev will pick up the artwork this afternoon." He continued to blather about painting gallery walls. "What do you think?"

Monica was thinking he should just get on with it, but kept that snarkiness to herself. She was grateful he was taking charge. "I'm thinking I love you, and whatever you plan will be perfect. And I'm also thinking I need to go home. Can you guys do without me?"

"Good grief, yes. I'll have Trev paint the two walls, then we'll hang the artwork. Sam talked to Ben about the food for opening night. The music is set. The kiddos were delighted to be asked. Now go. We'll be just fine." He walked over and hugged her, giving her shoulders a little rub.

"Thank you. See you tomorrow."

Chapter 34

Alex woke feeling better but not entirely rested. Grateful he hadn't run into Joi since his encounter with David. His emotions were raw. He loved her. How could she be a part of the scheme to take him down? And Kat. They had all become so close. He needed to tell David the whole story about the forgeries and let whatever happened, happen.

"David, it's Alex. If you have the time, I'd like to meet with you and Kat. I need to explain. Tell my story."

David was slightly stunned to hear from Alex so soon. "Alex, that's wonderful news. How about eleven this morning? Do you want Joi to be here as well? I can call her."

"No. I need to talk to her alone—if she'll see me at all. I may have lost her." Alex choked back an emotion new to him. "I'll see you both at eleven."

Alex nervously adjusted his shirt collar, feeling like he was being sent to the *directeur de l'école*—the principal's office. Taking a deep breath, he tentatively knocked on the door.

"Come in." Kat smiled and gestured for him to have a seat. "David will be out in a moment. I had *café* sent up. Would you like a cup?"

"Yes, thank you." Alex sat, then stood, beads of sweat erupting on his brow.

David appeared. "Alex! Good to see you." He squeezed Alex's shoulder while shaking his hand. "Have a seat."

Alex remained standing, nodding to Kat, and then faced David. His voice hoarse, he said, "I want to apologize for my behavior yesterday. Being confronted was both terrifying and . . . embarrassing. But today, it's simply a relief. I've been carrying around this weight for too long. I'm glad I can finally talk it through and take what is coming to me." He cleared his dry throat, searching for words. "We've become friends, but I'm not asking for special treatment. I'm ready to face what I deserve." Calmness held him, then gently allowed him to speak. "Where should I begin?"

"I guess my question is, when did this start? How many forgeries? And why?"

Alex nodded. "I was already involved in the art world socially, through my mother's connections, as I told you in Épernay. I knew then I wanted to buy and sell art as an agent."

Alex explained the beginning with his college friends and the three paintings. "It was all very innocent, a joke really. But I think a seed was planted—with Pierre's talent and where my career was heading." He settled onto the sofa.

"Fast-forward to your friend and the painting I sold two years ago. That was the first and only true forgery that I sold. The situation was like taking candy from a baby, to use a trite expression. Your friend's wife was insisting on owning a Derain, and I accommodated. It was way too easy."

David looked at his cup. "I've had enough coffee. I'm going to pour a glass of wine. How about you, Alex? Kat?"

"Sounds good. Thank you." Alex continued, now more relaxed. "I contacted Pierre, proposing he paint an 'unknown' Derain. He was hesitant, but I assured him the responsibility was all mine. He finally agreed, and I actually felt pretty confident." He paused. "And the thing is, it was a whim. Not something I planned on as a career— but I wanted to see if I could pull it off. I had credentials and status as a licensed agent. A good reputation. Who would connect me with a forgery? Bizarre, I know." Alex suddenly felt queasy. "What in the hell was I thinking? But I saw, in that situation, how easily it could work. Your friend's wife didn't ask questions. Basically clueless. She simply didn't know. And because it was an 'unknown' piece, I wasn't in jeopardy. There simply were no papers. The painting was delivered. Everyone was happy. I felt safe."

David sipped his wine and shared his side of the story. "Apparently my friends were hosting a dinner party shortly after they'd received the painting. They wanted to show it off. One of the guests inquired as to when and where they had acquired the Derain. He questioned the authenticity because of some small detail. He wasn't sure, just a question. No big deal. My friend took the opportunity to loudly proclaim, 'I was screwed, and I'll get that SOB.' Rather than seeing the situation for what it was. Which was that his ditzy, social-climbing wife had not bothered to inquire or research the art. He could have ignored his guest's comment and researched it on his own in private. But now, the whole room had heard him. He had to act. And act he did. He called me the next morning."

Alex couldn't help but smirk at the visual. David's account sounded like a scene from a documentary on forgery. "So that's it? He turned the quest over to you?"

"Yes. But I had nothing to go on. His wife couldn't remember the gallery where she'd met you, or even your name. She did recall that you were 'extremely handsome,' which ticked off her husband even more. She eventually found your card, giving me my one and only clue. I was able to pull up a poor-quality photo of you online. You were at an auction in New York, I think. So, for almost two years I've been sporadically playing detective. Mostly bored out of my mind with something I didn't care about personally. It wasn't until Monica mentioned you and Joi had met and travelled to Paris together. And then shortly after you contacted me about the Chagall. The timing couldn't have been more perfect."

Alex sat quietly, a little confused. "So, there are more than you and Kat and Joi privy to this drama? Monica and who else?"

"I'll backtrack a bit. Joi, Monica, Sam, and Phillip are all friends. They graduated from Pratt in New York, moved back to San Francisco, and eventually opened the art gallery and events planning company. They all know. That's about it."

Alex tried to take it all in. "Interesting. Pierre graduated from Pratt in the '80s. And did you say Sam? The accountant?"

"Yes, Sam is the accountant and office manager. And also, a very fine sculptor."

Alex continued. "Remember when I told you about running into an old friend from school? She told me that she lived in San Francisco, was studying art forgery, and was married to a wonderful man named Sam, who is an accountant. This whole crazy set of serendipitous facts could only mean that it's the same Sam. Am I right?"

David hung his head, then looked up at Alex with a smile. "One and the same."

"So, Jenny is in on all of this too?" He laughed out loud, shaking his head in disbelief. Alex said, "That is so Jenny."

David continued. "The Jenny part of this story is this: she came to Paris because she was concerned about Joi and also because of her specific studies on forgery. The fact that she attended the Sorbonne was an added bonus. As a former employee, she was easily given access to the Artcurial auction house. Her quest at the time was to meet you, Alex Marshal, and try to seduce you. Find out about the forgeries, but not connect to any of us. She didn't initially know that Alex Marshal and Alex Marchand, her old friend, were one and the same."

Kat refilled their glasses, curled up next to David, and put her hand on his shoulder.

Alex felt numb listening to the intricate and incredible details of David's story.

"Bottom line, Jenny's heart was broken, thinking you had moved to the dark side. She agreed to help because she cares about you. We all do, Alex. Everyone makes mistakes in life." David choked back a deep emotion and cleared his throat. "It's what we do about it that counts. Most of all, you have to forgive yourself."

Alex felt an incredible calm and relief—a heavy, dark curtain slowly being lifted by people who truly did care about him. "Thank you both for listening to me. For being here and helping me to make sense of it all. There's one more thing you should know. After I left here yesterday, I went to see Jenny. I was drunk." Alex recounted how Jenny had encouraged him not to submit the latest forgery for auction. And how his brother had agreed with everyone by simply destroying the painting. "And now, here I am."

"And we are happy you are," Kat said. "It certainly could have gone in a very different direction."

"There's one last thing. Telling Joi. My heart is breaking for her. I have never loved anyone so much in my entire life. When we met in Seattle, my head was thinking, 'She's perfect for my business.

The pizzazz on my arm.' But my heart was not buying that theory. Coming to Paris and watching this unique and lovely woman blossom before my eyes has been a joy. She's sweet, innocent, and yet very much a woman." Clearing his throat, he choked out, "I would do anything to keep her safe and protected." Overwhelmed, Alex began to sob, pressing his palms to his eyes. The last two days of discovery, drunkenness, anger, and reconciliation were finally breaking him. "I've lost her. What should I do?"

The room became still and silent. Joi walked out of the bedroom. "Alex?"

He looked up, not sure what was going on. "Joi? You heard . . . everything? Have I lost you?"

"*Non, mon chéri*. You couldn't lose me. I've loved you from the day we met." A sob caught her voice. "I couldn't help myself. Some people just belong together. *Oui?*"

They all stood in a group hug. All grateful for the outcome and the profound love they shared and treasured.

Alex turned to David. "This has been quite a day. Would you excuse us? I'll need your advice on the Derain situation. Tomorrow?"

"Why don't the four of us meet in the morning. Someplace private, but not the hotel. Any suggestions?"

Alex smiled, wanting to lighten the mood. "Dress casual. We'll take the bus to Saint-Ouen and the flea market at Clignancourt. Everything you can imagine is being sold there. And great places to eat. We can plan my fate, whatever that may be. My choice is an atmosphere of joy and great food and wine with the people I love. I would say we should invite Pierre, but not just yet. Another time."

David said, "Who exactly is Pierre? Business partner? Friend from school?"

"Pierre? He's my older brother. Quiet man. Amazing artist. And to tell you the truth, he actually saved my life yesterday by destroying that painting. He did it with love, and I owe him everything. As I do you."

"Tomorrow then. Flea market." David chuckled at how life kept throwing out every possible scenario, then leaving it up to them to figure it all out.

David called Geoffrey Reid. "Geoff, it's David. I have a proposition for you. Concerning the Derain. Would you consider accepting a payback in cash?"

"I don't give a shit about the Derain. My wife and I are getting a divorce. She's moved out. I told her to take the Derain with her. She's happy. I'm happy. What a joke."

"I'm so sorry to hear that, Geoff." He wasn't. "As a lawyer, do you recommend signing some kind of release?"

Geoffrey let out a big sigh, wishing the conversation would end. "Let me think about it. I'll need to talk to my soon-to-be ex-wife."

"Thank you. Take care, Geoff."

David had mixed feelings. Relief that Geoff didn't care about the painting anymore. Yet he didn't like the idea of Mrs. Reid coming back sometime in the future and causing problems. He needed to discuss this with Alex.

Alex and Joi returned to their hotel completely wrapped around each other. As they approached the elevator, he said, "I'll meet you up in your suite. I have something to take care of and won't be long. Order champagne, soak in the tub, and put on the dress I love. The lace one you wore when we met David for dinner that first time. We're going someplace special tonight, with an amazing view of the Seine and the Eiffel Tower." He held her close and kissed her forehead, the tip of her nose, and finally her soft lips. *"Je t'aime."*

Alex held the note he had found under his door that morning. *Meet me at four o'clock on Pont Alexandre III.* It was signed with a simple *J.* Alex smiled, remembering how Jenny used to send him notes at school signed with a *J.* He left the hotel and walked the few short blocks to the bridge. The sun gave the sky a marvelous peach-sorbet hue with abstract streaks of blue and purple, promising a lovely sunset later. He saw a blonde-haired woman standing at the center of the bridge and approached her, then realized it wasn't Jenny. She smiled and continued to walk away as he stopped to watch the barges glide underneath. He heard someone call his name and turned. Standing there was Joi. He hesitated and said, "*J*?"

"I didn't know if I would see you again. I put the note under your door first thing this morning. Then David called and asked if I would be at their hotel before eleven, before you were to arrive. He filled me in on the conversation you had yesterday. He also said you didn't want me there this morning. I understand that."

He laughed. "I'm glad you were there. It saved me from regaling that painful story twice."

"There was something wonderful about hearing the story that way. Your respect for David and Kat and the trust you have for each other." She hesitated, then changed the subject. "So. Where are we going tonight? We should head back so I can put together the outfit you requested." She gave him a playful smile and soft kiss on the lips.

Time stood still for a moment as they gazed at each other. In love. Grateful.

"It's a surprise. A quiet little place with a lovely ambience." He wrapped his arm around her waist as they walked back to the hotel.

Alex delivered Joi to her room. "I'll be right back." He went to his room and called room service. "Please send champagne and oysters up to suite 512. *Merci.*" He changed out of his suit and pulled on a pair of jeans and the faded gray "security blanket" shirt that had once belonged to Pierre, with the Seine and Eiffel Tower printed on the front. He smiled at the memory Pierre had shared with him, feeling the importance of it now. He walked barefoot back to Joi's room.

She opened the door, wearing the lace dress he had requested. Surprised, she said with a smirk, "Well, look at you. Did I miss something in regard to dinner tonight?"

Alex shut the door. "Here. Let me help you with that." He turned her around and slowly unzipped her dress, letting it drop to the floor. He placed his hands on her shoulders and kissed the back of her neck, then turned her around and kissed every beautiful feature on her face, finishing with her mouth. Sliding his hands down her body, he teasingly said, "You should put something on, dinner will be delivered shortly."

She pointed to his T-shirt. "Dinner with a view of the Seine and Eiffel Tower?" They fell on the bed in laughter, mixed with relief, then quiet intimacy, removing one garment at a time. She removed his shirt. He removed her lacey bra. She purred "Alex" just as there was a knock on the door.

"*Service de chambre, mademoiselle.*"

Joi slipped into the bathroom while Alex answered the door and retrieved the meal.

As they sat at the table, sharing bites of oyster and baguette, Alex regaled her with a short history of the T-shirt, which was now thin and revealing several small holes. He went on to explain that their father had died, but the hurtful memories of abuse were strong and had become an influence on his bad behavior. Not an excuse, but a reason.

Joi touched his cheek and leaned over to kiss him. "I'm so sorry."

Alex smiled, wanting to lighten the mood. "Just so you know, this shirt will always be with me. Don't even think about tossing it away on the sly!"

Joi grabbed his hand and the champagne as they retreated to the bed.

Chapter 35

Later that evening, David called. "Alex, I know we weren't going to see you until morning, but I have some news from San Francisco. Kat and I would like to come share a bottle of wine with you and Joi. We could be there in half an hour."

Alex looked around Joi's suite. Clothes tossed everywhere. The bed linen twisted and half on the floor, along with an empty bottle of champagne.

Joi walked out of the bathroom and softly mouthed, "Who are you talking to?"

Alex covered the phone and said, "It's David. They want to come over and share a bottle of wine."

She looked around and laughed out loud. "Nooo. See if we can meet them someplace." She scrambled to get dressed, slipping on jeans and a sweater. "Tell them we were just leaving for a walk, so we could meet them at . . . ?"

"Sounds great, David. We were just headed out for a walk. Why don't we meet you at Bords de Seine. It's at 1 Place du Châtelet, not far from your hotel."

"Perfect. See you in a bit."

David and Kat arrived at the café first. They had just ordered a bottle of champagne and were chatting about the news from San Francisco when Alex and Joi walked in. "You two look like a couple of teenagers." David stood and pulled out the chair for Joi.

The waiter approached with the wine, opened it, and filled their glasses.

David raised his glass. "To good friends and good karma."

"What's the news from San Francisco? Your phone call obviously garnered results of some sort."

"I spoke with Geoffrey. I told him the situation and asked if there was a way we could come to an agreement. A cash settlement, with a legal document dropping all charges. I did not expect his response. It completely threw me for a loop. He said that he and his wife were getting a divorce and that she took the Derain and didn't care about any damn papers. It's over. He doesn't care. Or in his words, 'I don't give a shit.'"

Alex grinned, and Joi shook her head in disbelief. More champagne was poured, toasting the end of the two-year quest.

"I still want to take you both to the flea market tomorrow. Are you game? We can enjoy the day without talking about forgery. By the way, David, how did you convince Geoffrey not to press charges, regardless of the divorce?"

"Well, when you grow up in a large family like I did, you tend to learn strategies of negotiation." David grinned, thinking of growing up the middle child among his five brothers.

They all cheered. "Bravo, David. *Santé.*"

David added, "You're going to love this, Alex. One more amusing fact. Geoffrey happens to be Jenny's boss at the law firm. She didn't know the connection with the Derain until she arrived here a few days ago."

Alex stood, closed his eyes for a moment, then became serious. He held his hand out to David.

David stood. "What is it?"

"I owe you my life. I can't thank you enough."

The two men hugged, patting each other's shoulders, speechless for a moment.

"Okay, you two. See you in the morning for our trip to the fleas in Clignancourt." Alex smiled at Kat. "Bring a shopping bag. I guarantee you will find must-have treasures."

Alex and Joi strolled along the Seine, both feeling overwhelmed by the last two days of revelations. They stopped and quietly embraced.

Alex hesitated, then smiled. "There's something we need to do. If you don't mind, I'd like to call Jenny. Ask her to meet us for a drink."

"Absolutely. Do it. I can't wait for her reaction."

Willi's Wine Bar on rue des Petits-Champs began to fill with tourists and locals alike. The popular bar had a modern, pristine feel, the walls covered with the famous Willi's posters, displayed in simple black frames.

Giddy over how their lives had changed in the last few hours and the complete love and respect she felt for Alex, Joi winked at him. "I'm a little hungry—all that afternoon activity. Let's have a snack and go to a jazz club later. I want this to be a crazy, fun night."

Alex ordered a bottle of pinot noir just as Jenny walked in.

She approached and pretended not to know Joi.

Alex stood and kissed both her cheeks. "Jenny, this is Joi." He wanted to put her at ease as soon as possible. "We haven't ordered yet. Thinking a snack and a jazz club later. Maybe in Pigalle?" He and Jenny had first gone there during their school days. "Shocking" was all she could say then, even though they'd both loved it. Moulin Rouge and the *louche* nightlife of Paris.

She crossed her eyes at him and burst out laughing, then looked over at Joi, who was enjoying the whole scenario.

Joi could hardly contain herself. "Jenny, we have something to tell you."

The waiter appeared, asking for their order.

"Prawns and *frites* for now. *Merci.*"

Alex added, "After I left your apartment yesterday, I managed to make it to Pierre's apartment with the intention of picking up the painting—the forgery. Bottom line, Pierre agreed with all of you about not putting it up for auction. And to make sure of it, he destroyed it right before my eyes."

Jenny stared at Alex in shock. She lifted her glass of wine in a toast. "Bravo. Here's to Pierre!" She took a sip. "Damn." Then, patting his shoulder, she added, "You were pretty wasted, Alex. So, what then?"

"After sleeping it off, I came clean to David, told him the whole story. David connected with Geoffrey. Turns out he's in the middle of a divorce and doesn't 'give a shit' about the painting."

Jenny laughed. "Geoffrey Reid's wife is a total ditz. He's lucky, if you ask me." Jenny looked at Joi, wondering why she hadn't said anything. She waited for Alex to continue.

"So, my dear Jenny, I know the whole story. I know about you and your reason for being here. And I absolutely love that we both thought we were just friends from the Sorbonne and not at all connected to this other caper going on."

Jenny shook her head at both of them. "I'm completely blown away."

They all burst out laughing, finished the bottle of wine, and talked about going someplace else for a night out.

Jenny declined the invitation, saying she needed to call Sam, make travel arrangements, and pack. "I can be an insensitive bitch at times. I've gotten so wrapped up in the 'Paris Affair' that I'm afraid my dear Sammy has suffered. I need to make things right. Alex, I'm sure you'll meet Sam at some point. He's a great guy. You'll like him." She stood. "I'll call David to let him know I'm leaving." She looked at the two of them, kissed their cheeks, and said to Alex, "Looks like I'll be seeing you in the future. Not a doubt in my mind. I love you." She wrapped her scarf around her neck and playfully flipped her hair in a dramatic move. "That's it. It's time for me to go home. My work here is done. *Bonne nuit.*"

Alex and Joi stayed at Willi's Wine Bar and ordered a light dinner. They had to make some decisions. Their conversation turned somber.

"I need to go home. I can't put it off any longer." She pushed the food around on her plate. "When we first met, you told me you spent half your time in New York and half in Paris. Is it auction business? You haven't mentioned the Big Apple since we arrived here."

"I bought an apartment there years ago, thinking it would be my home base. But Paris is where I prefer to be. I'm thinking of putting it on the market and purchasing a larger place here. Since I travel so much, the apartment I live in now is very small. What do you think?"

Joi felt in limbo, like she was floating above, untethered. San Francisco? Paris? New York? Where would her place be?

Alex took her hand. "Let's go back to the hotel. We need to talk in private."

Chapter 36

Alex opened the door to Joi's suite, pulled her inside, and held her. He could smell the faint scent of Moroccan oil in her hair as he kissed her forehead and then her tear-streaked cheeks.

"How can I leave you now?" Joi asked, leaning her head on his shoulder. "San Francisco is another world and life away. I can't wrap my head around going back and not being with you. I'll go, but my heart will be here with you." Tears again filled her eyes. "Will you take care of my heart?"

"Shh. We'll work this all out. I have some things to take care of, and I need to go see my brother. I would like you to go with me. It's important that he understand what has happened the last few days and that the forgery situation has been taken care of. He's a good man, and I want him to know how much I love you and that you're in my life. And yes, I will take care of your heart, *ma chérie.*"

Alex caressed her hair. "There's something else. I still feel restitution needs to be made to Geoffrey Reid, regardless of his desire to be finished with it all—including divorcing his wife. I did something very wrong, and I can't let it hang over us for the rest of our lives. I need to make it right."

Joi snuggled against him. "I understand and agree. I'm very proud of you. You know that, right?"

Alex kissed her. "Yes. I'm going back to my room to call Pierre. Back in an hour."

Feeling anxious, Joi poured a glass of wine and called Monica "Hi, it's me. How are you feeling?"

"Good. I'm spending time at home, the office, and the bathroom. Business is okay for now."

"I'm making plans to come back soon." Saying it out loud made her feel dizzy. "How are things with the new exhibit? Phillip in his take-charge mode?"

"Yes, thank God. He could run this place by himself, blind-folded. Sam has been in a funk the whole time Jenny's been away. I find myself prodding him as if he were a turtle in a race. And then I run to the bathroom and throw up while Phillip flits around with swatches and paint chips, ranting about flower arrangements. It's quite a circus."

Joi burst out laughing. "I miss you guys. I have so much to tell you but won't on the phone. Just know that everything is fine. We're all fine. Jenny is flying back tomorrow. David and Kat are staying here for a while longer, visiting friends in Provence. Anyway, I'll let you know when my travel arrangements have been made. My love to Ben, and big hugs to Sam and Phillip. I love you, sweetie."

Alex returned with a cold bottle of rosé and a snack of grapes, pâté, and a baguette. He found Joi sitting by the fire, wearing a short, pale green satin slip and rubbing oil on her legs.

"You're early. Want to rub some oil on my back?" She let the straps slide off her shoulders, her body glowing from the firelight, and began rubbing oil on her arms, looking back at Alex, teasing him to join her.

Michel Gaudet called his PI friend in New York. "Nick. It's Michel. Find out where Alex Marshal's apartment is. That's Marshal with one *l*. I think it's in the west 80s, close to Central Park. Alex is an art agent I've been keeping tabs on for a client."

Nick said, "Tall, handsome Frenchman? You're not going to believe this, but he has an apartment where I live. My family recently bought the building and I moved in last week."

Chapter 37

Alex's phone rang at eight the following morning. He untangled himself from Joi, opened the window shades, and looked for his phone. *Merde.*

"Good morning. Are you two up and ready to go? Kat and I had *café* and croissants, and we're ready whenever you are."

"David. *Bonjour.* I'm afraid we overslept. Yes, um, give us half an hour. Meet us at the Louvre–Rivoli bus stop on rue de Louvre. It's next door to DuChat Detective."

Sitting at the bus stop, David glanced up at the DuChat sign and realized he hadn't talked to Michel about ending his services. Afraid Alex and Joi would arrive seeing him enter or leave the building, he made a quick call instead. "*Bonjour,* Michel. It's David Waters. I wanted to let you know your services are no longer required. Yes. What? New York apartment? Okay. You're positive?" David glanced at Kat. "Michel, I need for you to remove the bug app from Alex's phone. And I'll stop by the agency tomorrow and pay my bill. Thank you again. You've been a great help."

Michel suggested they wait a bit on the bug, just to make sure all information had been gleaned.

David agreed. He looked down at his hands and frowned. He didn't want to spoil the day. "The PI heard a phone conversation last night. Alex and someone in New York and something about the paintings." He gave her a weak smile and patted her shoulder. "I'm sure it's okay."

Alex and Joi arrived just minutes before the bus pulled up. After boarding, they found four seats toward the back of the bus and scrambled like teenagers on a field trip, laughing and teasing each other.

David said, "What do you mean my socks don't match? They're both gray."

"But one sock has stripes, darling. And the other small dots." Kat and Joi giggled and nudged a grinning David.

David would deal with the new information from the PI later. Today they would have fun and simply enjoy each other's company.

Fifteen minutes later, they arrived at Marché aux Puces and walked the short distance to the acres of buildings that housed the flea market's stalls and showrooms. Outdoor vendors, selling T-shirts, running shoes, backpacks, and cheap trinkets, formed a gauntlet outside the main market of small booths offering antiques, vintage clothing, and small treasures.

Alex said, "Everyone keep your cell phones on. It will be easy to get lost if you all go wandering off. Best to stay together. Better yet, take a photo of the map posted over there on the fence."

Kat and Joi immediately went in opposite directions, picking up old keys, small dishes, and antique buttons.

"You know this is going to be like herding cats, David. We'll follow along behind. But enjoy yourself. We can explore and stop for lunch later."

After a good hour, they regrouped and found Chez Louisette. Alex said, "This is a wonderful Paris experience. And the food is quite good."

They entered to a packed house and the sound of a chanteuse, well past the age of Brigitte Bardot sexy, singing "La Vie en Rose." Her look and earthy voice added to the bizarre ambience. Long plank tables sat on the black-and-white tiled floor and encouraged diners to socialize with friends and strangers alike. Every inch of wall space was covered with memorabilia and autographed photos of visiting celebrities. Tinseled garlands from Christmases past draped the ceiling in between crystal chandeliers and cheap shiny ornaments. Patrons held their beloved dogs, laughed, and toasted life in general.

They were seated beside four other people, with just enough room for David and his large frame to squeeze in.

"It's good to sit down. I can't wait to show you some things I found," Kat said to no one in particular as she rummaged in her shopping bag. "Oh, I'll show you later. Let's eat." The pale pink vintage satin bra trimmed in lace would be for David's eyes only.

The waiter appeared with menus and asked for a wine choice. He was animated and charming, with an in-your-face kind of playfulness. Joi recognized him from an old newspaper clipping posted outside the restaurant, mugging with Charles Aznavour.

Alex said, "Chardonnay?" They all agreed and quickly decided on their meal, salmon with *salade verte*.

"This is fabulous, Alex. David and I have never taken the time to come here on our visits to Paris." Kat was delighted to see yet another side of Paris. And of Alex.

"Just wait until later. I'm taking you to the most amazing place for jazz manouche. You won't believe the talent. And I'm delighted to introduce you to so many of my favorite places." He took Joi's hand and kissed her fingers. "I love you." He turned to David and Kat, raising his glass and smiling. "And I love you too." They all sipped their wine and melded into the din of celebration around them.

David sensed something more than just happiness in the moment. Something deep-seated and painful for Alex to express. A tacit yearning. Hopefully, a conversation for another time.

They finished their meal and wandered back to the buildings housing high-end decorations and furnishings. Antique sideboards, large kitchen worktables, and copper pans. Carved side chairs upholstered with satin and velvet were on display alongside modern furniture, huge abstract paintings, and glass sculptures.

Shopping was successful. Both David and Kat found small items to adorn their home. Joi purchased a few small trinkets, jewelry, a small gold-framed painting of the French countryside, and an old print of a hen strutting along with baby chicks scampering behind. This would be a gift for Monica, their mother hen.

Alex said, "How about a break? Let's go to La Chope des Puces— the place I told you about earlier. We'll have wine and listen to gypsy jazz."

They entered the small café, already packed with visitors, and found a table along the side wall with a good view of the two musicians. They ordered a bottle of rosé and sat enraptured by the talent of the two men. The lead guitarist was a young and handsome man, reminiscent of Django Reinhardt from the 1930s, dressed in jeans, a black leather jacket with no shirt, and slip-on shoes with no socks. Kat and Joi raised their eyebrows and smiled at each other without saying a word.

Michel made a call. "Nick. Something's going on. Check with the high-end galleries. See if they know Alex Marshal."

Chapter 38

Alex knocked, and Pierre opened the door immediately. They embraced, and for the first time in a very long time, Alex could let his guard down—his professional persona—and simply be a brother. Their last encounter had been quite the opposite. Alex took Joi's hand and said, "Pierre, I want you to meet the love of my life," as though it was a first-time introduction.

They sat at the table, drinking wine. Alex told Pierre the facts of the last few days and how grateful he was for his brother's wisdom and insight. "Thank you for stopping the final forgery sale and making me face myself."

Joi watched two grateful men make sense of a situation that could have potentially been a disaster. She didn't speak but kept hold of Alex's hand.

"Alex, I've always tried to watch over you. I knew things weren't right with our parents. Our father's romantic affairs and frequent absences. He was never there for us." Pierre was pained with memory. "Any interest or success we had was arrogantly responded to with, 'Who do you think you are?' I can still hear him!"

"It doesn't matter now. He's gone. But sometimes I, too, feel like that old bastard's still lurking about." Alex shook his head.

After a moment of quiet, Alex turned to Joi. "I haven't talked to my mother for a while. Now I have someone for her to meet." He kissed her hand. "She will love you."

Alex turned to his brother. "Pierre, we need to go forward now. You are an incredible artist, and I will promote you as much as I can. The forgery situation is not your concern. You have my word on that."

While Alex and Pierre continued to talk, Joi walked around the small apartment. "Pierre, do you mind if I look at the canvases stacked against the wall?"

"Please do. Some aren't quite finished. They sit for a while, you know, before I add more paint or finally say *fini*."

Paintings hung on every inch of wall space and sat stacked against chairs and tables. One canvas on an easel caught her eye. It was of a woman looking out over the Seine, her face slightly obscured by the shadow of the trees. "It's me, before my haircut." She glanced over at Pierre, who simply smiled back.

"When did you paint that? How?" Alex was in awe.

"From memory." Pierre looked down, slightly embarrassed.

Joi spent more time examining the many canvases, revisiting several to consider them more closely. Turning to Pierre: "I wonder if you'd be interested in showing your work in a solo exhibit at my gallery in San Francisco. We'd be honored. Your art is—it's remark-able." She slowly turned, like a windup toy gone awry, pointing to several pieces. "Your brush technique, the color and detail—breath-taking. If you agree, we could choose several and arrange for ship-ment before I leave Paris."

Alex chimed in, "I agree, Pierre. You have quite a collection here. Could you pick out some canvases you consider finished?" Alex enjoyed watching Joi take charge of something he had wanted to do himself for a long time—promote his brother's exceptional talent. "Once a date is set for the exhibit, we can invite *maman* to fly out to San Francisco. What do you think? A celebration all around."

Pierre was touched by their enthusiasm and appreciation of his original artwork. "Yes, I can do that."

"I'll come by tomorrow." She gave him a hug. "I'm so happy, Pierre."

They returned to their hotel, thrilled about promoting Pierre's work.

"I'll be back in a while. I have a couple of calls to make."

"I'm really excited about this, Alex. I'll call Monica now." She pushed him toward the door. "I'm starving, by the way. Any ideas for dinner?"

"*Oui.* I'm taking you to Aux Lyonnais."

Alex made his first call. "*Bonjour, maman.* Hope you weren't sleeping." He listened for a minute. "Yes, I'm good. More than good. I have some great news. Actually, two things." He told her about Joi, her art background and gallery business, and the fact that he was in love. He told her about plans to exhibit Pierre's work in San Francisco. "And we want you to be there. I'll let you know when. Yes. Me too. Can't wait to see you. *Je t'aime, maman.*"

His second call was to David. "Are you busy?"

"Just reading a book I bought at the flea market. What's up?" David whispered. "Yes. Why don't I meet you someplace. Kat is taking a nap."

Ten minutes later, both men stood in David's hotel lobby. "We could have a drink here in the bar, if you'd like. What's going on? You sounded a little serious on the phone."

Alex let out a deep breath. "We need to talk about Geoffrey Reid and the Derain. I would rather not stay here. Let's try Bar Hemingway. It's almost a cliché, but it may be quiet now. Let's check it out."

They entered the small bar, furnished with cozy overstuffed chairs, warm wood paneling, and displays of old photos of celebrities, highlighting Hemingway. The bartender was friendly and deft at mixing the bar's famous concoctions. They found a small table away from the other patrons and both ordered the Red Nichols Manhattan.

"This drink will knock your socks off." Alex grinned. "The best booze—rye and French vermouth—and they make their own cacao bitters here at the Ritz."

David held up his glass. "A drink named after the great Red Nichols has got to be good. An amazing jazz musician. What's up?"

"I'm so grateful to you, David, for speaking with Geoffrey. My concern, and what I need to do, is pay back the money. It's the only way I can be done with it. The other thing is a legal release document stating that once he receives compensation, no further charges would be made. Is that even possible? I mean, Geoffrey would know, being an attorney."

"He certainly would know, but he's also a bit of a bastard. Since he was the one bilked in the first place, he could turn it around and cause a lot of problems. I actually mentioned such a document to him. He said he needed to talk to his soon-to-be ex-wife. Maybe the time will be right while he's dealing with that money-grubbing woman. This situation could very easily mean nothing to him." David sipped his Manhattan. "My God. You may have to carry me back to the hotel. I won't soon forget this drink."

They laughed at the image of Alex bolstering David along the streets of Paris. Soon their conversation turned to David's life in San Francisco, his two children, and how he and Kat would spend the rest of their time in Paris. As they finished their drinks, David's phone rang. He smiled at Alex and mouthed, "Kat."

"Where are you? I woke from my nap and waited, thinking you were out on a quick errand. Are you okay?"

"I'm actually out having a drink with Alex. You were asleep when he called, and I didn't want to wake you. We had some things to go over regarding Geoffrey. We're almost done here. Back in a bit. Okay. I love you too."

Alex excused himself. "I need to use the loo. Be right back."

David noticed Alex's phone on the table. Bolstered by Manhattan courage, he glanced around, grabbed the phone, and slid it onto his lap with the hope of removing the bug even though he had no idea how to do it. His own phone rang again. Thinking it was Kat again, he said, "Yes, darling. On my way."

"David? It's Michel. I wanted to confirm that we leave the bug in Alex's phone for a bit longer. I can take care of it later."

David was about to tell Michel that more information was no longer necessary when he saw Alex on his way back. "Yes. Okay, Michel. Thanks." He quickly slipped Alex's phone back on the table.

"I've cleared our bar tab. Nice to chat. I feel better. Let me know how Geoffrey responds to my request. I'd better get back to the hotel. Joi is busy making plans for a solo exhibit of Pierre's work at her gallery."

"That's fantastic. Kat and I will finally get to meet him. Looking forward to it."

"Pierre is extremely grateful, although it's hard to tell with him. He's so quiet and reserved. But I know this is a big deal for him, and the beginning of long-due recognition of his work."

Joi had spent the last hour detailing some sketches she had drawn earlier, wishing she had done more. Alex seemed to consume every minute, leaving little time for her art. And now she needed to dress for dinner. She chose a red boat-necked short shift dress with three-quarter sleeves and black pumps. She held up a pair of earrings, trying to decide, when Alex walked in. He looked tired but less anxious than when he'd left.

"There you are. Do we have reservations, or are we winging it? And am I overdressed?"

"No reservations. And yes, you're overdressed. Too many clothes. Come over here."

"Oh no you don't. I said I was hungry almost two hours ago. I've been waiting patiently. And I'm ready to go. We can discuss how overdressed I am later."

"Okay. I give up, reluctantly. Be back in a few minutes. I'll return dressed appropriately and eager to take my love to dinner. I'm anxious to see if you'll recognize the restaurant."

They walked toward Opéra Garnier as the afternoon sun began to set, giving the elegant building a magical radiance. Beautifully dressed patrons arrived early to partake of champagne before the evening's opera performance.

Alex said, "Would you like to go there before leaving Paris?"

"Let's save it for the next trip. I don't want to start packing in experiences just because I'm leaving." She gave Alex a lusty smile and with an inflection said, "Yes, my dahling, an evening at the ah-per-ah would be lovely when we return."

They crossed Avenue de l'Opéra and found Aux Lyonnais a few blocks away on rue Saint-Marc. The small restaurant was painted a dark burgundy. Inside, the decor consisted of cream-colored walls and rugged tables draped with linen.

As the waiter served their champagne, Alex put his arm around Joi. "Does this place look familiar to you?"

"It does. It was in a wonderful scene in the movie *Midnight in Paris,* wasn't it?" She was delighted to be sitting in the same place, at practically the same table. The giveaway was the hand-painted tiles above the wainscoting. Light green, with pink roses and pale blue satin ribbons. Beautiful and unique. "Actually, this venue has been in many films." She leaned into his embrace. "You are the best, Mr. Marshal."

Alex ordered *fritots de Saint-Marcellin* and the monkfish with potato for both of them.

Their conversation focused on Pierre.

Joi pulled a notebook from her purse. "I need to write a short bio on Pierre for the exhibit. Help me here. Name: Pierre Marshal. Resident of Paris. Studied art at . . . ?" She looked to Alex for information.

"First of all, our last name is Marchand. I changed my name years ago to create a new persona for myself in the art world. Basically, to distance myself from my father."

Joi stared at him, hearing his words in slow motion. "Marchand? Pierre Marchand?"

"Yes. Pierre Marchand."

"And he studied at Pratt Institute in New York, right?"

"Yes. How did you know that?"

"Because Monica, Sam, Phillip, and I studied art there. We graduated much later than Pierre, so we never met him. But the school had a glass case in the lobby dedicated to Pierre and his art. We all aspired to become like him. We did this silly thing of nodding at the case in reverence as we passed by. And the thing is, Monica and I both thought he looked familiar at the Seattle auction. He looks so different now."

"In his desire to get away from our father, he went through quite a period of 'finding himself.' Like a bird leaving the nest. Being gay meant freedom for him. Experimenting with drugs didn't last long, but he did have a certain 'look' going on when he grew a beard and let his hair grow long." Alex shook his head at the visual. "But now here he is, back in Paris, creating fabulous art and living a quiet, happy life."

"I'm blown away. This changes everything. The exhibit will be an extravaganza!" She couldn't wait to tell Monica, Sam, and Phillip.

Alex reminded her, "I still have some things to clear up, with David's help. Oh, and I spoke with my mom earlier and told her about you and what you're doing for Pierre. She's very eager to meet you and to see the exhibit. It's all good. All so very good." He tilted her chin and kissed her softly.

They strolled back toward their hotel. Both quiet. Both deep in thought. They turned down a narrow, cobbled side street, lit only by the lights of two upper apartment windows.

Alex stopped, grabbed Joi, and pulled her into a darkened doorway. He kissed her neck and whispered, "Now let's discuss how over-dressed you are." He lifted her up as she wrapped her legs around his waist—their lovemaking passionate and yielding, desperate. Thoughts faraway and yet close. They seemed to meld into one.

Breathless, all she could murmur was "Alex," over and over again.

Chapter 39

Monica arrived at the gallery feeling tired and nauseated. Her gynecologist had told her yesterday the morning sickness would ease off at around three months, and she was anxious to see some kind of progress in that direction. With a snack of tea and soda crackers, she plopped down at her desk. Within minutes, her phone rang, showing Joi's number.

"Hey, Monica. I just made my reservations. I'll be home in four days. How are you feeling?"

"Feeling? I feel like crap, that's how I'm feeling."

"I'm so sorry. And I'm sorry for being gone so long. I haven't been a very good friend or business partner. I'll make it up to you. Give you a break. Is Phillip around?"

"No. Why do you ask?"

Joi hesitated, knowing what Monica's reaction would be. "Something has come up, and I had to make a quick decision. I need Phillip's help to make this work, and as soon as possible."

"What are you talking about? Spit it out."

"I want to have a solo exhibit for Alex's brother, Pierre, at the gallery. I'm shipping an array of canvases to the gallery. We need to schedule it as soon as possible." Joi held her breath and waited.

Monica sat stunned, looking down at her phone like it was a small dead animal. "What?"

"Monica, his work is incredible, and you won't believe—"

"Stop! Just stop!" She closed her eyes and took a moment. "First you run off to Paris with two questionable characters. Who, am I correct, are brothers? Brothers!"

"Yes, I know. But I just found out that—"

"Then you hook up with David. You're both hell-bent on catching the bastard. Jenny arrives to seduce said bastard. Now you're all lovey-dovey and promoting the actual forger? What in the *hell* is going on?"

"Monica, you don't understand. Everything has changed—"

"That's questionable. You know, I've been here alone trying to hold this business together. I'm exhausted. If it weren't for Phillip, I would have put an Out of Business sign on the door."

"Monica, Pierre is Pierre Marchand!!"

"What?"

"Alex changed his name to Marshal years ago, and I had assumed Pierre's name was Marshal. Didn't give it a second thought. Last night Alex told me. I told him about Pratt. It's all so amazing. And Monica, David has taken care of the situation with Geoffrey. It's over! You have to trust me."

"If the law comes knocking on our door because we're promoting a forger, I'll be stepping aside. I'll have no part of it. I may talk to a lawyer today, just in case." Monica felt faint thinking about it. "And another thing. Dani and Trev are leaving. We need to make some decisions fast."

Joi took a deep breath, suddenly feeling confident and in control. For the first time. "Monica, calm down! First of all, I would never put our business at risk. In the meantime, Pierre deserves recognition as an artist. I'm going to call Phillip with a heads-up. The planning can occur when I get home. This is a good thing." She took a breath and switched gears. "And about Dani and Trev—we all knew this was coming. See you in a few days."

Sam called Monica from home. "I'm not coming in today. Jenny's plane arrives late this afternoon, and I'm attempting to make sense of this apartment I so deftly managed to turn into a disgusting bachelor pad."

Monica, still stunned from Joi's phone call, offered her help. "Let me call my housekeeper. She can do magic in a very short period of time. Just relax. Start by gathering up garbage: pizza boxes, empty beer bottles, candy wrappers. What is it with you men? Why do you find it so difficult to actually put garbage *in* the garbage?"

Sam assumed that was a rhetorical question. "If your housekeeper could come, that would be great. Call me back with a time. Thank you, Monica. I owe you."

"Wait, Sam. I just got off the phone with Joi. She'll be back in four days. We need to talk. I feel like everything is falling apart. She said—"

"Relax. When she gets back, we'll have a meeting. Go over the books, see how the business is doing, and what we need to do to make it better." On a roll, he continued. "Also, the staffing issue and bringing Phillip in as a partner. We have a lot of decisions to make. For now, take care of yourself and your baby." Sam was beginning to feel his old self again and in charge. Both at work and with his marriage.

Monica's head reeled from the last two phone calls, only minutes apart. Joi was promoting forgers, Sam was living like a homeless man in his own apartment, and Phillip was constantly making decisions for floral arrangements, paint, and fabric. "Thank God I'm okay," she said aloud, as she leaned over and puked in the wastepaper basket.

Monica called Sam back a few minutes later. "The housekeeper—her name is Felicity—will be there in half an hour. I asked that she bring fresh flowers to pretty up your apartment. As soon as she arrives, go to the store, and buy groceries. Fresh fruit and vegetables, a nice bottle of wine, and something you can easily cook. Steak, salad. Simple. Jenny's not going to want to do anything but be home with you. Make it special."

Sam grinned. "Yes, Mother."

Felicity arrived at Sam's apartment and immediately told him to go away. Short and stocky, she wore jeans, a yellow cotton blouse, and a bright, flowered smock with large pockets. She carried a plastic bucket with the products she liked to use for cleaning. In her other hand, she carried the bouquet of mixed flowers. "Here, take these flowers. Put them in water. I've got lots of work to do here. Go. Go. And don't come back for two hours."

Sam was glad to get out of her way. He walked toward the market but decided to stop for lunch before buying groceries. He sat at the counter facing busy Church Street and thought about the gallery and events business. Both were successful, but he sensed big changes were about to happen. Phillip wanted in, but he suspected Monica wanted out. With Dani and Trev leaving, they would be down to bare bones. Maybe it was time to add the bistro like they'd talked about for so long. Then a light went on in his head. He knew exactly what they should do. He smiled and mentally praised himself for his genius. He called Ben at the Purple Puffin!

He returned to the apartment, groceries in hand, opened the door, and almost thought he was in the wrong place. Everything was organized, shiny clean, and fresh smelling, and there on the table were the flowers.

Felicity had packed up her supplies. She looked up at Sam without smiling. "Your wife coming home? She be glad I was here."

Sam pulled out his wallet to pay her.

"No, no. Ms. Graham already paid. Goodbye." She scooted by him and out the door, anxious to get to her next, and last, cleaning job for the day.

Sam looked at his watch and panicked. Not having time to drive and park, he called a cab and arrived at the airport just in time. Jenny was standing by the luggage carousel, scanning for her one suitcase and small duffel.

"Jenny." Sam suddenly felt weak. His beautiful wife was home at last. Two weeks apart seemed more like two years to him. He scooped her up for an embrace and then a long, lingering kiss.

"Ooh. I should go away more often," she cooed. She stepped back and looked him up and down. "You look like you've gained a little weight. Let me guess. Pop-Tarts, pizza, ice cream, and copious amounts of beer." She gave him a little hip check. "I think we can figure out a way to work off those extra pounds."

Slightly offended, even though she was right, Sam mumbled, "Nice to see you too."

Jenny ignored his remark as she scanned the carousel. "Oh good, my bags."

As they walked to the curb to flag a cab, she said, "Why so glum?"

"You know, you've been in Paris for two weeks, doing God only knows what. You rarely took the time to call. I had no idea if you were in trouble, lonely, missed me, or just didn't give a shit."

She stopped and turned to him, completely surprised by his outburst. "Sam. I'm sorry." She wrapped her arms around him, his body stiff and unyielding. She stood back again. "Sweetie, I'm exhausted. Let's talk about this when we get home."

The cab ride home was in silence.

Sam opened the door to their apartment and let Jenny walk in first. He carried in her bags and dropped them in the hallway. He was no longer angry, but he did know they would have a discussion about their relationship—a marriage that seemed to him to be faltering and one-sided.

"Sam, it's beautiful in here." She added teasingly, "What did you do? Hire a French maid?" She peeked around the corner to see a pristine kitchen. Fresh fruit in a bowl, a nice red wine on the counter. The little patio off the kitchen had been swept, plants trimmed, weeds pulled. "I'm impressed. Can't wait to see the bedroom." She smiled and grabbed his hand.

"I have some things to take care of at the gallery. I won't be long. Take a nap. I'll fix us dinner when I get back." He didn't kiss her. He simply strolled out the door.

Chapter 40

Alex watched Joi pack her things, taking her time and choosing an outfit for the flight tomorrow. "We meet David and Kat in half an hour. Are you almost ready?"

"Five minutes." Distractedly, she said, "When are Pierre's paintings due to arrive in San Francisco?" She wrapped the last pair of shoes in a bag and tucked them in the large hard-sided suitcase she had purchased the day before. To herself, she said, "All that's left are my toiletries in the morning, and I'm set."

Alex ignored her question since he'd given her the shipping information a mere fifteen minutes ago.

"Okay. Ready." She kissed his cheek as she straightened the sleeves on her jacket. "Now where's my purse?"

Amused, he turned her around and held her without saying a word, then admitted, "I'm going to miss you, even if it's only for a week or so."

They arrived at Les Halles minutes after David and Kat, who stood waiting by the door.

David kissed Joi's cheek. "We're sorry you're leaving Paris. It's been quite an adventure, hasn't it?" His eyes twinkled.

"Yes, it has. I'm packed but certainly not ready to leave." Dewy-eyed, she choked back emotion, not wanting to cry. "Let's have champagne. I want this evening to be special. And being with you is definitely special."

Alex had emotions of his own and something important to tell all of them. Wanting privacy, he asked the waiter to seat them in a quiet corner.

They ordered champagne and foie gras with chutney and nut bread. Alex struggled to begin his story. "I have something to tell all of you. And David, I need your advice."

Not knowing what he was about to say, Joi simply put her hand on his shoulder. They all leaned in and looked at Alex with concern.

"I mentioned to Joi when we first met that I live part-time in New York and part-time in Paris. Actually, I don't spend much time in New York, Paris being my preference. I bought an apartment there years ago, then sold it recently to one of the residents. A single guy."

He paused while waiters opened the champagne and served the foie gras.

"I use the New York apartment mostly for storing artwork."

David asked, "A private collection? Art to present at auction?"

"Yes, a collection." Alex looked around the room then lowered his voice. "They're all paintings. Forgeries done by Pierre."

David and Kat looked at each other, and Joi removed her hand from Alex's shoulder like it was a hot stovetop.

"They've been stored there for the last couple of years. My intention was to slowly put them out for auction, but I just couldn't do it. Pierre would produce another painting, and I would ship it to New York and simply add it to the collection."

They sat stunned, no one more than Alex. After all this time, he was finally able to say it out loud.

"I have no intention of selling them, that's definite, but—"

David interrupted, "Alex, I . . . I'm speechless. What's your plan? You can't—"

"No, David. Of course not. That's what I'm saying. They can't and won't be sold. The strange thing is, Pierre doesn't even know. He would produce a painting, turn it over to me, and assume that I had sold it. I would pay him a nice amount. No questions asked."

"So, you want my advice?" David shook his head. "I'm not sure what you're asking."

"I don't know." Alex became quiet. He took a sip of wine, then said, "The thing about the paintings is that they are extraordinary. Pierre studied the techniques to make his own paint and age the paintings once they were complete. His technique is perfection. He even collected old frames from around Paris." Alex cleared his throat. "I'm sorry. This has been a hard one for me. Holding this inside. Struggling with—"

David leaned in. "Alex. It's okay. Continue."

"This is the problem—the paintings are masterpieces. I can't destroy them. I can't sell them. What should I do?"

They all looked at each other. No one said a word.

Finally, David spoke. "Well, for now, do nothing. It's a strange circumstance. For the last couple of years while tracking you, I've read a lot of books on forgery. Watched documentaries. There are forgers openly selling their work and proclaiming that the pieces *are* forgeries. People don't care. They pay the money and take home the art. It's crazy."

"That's not what I want. I won't do that."

Kat spoke up. "You should display them in your own home. Not hide them away. Enjoy the art your brother created. This is a turning point, Alex. You're not hiding any longer, and you have the love of your friends and your brother and this lovely woman sitting beside you. Nothing illegal has occurred here. Only the Derain, and that's no longer an issue."

After a long silence, Alex raised his glass to Kat. "Thank you."

David leaned over and kissed her cheek.

The waiter returned with their meals. Roasted lavender rack of lamb with eggplant, duckling with potatoes and carrots, cod with asparagus and grated truffles, and chicken with artichoke and lemongrass sauce.

Then, practically in unison, they declared, "I'm starving!" and "Me too!"

Alex looked at each person at the table with gratitude. "You'd think we hadn't eaten for a week. I believe the jazz group begins playing soon. This is one of my favorite restaurants. Intimate." He raised his glass. "*Bon appétit!*"

David and Kat chimed in, "Amen."

Chapter 41

Michel paced in his tiny Paris apartment. He finally called Nick. "Ten forgeries are stashed in Alex's apartment. We need to talk!"

Chapter 42

Joi finished packing. Nervous about the flight home and not wanting to leave Alex, she was in limbo, like a child sad when summer vacation ends. She opened her small carry-on bag and packed her computer, a couple of books, and some personal items. As she unzipped the inside pocket, she felt something. Her phone!

Alex arrived just then and asked if she was ready.

She waved the phone. "Look what I found. My old phone. It's been here all along," she said, shaking her head at the absurdity.

"The Uber will be here in fifteen minutes."

"I'm ready, but not ready to leave you." She wrapped her arms around his waist and rested her head on his chest. "I'm not going to let this magic end—ever. No matter where we are. San Francisco, here, or anywhere."

The drive to the airport was quiet. Both of them deep in thought, with agendas of their own, and a mix of sadness and relief.

"As soon as I set the date, promotion will begin." Joi jotted down some notes. "And then, my love, you and Pierre will be on your way to San Francisco."

Alex watched her switch to gallery-owner mode, proficient and professional. He looked forward to seeing the gallery and finally meeting Monica, Phillip, and Jenny's Sam, the accountant.

David also sat in deep thought. Anxious and wanting closure for Alex's sake, he needed to know Geoff's intentions.

"Hi, Geoff. Sorry to bother you. You said to call back. I'm wondering about the status of the painting and the release document."

Silence.

"Geoff?"

"My wife." A sob. "David, my wife was killed in a car accident last night. Out with her friends. Coast highway. Too much to drink."

David was stunned. "Oh God, no, Geoff. I'm so sorry. Is there anything I can do? We can take the next flight home."

"No, no. Not necessary. Thanks, no." Geoffrey hesitated and took the last sip of his second double Scotch whisky. His speech was broken and slow. "So strange, you know, going through a divorce—everyone angry and bickering, hating each other. And then this happens. I feel like I've been hit in the stomach. I can barely breathe."

David said, "What can I do for you?"

Geoff poured another whisky and added ice. The clinking sound seemed amplified and raw on his nerves. "You think about the person you once loved. Shared your life with." He looked around the room, remembering how they would sit there at night and read, make plans, laugh. Enjoy a glass of wine. "I hadn't filed papers yet. We were both sorting through things. We never had children, as you know. No close relatives." He paused, deep in thought. Numb and baffled as to what to do next.

David took a moment. "Geoff, I realize you're in pain. Please hear me out. I think you should—"

"What? What, David? What should I do?" He felt annoyed, but mostly overwhelmed, not following David's train of thought. Standing in the middle of his den with half-filled boxes and items his wife had set aside only yesterday, he looked down at the painting, which lay on his desk. His wife had brought it back the day before. She'd had questions about papers, had obviously been encouraged by someone to ask. He took another long swig. Overcome with a sudden rage, he picked up the box cutter he had been using earlier. He slowly and methodically made one long cut down the center of the canvas, then slashed the painting over and over again, hot tears streaming down his face.

David could hear the commotion, but didn't know what was happening.

"Destroy it. That's what you wanted to say. Right?"

"Geoff?"

Shreds of vibrant colors drifted down, landing on the floor like confetti.

"Done! It's already done."

David made another phone call. "Alex. I just spoke with Geoffrey."

"And . . . is he going to sign a release?"

"Alex. His wife was killed in an accident. He destroyed the Derain. It's over, Alex."

Chapter 43

Two weeks later, Joi was unpacking the boxes from Paris, gently unwrapping paintings and placing them on the floor against the walls around the gallery.

"You certainly were right about the talent. Remarkable." Monica walked from piece to piece, examining the artwork and the frames carefully chosen by Pierre. She was still uneasy about the situation but trusted Joi and certainly trusted David. He had assured them that the forgery situation had been taken care of. Forever.

Sam called Monica and Joi into a business planning meeting. "I have some ideas to share, along with a financial plan. First, Phillip comes in as an employee and, hopefully soon, as a partner. Second, Dani and Trev are leaving us at the end of the month. They have a recording contract and are in a good place financially. It also means we need to work quickly to replace them. I suggest posting those two positions at a few local art schools to inspire fresh, energetic students with a passion for art to join us. And third, thanks to Ben"—he nodded to Monica—"the Purple Puffin will install a full bistro kitchen, with staff, as a paying entity. They pay *us* to be here!"

Monica and Joi were relieved and impressed with Sam's proposal. "Let's do it."

Sam grabbed his water bottle and bag of carrots and announced, "Headed to the gym. See you both tomorrow. Oh, I forgot to tell you: Jenny takes her bar exam next week. Fingers crossed!"

Monica said, "I'm going home. Ben's fixing lunch. I may take a nap. Back later."

Monica stood in her kitchen with Ben. "I don't think Sam's plan is going to work at the gallery. It's all happening too fast."

"Let it go, Monica."

"I can't."

"Yes, you can. Let other people shine. Support them for a change."

"Ben."

"Joi is beyond capable. It's her turn, sweetie. And Sam? He's a genius!" Ben tossed the salad and refreshed Monica's herbal tea. "So, I was thinking. Should we get married now?"

Monica's eyes widened. "What? No! If anything shouts shotgun wedding, it's a pregnant bride standing at the altar with swollen ankles and needing to pee." She rubbed her tummy. "This little muffin here will be present at our wedding after her birth!" Monica described a miniature version of herself, dressed in pink fluff. "And I don't care if it's at an altar. City Hall works for me!"

Ben laughed out loud. "I can see it, and I love it!" He plated their lunch of chicken, roasted red potatoes, and green salad. "I have a surprise. I'm going to name the new Monterey restaurant Le Petit Poulet in your honor. You are so loved by your friends, and their Mother Hen endearment for you is perfect. Especially now."

Monica grinned. "Oh, for God's sake!"

Two hours later, Monica arrived back at the gallery and approached Joi. "When I made the solo drive from Seattle, I stopped at an all-night diner for coffee. I had an interesting conversation with a woman named Wanda. I kind of unloaded my frustration on her about your staying in Seattle and leaving me to drive home alone. As I left the diner, I grabbed a matchbook, like I always do, and I found it in my purse the other day. It reminded me of Wanda's words of wisdom about friendships. She said something like, 'If she's your best friend, be careful not to turn away.' And then something about 'sticking together.'" Monica gave Joi a hug. "I don't want to ever lose you as my best friend. I love you. Let's make this exhibit the best ever."

Patting Monica's back, Joi said, "Thank you. And I love you too." She gave her friend a squeeze, then said, "We need to leave soon! Alex and Pierre will arrive in less than two hours. Phillip is going with me to the airport. Do you want to come too?"

"Yes, of course. Let's do it!"

"Kat! I forgot about the bug in Alex's phone! Dammit! And now he's headed to San Francisco. And when I called DuChat Detective, they said Michel no longer works there. But he sure as hell is still monitoring Alex's activities." He hesitated. "Oh God! That means he knows about the forgeries at Alex's apartment in New York!"

"Sweetie, call Alex. Let him know. He can take care of the bug."

"Kat, he doesn't *know* about the bug." David shook his head. "Well, this is awkward."

Arriving at the airport half an hour early, Phillip paced around like a coach ready for the big game to start. Not exactly a Phillip persona. "Let's get an espresso. I'm so nervous. No, wine. How about a whisky?"

Joi put her hands on his shoulders. "It's fine. You are going to love Alex, and, well, Pierre. Maybe he's the one for you." Smiling, she kissed his cheek and smoothed out his collar. "He's very quiet and reserved. And you've seen his work at the gallery and, of course, at Pratt."

"Oh, please. He's going to look at me and roll his eyes."

Monica stood nervously off to the side, feeling out of place and certainly out of control. Her solid stance against forgery and the fact that they were now promoting a forger was beyond comprehension. She glanced over at Phillip. And yet, here they were both acting like a couple of starstruck groupies finally meeting their idol.

Tired passengers began to emerge, grateful to be on the ground. Within minutes, Alex and Pierre approached.

Phillip blushed and said, "Oh my!" He approached Pierre. "It's an honor to meet you." He put out his hand. "Phillip. I'm Phillip."

"Nice to meet you, Phillip."

Sweat beaded on Phillip's forehead. He began to babble. "I, we— Joi, Monica, and Sam—we all graduated from Pratt, a few years after you. You were our hero. Our muse. Your art, photos, and awards are displayed in a permanent case. Did you know that?"

Pierre looked down, embarrassed, then back at Phillip. Smiling, he confessed, "I didn't know."

Monica took a deep breath and approached Alex. She nervously offered her hand. "I'm Monica."

Alex, always gracious, kissed both of Monica's cheeks. "It's so nice to see you again. We actually met briefly at the Seattle auction. Hope you're feeling well. I know a lot has happened in a very short period of time."

Monica blushed. Surprised by her reaction, she said the first thing that popped in her head. A famous quote by Yogi Berra. "When you come to a fork in the road, take it."

"Pardon me?"

Laughing, she said, "Oh, it's a quote by a famous American baseball icon."

Alex, still not understanding, simply smiled and stared at her.

"Okay, I was thinking of you as a young man and the path you took. Now back at the fork, you've obviously taken the right road." She nodded at Joi then smiled at Alex. "I'm so happy for you both."

Fin

Epilogue

Having discovered the existence of a cache of potentially valuable forgeries in Alex's apartment, Michel Gaudet, former PI with DuChat Detective Agency in Paris, embarks on a quest of his own. He, too, has decided on a new career and lifestyle in the art world. The bug in Alex's phone is, of course, still intact.

Coming Soon!

Forgery Redux

"Many a dangerous temptation comes to us
in fine gay colors that are but skin deep."

MATTHEW HENRY

Fini

"To an untrained eye, need and love were as easily mistaken
for each other as the real master's painting and a forgery."

DEB CALETTI

Find out more, and sign up to be the first
to know about new releases:

WWW.DIANENAAB.COM

Acknowledgments

I cannot begin to name everyone who has, in some way, encouraged me on this journey with *The Paris Affair*. It would be too humiliating to leave out a name. I will simply say "thank you" to my family, my writer friends, and countless strangers observed on the street or in cafés, who have given me a visual for many of the scenes, especially in Paris.

I am especially indebted to my insightful and amazing editors, Kathy Burge and Kara Aisenbrey. To Caerus Kourt, whose eye for detail in formatting and cover design brought my book to life. And to my publishing consultant, Beth Jusino, whose wisdom and encouragement have taken me through the final steps of this project.

My husband, Michael has been with me throughout. His input, insight, and humor have made this first novel writing project an adventure in itself. Imagine, if you will, the following scenario:

It's 2 a.m. I'm pacing and pondering with pen and pad in hand. Finally, I shake his shoulder. He's been in a deep sleep for hours. "I changed that part in Chapter 3. What do you think?" as I hand the pages to him for consideration. I then go back to bed—feeling quite content.

Thank you, mister man.

About the Author

Diane W Naab is an artist and writer. Her love of travel takes her often to Europe, and always Paris.

Her poetry and short stories have been published in *Inside Passages,* Southeast Alaska's annual literary review; *Poetry Corners,* published by the Arts & Humanities Bainbridge; and featured in *The Poet's Corner* of *My Edmonds News.* Her visual art and poetry are often a part of the *Ars Poetica* event promoted by the Bainbridge Artisan Resource Network (BARN) on Bainbridge Island, and her artwork has been displayed at the Bainbridge Island Museum of Art.

When not choosing the perfect white wine to accompany raw oysters in Paris, attending cooking classes in Spain, Italy, and France, or hosting a writing critique group, Diane lives the creative life a ferry ride from Seattle. She counts owning an art gallery and bistro in Ketchikan, Alaska as one of her favorite adventures.

Diane lives near Seattle with her husband, who shares her passion for good books and great travel.

The Paris Affair is her first novel.

Find out more at

WWW.DIANENAAB.COM

Printed in the USA
CPSIA information can be obtained
at www.ICGtesting.com
CBHW03202610123
1797CB00003B/24